The Bootlegger's Legacy

Denise Devine
USA Today Bestselling Author

A Sweet Historical Roaring Twenties Novel

Moonshine Madness Series – Book 3

Wild Prairie Rose Books

The Bootlegger's Legacy

(Moonshine Madness Series - Book 3)

Print Edition

Also available in audiobook

ISBN: 978-1-943124-39-8

Published in the United States of America

Wild Prairie Rose Books

Edited by L.F. Nies and J.A. Dalton

Cover Design by Raine English

Chapter One

CHAR

My Coco Chanel dress rustled softly in the warm, balmy evening as I slid out of the limousine, clutching the hand of my beau. Will stood patiently as he assisted me, looking extraordinarily dashing in a black tuxedo with a long-tailed cutaway coat.

Will had purchased tickets to a glamorous charity ball sponsored by the St. Paul Women's Friendship Club to celebrate his birthday. The annual event had been a family tradition, dating back to his youth when his late mother had served on the club's executive board. I'd never attended a black-tie ball before, but I'd read articles in the society section of the newspaper about fundraising galas. For days, I had looked forward to a wonderful evening of dining and dancing with Will and my friends.

As we stepped onto the sidewalk, Will paused and smiled at me. He stood well over six feet tall with broad shoulders and muscular arms. His thick black hair glistened in the bright June sun. His deep blue eyes gazed into mine. "You look wonderful tonight, Char."

"Thank you." My heart fluttered at the tenderness in his deep, throaty voice. I'd purchased a shimmering black dress with cap sleeves purposely for this occasion. The skirt's hem brushed my ankles with an overlay that sloped upward toward my right side. The two-tiered, draping bodice slanted toward the opposite side. I'd finished my outfit with matching T-strap shoes, elbow-length gloves, my favorite black beaded shawl, and a platinum and diamond necklace set.

"Ahem," Will's sister, Madeline, said loudly.

Glancing past my shoulder, I caught Madeline prodding Will's back with the tip of her red-lacquered fingernail to make him stop flirting and get moving.

"Peter, tell your girlfriend to stop poking me," Will said with mock irritation to the fellow at her side.

"Tell her yourself," Peter replied with a wry chuckle. "She won't listen to me."

Laughing, Will offered me his arm and escorted me to the canopied front entrance of the elegant Saint Paul Hotel.

Will had convinced Madeline and his best friend, Peter Garrett, to accompany us using the excuse that the couple he'd originally purchased the tickets for had canceled at the last minute and he couldn't find anyone else. Madeline and Peter accepted his story, but he hadn't fooled me.

Once upon a time, Madeline and Peter had been the talk of the town. Back then, she'd found the handsome, eligible bachelor with a Harvard law degree and impeccable manners irresistibly attractive. She eventually became bored with him, however, and though they'd parted friends, nowadays their paths rarely crossed. I suspected Will hoped his sister and his best friend would renew their romance. I couldn't fault Will for trying, but I worried his good intentions were doomed to fail.

Peter, a successful attorney, wanted to settle down and raise a family. Maddie, as she preferred to be called, considered herself a "free spirit" who drank bootlegged whiskey and danced the night away. Whenever they were together, Maddie and Peter fought like cats and dogs. I hoped they were too distracted by all the gaiety tonight to disagree on anything, but I had a feeling this little reunion was a huge miscalculation on Will's part.

We walked through a spacious, European-style lobby furnished with leather furniture, marble columns, and palm trees. Waterford crystal chandeliers showered the room with sparkling light. The room held such an enchanting atmosphere, I couldn't wait to see what the ballroom looked like.

We approached the elevator, operated by a young man wearing a red bellhop uniform and a round, brimless cap with a leather chin strap. His cropped coat narrowed at the waist, embellished with three vertical rows of gold buttons. A matching gold stripe accentuated the sides of his trousers.

He nodded solemnly at Will. "To the ballroom, sir?"

"Yes," Will replied as he ushered us into the elevator car.

I stood quietly by Will's side, our fingers tightly entwined as the bellhop extended his gloved hand, pulled the glass door and metal scissor gate closed then pressed the lever on the manual control. We slowly glided up to the ballroom floor. Once there, we stepped out of the car and walked to the wide-open doors of the Promenade Ballroom where a silver-haired gentleman in a tuxedo stood behind a wooden podium. The man perused Will's tickets and slipped them inside a flat leather pouch. "Your name, sir?"

Will smiled. "William Van Elsberg."

The man uncapped his fountain pen and crossed Will's name off his list. "Very good, sir. I'll show you to your table. Right this way please."

Laughter and lively banter echoed through the softly lit ballroom as we followed our host to a round table covered with peach linen, gold-rimmed dishes, and crystal stemware. The gentleman wished us all an enjoyable evening before departing.

Peter pulled out Maddie's chair to seat her. Will stood patiently as he assisted me. I sat down and promptly moved my chair closer to his before slipping my shawl off my shoulders.

Maddie ignored Peter as she sat down and instead glanced around, waving at a young woman she knew across the room. "Don't look now, but, the old biddies of the Friendship Club are on their high horses tonight," she announced with a droll smile as she turned back to us, placing her black sequined clutch on the table. "Faye Delacorte and her friends on the board must be on fashion guard duty. Not that I care, mind you, but she's apparently taken issue with my outfit. She's gossiping about it with the other fossils—I mean, board members—right now."

I had been too focused on following Will to our table to notice anyone watching us. Still, the name Delacorte sounded familiar. Where had I heard that before? "Perhaps they were merely curious," I replied, unconcerned.

"Not *these* ladies." Maddie's kohl-lined eyes flashed. "The

Friendship Club disapproves of anyone who dares to be fashionable." She snorted. "It violates their ancient dress code."

Maddie's taste in evening couture was a dazzling black shift in fine silk, hand-embroidered with glass bugle beads and shimmering sequins. The sleeveless, body-baring fashion had a knee-length hemline to show off her curvy legs when she danced. She wore a matching cloche hat over her black, chin-length bob, adorned with a satin ribbon above the brim and accented with an ostrich feather. And of course, she wore her signature rope of pearls. The outfit looked terrific on her, but a flapper dress was unconventional and a bit risqué for a formal dress ball.

"Pipe down, Maddie," Peter whispered as he sat down and glared at her, unimpressed with her opinions. "The people around us hear your criticism of our hosts. It's rude and embarrassing."

"I'm a modernist," she responded matter-of-factly as if the proclamation alone was sufficient to counter his rebuke. "I'm not afraid to speak my mind."

My gaze swept the ballroom, noting a sea of gray-haired attendees. Some of them *were* looking our way, especially that small crowd of ladies huddled together by the dance floor. A few women scattered about the room reflected our age group—Maddie was twenty-eight and I was twenty-six—but this event overwhelmingly favored a mature crowd. Older women tended to be traditionalists who believed in long-held cultural and religious values. Simply put, their view maintained that a woman's place was in the home raising children, not exercising her independence with loose morals. And that included exposing her knees.

"I don't understand why you paid a sack full of money for tickets to this yawner to celebrate your birthday, Will," Maddie continued as she raised one finely penciled brow. "We could be having more fun at a gin mill, kicking up some dust! This was fine entertainment for our parents when they were alive, but we don't have anything in common with such a stuffy crowd."

Will gave his sister a stern look. "You're right, I did spend a lot of dough on the tickets so behave yourself. We're not leaving early to get sozzled at your favorite *gin mill*."

He plucked a small cluster of miniature peach roses from a round glass vase in the center of the table and tucked the stem behind my ear. "I thought it would be nice to donate to a worthy cause, Char, and at the same time, introduce you to some of the members of the club. Many of them live near you."

"I love that idea, Will," I replied, anxious to change the subject and ultimately the mood around the table.

My late husband, Gus LeDoux, had built a palatial mansion for me on Summit Avenue in St. Paul but in the three years I'd owned it, I'd never had an opportunity to meet any of my neighbors. Gus and I had been so busy establishing our nightclub, La Coquette, that we never had time for socializing outside of our business clientele. After he died, I'd had my hands full raising my infant son, Julien, and overseeing Gus' business empire.

Except for La Coquette. The nightclub had been problematic since the day it opened, and the Feds shut it down before Gus passed. Since then, I had reopened the building as a shelter for homeless and abused women. I'd renamed it "Anna's House" to honor the memory of my late mother.

Thinking about La Coquette suddenly jogged my memory, reminding me why the name Delacorte sounded so familiar…

A waiter appeared, interrupting my thoughts as he filled a stemmed glass with ice water. "Would you like coffee or perhaps an iced tea?"

I looked up. "I'll take an iced tea, please."

"I'd like a ginger ale," Maddie said as he filled her water glass.

The men ordered coffee.

The waiter returned quickly with our beverages. After he left, Maddie slipped her fingers into her handbag and retrieved a small silver flask, the one she always carried with her.

Peter's jaw clenched. Behind his wire-rimmed glasses, his brown eyes pierced hers. "Really, Maddie," he complained under his breath, "must you do that *here*?"

"Don't be such a flat tire, Peter. I'm thirsty." She rolled her eyes and quickly poured a generous amount of whiskey into her glass then buried the flask back inside her clutch. "Besides, I doubt I'm the only person in this room spiking my soda with a little giggle water."

I took a sip of iced tea to conceal my amusement as I wondered about that. It was no secret that prohibition hadn't stopped the illegal manufacture, sale, or distribution of bootlegged liquor in St. Paul. Gus once told me that there were tunnels below the hotels in St. Paul where bootleggers transported booze to the kitchens for guests to consume discreetly in the privacy of their rooms. I didn't know if that was true at this hotel, but I didn't think it would be difficult to obtain liquor if a guest wanted some.

Will held up his water glass. "Cheers."

Everyone followed suit, clinking their glasses together in agreement.

Our waiter appeared with our first course of tomato bisque soup with a side dish of cheese straws. He also set a dish filled with celery, salted nuts, and olives on the table.

The previous discussion fizzled in favor of enjoying our meal. I dismissed all curious thoughts from my mind and began to relax as my apprehension over Maddie and Peter subsided, giving way to the merriment of dining with dear friends.

We were enjoying our soup when Maddie glanced up. Her smile faded. "Oh-oh. Here they come," she said wryly.

The conversation abruptly ceased as a small army of footsteps approached the table.

A stately woman wearing a black, floor-length gown, wire-rimmed glasses, and heirloom diamonds suddenly stood next to my chair, looking down at me with a grim frown. Her stone-gray hair was twisted into a bun on the crown of her head and accentuated with a tortoiseshell comb. Her three companions stood behind her. "Are you Charlotte LeDoux?" she demanded with an official, duty-first tone in her voice.

Everyone at the table froze.

"Yes," I said, tense with uncertainty as I encountered the woman's stern gaze. "What can I do for you?"

"You must leave," she announced then glanced sternly at her companions for reinforcement. At their nod, her expression grew cold. "Immediately."

I stared at her in shock. My spoon clattered into my bowl. "I—I don't understand."

"What's going on?" Will slid his arm around me. "What's the meaning of this, Faye?"

"I'm sorry, William," Faye Delacorte replied stiffly, "but only members and their families are allowed to attend this event. You know the rules. It's a private affair."

"This is ridiculous!" Maddie slammed her glass on the table. "Both Peter's mother and mine were board members of this club. I'm a lifetime member. Char is my guest."

Faye ignored Maddie's protest, focusing on me. "Let me be frank, Mrs. LeDoux, so there is no misunderstanding on your part. We are a Christian organization of law-abiding citizens," she stated crisply. "We don't approve of people like you and your husband."

Suddenly, Faye's reason for expelling me became crystal clear. It never dawned on me that Gus' reputation as a notorious bootlegger was still alive—even though he wasn't. About a year ago, he had been killed during a shootout with federal agents.

"You mean my *late* husband, Gus," I replied defiantly.

"Yes." Her lips formed a tight line as though the mere mention of my husband's name in public was so scandalous—gasp—she could barely acknowledge it.

"With all due respect, Faye, you're wrong." Will's lean face darkened with anger. "Her husband was involved in that business. *She is not.* You have no excuse to insult my guest like this and I'd like you to apologize immediately."

Faye stood her ground, holding her head high. "I disagree." She glanced over her shoulder at the rest of her posse. Once again, they nodded in support. She turned back to us. "Her status in the community has been tainted by his criminal activities. Allowing her to be here damages *your mother's* legacy and the good name of The Women's Friendship Club. Now, if you please—"

"Fine." Will pulled his napkin off his lap and tossed it on the table. "Have it your way. We'll leave." He stood up, glaring with disgust as he pulled out my chair.

Peter followed suit. Maddie gulped the rest of her ginger ale and stood. "I've been kicked out of better places than this." She grabbed her clutch. "Let's go!"

Well, that was that. I had been foolishly naive to think the notoriety surrounding Gus' life and death wouldn't affect my future. This painful encounter, however, made me realize it would always be a curse upon me. Worse yet, I had embarrassed my friends. I didn't care what anyone thought of me, but I cared deeply that my friends had been subjected to public humiliation *because of me.* I rose from the table, clutching my shawl. The sooner we left, the better.

It was so quiet in the ballroom you could hear a pin drop. I turned away from my sanctimonious accusers, wishing I had some way to wipe that triumphant sneer off Faye Delacorte's wrinkled face.

A man's deep chuckle prompted me to look up. Across the room, I saw a familiar face staring back at me. He appeared just as I remembered him—florid, stout, balding. And as arrogant as ever. A slight curve at the corner of his bluish lips indicated he was reveling in my misfortune. Was this his way of getting revenge for the small fortune he'd lost gambling at La Coquette? Whatever the cause, the glare in his eyes indicated he thought he was better than me. Him and his nasty wife…

Something inside me instantly changed. I couldn't stop them from ordering me to leave, but I didn't have to go quietly. Or with my tail between my legs.

I whirled around, confronting Faye Delacorte with a renewed surge of energy and a clear sense of purpose. "You know, if I were you, I wouldn't look down my nose at people who didn't measure up to my rigid standards," I said loudly. "You never know, someone in your family might get caught with his pants down and embarrass you, knocking you off your self-righteous throne."

Will slid his fingers around my arm. "Come on, Char. Let's go."

I shrugged off his hand. I wasn't finished yet...

"Oh, and just so there is no misunderstanding on *your* part," I continued, raising my voice, "many of the so-called upstanding, pillar-of-the-society husbands in this room were regular customers at my husband's nightclub. They drank, they gambled, and at the end of the evening, they left with glamorous young chorus girls hanging on their arms."

Faye's eyes widened with shock as a collection of gasps echoed around the room. Her face blanched. "How dare you..."

"Char—"

I treated her to a triumphant smile as Will grabbed my arm again and pulled me toward the door. "Every weekend, rain or shine," I shouted, "drinking, dancing, and cheating on their wives like there was no tomorrow." My gaze swept the room, catching more familiar faces. "The Bible says that your sin will find you out. Right, fellas?" I cut a sideways glance at Faye's husband, Charles, enjoying watching him sweat. "Right, *Charles*?"

The gasps turned to snickers.

"Get out," Faye screeched, her face now flaming with anger. "Get out, now! Or I'll have you thrown out!"

Will managed to pull me out of the room and into the hallway just as the doors to the elevator opened. He pushed me inside and pressed me toward the back of the car. Maddie and Peter stood in front of me, presumably to keep me from charging back out to have another go-around with our imperious host.

As the doors closed, a rush of conflicting emotions washed over me. On one hand, the Delacortes—Faye and her odious husband, Charles—deserved to have their dirty secrets made public after the despicable way they'd behaved toward me. On the other hand, I regretted embarrassing my friends by reacting like an impetuous schoolgirl who'd been picked on one too many times by the class bully. Regardless of who was at fault, the glaring fact remained that because of my husband's notorious legacy,

I would never be accepted by my wealthy peers.

The realization that I'd been unfairly judged angered me, but it also made me see the indisputable truth. Even in death, Gus's reputation overshadowed me, controlling my life. I knew of only one way to change that. Go my own way, create my own legacy, one that upheld the person *I* was, not the person I'd married. It sounded impossible, but I had to try.

But first, I had to make things right with my companions. I took a deep breath. "I'm sorry I lost my temper. I embarrassed you all."

Maddie burst out laughing. "Don't be—she deserved it, Char. I'm glad you put that old hag in her place." She looked back at me. "That was the best show I've seen in a long time!"

Will didn't answer me or acknowledge my heartfelt apology. He stared at the floor, frowning.

I couldn't tell what was going through his mind. Was he rethinking our relationship?

His silence worried me. A lot.

Chapter Two

WILL

As the elevator car slowly descended to the lobby, I stared at the floor, filled with so much anger and frustration I could barely contain my temper. I knew how snobby the old biddies of the Friendship Club could be. I'd been attending their functions all my life. It wasn't the first time I'd seen them eject a guest that didn't measure up to their standards, but I never suspected they would treat a guest of mine that way!

We exited the elevator and made our way through the lobby to the front entrance where I requested the valet to inform our driver to bring the car around. I avoided speaking to anyone until Char's new limousine pulled up to the curb and Errol, her liveried driver greeted us.

I expected her to scramble into the car, but she held back, allowing Maddie and Peter to get in first.

"I shouldn't have lashed out at Faye Delacorte in front of everyone," she said contritely, placing her palm on my chest. "It was beneath me. You have every right to be angry with me."

"I'm not angry with you, Char. It wasn't your fault," I whispered into her ear.

Her eyes widened with surprise. "But Will—"

"I blame myself for what happened. I owe *you* an apology." I silenced her by framing her heart-shaped face with my hands. Slipping my fingers through her soft, mahogany curls, I tipped her head back to gaze into her wide, troubled eyes. "If I'd known the ladies in the Friendship Club were going to act like that, I would never have taken you there."

She sniffled. "Faye simply said what everyone was thinking."

13

"Never mind what she said, darling. *I* think you're the cat's meow," I murmured, trying to make amends though I knew nothing could erase the sting of Faye's public humiliation. "And my opinion is the only one that counts!"

Errol stood at the door waiting patiently to assist Char into the car.

We slid into the vehicle's spacious interior, and I stretched out my legs, making myself comfortable as I tried to put the evening's fiasco out of my mind.

Errol jumped into the driver's seat and eased the automobile into the flow of traffic. I suddenly wondered where he was taking us.

"Shall I have Errol drive you home, or would you like to spend the evening at my house?" Char asked. "Adeline will make dinner for us," she said referring to her cook. "Afterward we can play cards in the drawing room."

Peter stared out the window, looking grumpy and I wondered if he and Maddie had exchanged unpleasant words. I sensed he was putting up with her for my sake. Regretting my mistake, I vowed never to get involved in matchmaking again.

Maddie smiled in that mischievous way of hers that always informed me she had something up her sleeve.

"Oh, it's too early to go home," she said with a dismissive wave of her hand. "Errol is taking us to the perfect place for dinner. Since you two were…um…distracted, I told him it was Char's idea and swore I was just relaying her instructions."

Char and I glanced at each other warily.

"Maddie," I replied with impatience, truly suspicious. "Where are we going?"

She grinned. "You'll see."

Thirty minutes later we stood in the lobby of The Oasis, the newest speakeasy in St. Paul. Soft lighting, life-sized palms made of paper mâché, and Persian tapestries covering the walls gave the dining room a unique Middle Eastern flair. Small lights in the high ceiling replicated a starry nighttime sky.

On the corner stage at the opposite end of the room, a jazz band played a melancholy tune.

Following the host to our table, I took note of all the exits, glad that I had a knife strapped to one ankle and a handgun strapped to the other. I scanned the busy room and saw a veritable *who's who* of the St. Paul elite representing both sides of the law. An establishment like this always made me uneasy, especially when I had Char with me. Her former husband had racked up enemies like most men accumulated spare change and I never knew who might be lurking in the shadows, waiting for an opportunity to settle an old score.

I regarded the flipside of that coin, however, equally as dangerous. Char had devoted admirers and many of them wanted to take my place, but it wasn't just her wealth that made her so attractive to the men in this town. Though she stood a little over five feet tall and weighed about a hundred pounds soaking wet, underneath that petite, feminine exterior was one smart, witty, and fearless woman.

"Good evening, Miss Van Elsberg," our waiter said to Maddie with a smile. "Welcome, ladies and gentlemen to The Oasis. Would you like to start with a special beverage this evening?"

It didn't surprise me that the employees here knew my sister by name. However, it didn't make me happy, either. Maddie spent too much time in places like this to suit me.

"Yes, Ivan," Maddie said as she placed her clutch on the table. "I'll have the manager's special. We'll all have one." She glanced at us. "You're going to love this."

"None for me," Char said quickly. She sounded exhausted. "I'll just have a glass of water, please."

Her wide green eyes always sparkled when she laughed, and they glittered like fireworks when something made her mad. Tonight, they were underscored with dark circles, and her cheeks were flushed. The incident at the Saint Paul Hotel had impacted her more than I'd realized. Worried, I took her soft hand in mine. "Darling, are you all right?"

She winced. "My stomach is queasy. I was so busy getting ready this afternoon to go out that I skipped lunch. At the ball, I'd barely started on my soup when we were forced to leave."

The weariness in her voice suggested she needed more than just a good meal. Her condition greatly concerned me, but I didn't want to embarrass her by voicing my opinion in front of Peter and Maddie, so I kept my thoughts to myself. I'd already made up my mind to take Char home right after dinner, no matter how much my sister protested.

The manager's special turned out to be a pitcher of sweetened iced tea laced heavily with bootlegged whiskey and spices. I didn't know what to make of it at first, but after a couple of sips, I had to admit, the cinnamon-and-whiskey-flavored drink wasn't bad. The first glass went down faster than I'd anticipated, and I poured myself another.

As if on cue, our waiter appeared with another pitcher of tea. He gave each person a menu.

At his suggestion, we decided upon chicken curry for our dinners. For an appetizer, the waiter suggested hummus, a smooth dip made with chickpeas, olive oil, and spices accompanied by a basket of flatbread. As soon as he returned with the hummus and flatbread, I dived in.

"Take a bite of this," I said to Char as I covered a triangular piece of flatbread with a generous amount of the dip and held it to her lips. I needed to get some food into my gal.

She hesitated at first then took a small bite. Her face lit up. "This is very good," she announced as she took the flatbread from my hand and stuffed it into her mouth. "I'm starving!"

After we finished our appetizer, Maddie picked up her clutch and pushed back her chair. "I'm going to the ladies' room. Want to come along, Char?"

As soon as Char and Maddie departed, I stared at Peter, my oldest friend, and the person with whom I shared an office. "You've been rather agreeable since we got here, Garrett. You must be enjoying yourself."

"Not really." Peter topped off my glass with more iced tea. "I'm putting all my energy into this." He held up the pitcher. "It beats arguing with Maddie all night."

"Whoa," I said, holding up my palm. "This stuff is pretty potent. If

I drink much more, I'll be cross-eyed by the time we stumble out of here."

Peter grinned, his reddish pencil mustache widening to a thin line. "I think that's the point, old boy." He touched the rim of his glass against mine. "To our health!" He took a generous swig of his drink. "How are you feeling tonight? You haven't spoken much since we left the club. Is your injury bothering you?"

My right side *was* a little sore tonight, but I didn't want to admit that out loud. I was still recovering from a serious gunshot wound that I'd received two months ago while protecting a client, and though my health had made remarkable progress, my body still hadn't returned to normal yet. This evening marked my first outing with Char since the incident happened. We'd already experienced one setback tonight. I didn't want anything else to spoil our evening.

"Don't worry about me." I sipped my tea, noting that the alcohol in it was already dulling the pain. "I'm doing fine."

Peter set down his glass. "By the way, happy birthday. In a couple of hours, you're officially thirty-five and a rich man. How does it feel to finally get your hands on your trust fund?"

I stared at him. "I couldn't care less."

"Of course, you care." Peter's golden brows knit together as his brown eyes studied me in puzzlement. "That money is your inheritance, and you deserve it," he argued, adjusting his oval, wire-rimmed glasses. "You've waited a long time for it. Besides, you've got a rich girlfriend. Don't you want to step out with her in the style she's accustomed to now that you have the dough?"

"She loves me just the way I am." I pushed my glass away and rested my arms on the table. "I don't see the point in changing anything."

"Are you..." Peter blinked in astonishment. "Are you saying you haven't told her about the money yet?"

"What's there to tell," I argued. "That my father was a tight-fisted and cruel old bas—" I checked myself and glanced around hoping the ladies at the next table hadn't heard that. "—who withheld his money to punish his son?"

"Hey, take it easy," Peter whispered patiently as he leaned forward. "Look at it this way. You outlasted his plan to force you to comply with his will." He pushed my glass of iced tea toward me. "You won."

"I prefer to think that I never rose to the bait." I leaned back in my chair with a tired sigh. "The old man got one thing out of me, though. He always wanted you and me to become partners like him and your father. We finally got around to making the move, but on *our* terms, not his."

Peter picked up a leftover piece of flatbread. "Yeah, well, I used to wish you'd gone to law school and become my law partner. Now, I'm glad you didn't." He dipped his bread into the nearly empty bowl of hummus. "You're the best private investigator in town, Will. I can't imagine trusting my most sensitive cases to anyone else."

"That means a lot to me," I said honestly and cleared my throat. Peter and I didn't have emotional conversations. It wasn't our way, but this time I wanted him to know how much I valued our friendship. "I wouldn't share an office with anyone else but you. I trust you, too. And that means I'm counting on you to keep quiet about my inheritance when you're around Char. All right? I want to tell her about it in my own way and on my own time."

"Agreed. It's not my secret to tell," Peter said and stuffed the flatbread into his mouth.

I breathed a sigh of relief. I didn't want to keep secrets from Char. I wanted her to know about the money, but to do so meant I also had to recap the sordid details of my childhood, something I wasn't keen to talk about. That part of my life died with the old man and that's where it belonged. I had no desire to revive the past, but I knew I couldn't keep it buried forever.

Why did life have to be so blasted complicated?

A couple of minutes later, the girls returned. I pulled out Char's chair for her, noticing she looked even more tired than she did before she left the table.

I cheered when our food arrived. We were starving and the chicken curry practically melted in my mouth. We had finished eating and I sat waiting for the check to arrive when I heard Maddie clear her throat. "Behind you, Will—"

I spun around as a tall, regal blonde wearing a long, sleeveless dress in shimmering ivory satin sauntered toward the table, her slender hips swaying to the music. She looked as beautiful as ever, but to me, her attractiveness was merely a façade. As our gazes met, my hands clenched. She was the last person I wanted to run into here—or anywhere.

"Well, hello there," she said slowly in that sultry tone she always used when she wanted to charm me. She stood like a Hollywood film star with one gloved hand on her hip and a beguiling smile on her bright red lips. The other gloved hand clutched a slender black cigarette holder. I noticed she wasn't wearing an engagement ring on her left hand. "Happy birthday, Will," she said. "How have you been?"

"I thought you moved to New York with your *fiancé*," I said brusquely to show my disinterest in answering her question. "What happened? Did you get bored with him, too?" I raised my hand, snapping my fingers for our waiter to hurry with the check.

"I love New York City. There's no other place in the world like it," she replied, ignoring my question about her fiancé. "But there's no place like home." Her evasiveness all but confirmed she and her Wall Street tycoon weren't together any longer. Frankly, I didn't care.

Char shot me a sideways glance, silently questioning who this woman was and why I hadn't immediately made introductions.

Because she's not sticking around long enough to warrant it... I thought irascibly. Where the heck was that waiter?

Without waiting for me to speak, Char raised her hand in a friendly gesture. "Hello, I'm Charlotte LeDoux," she said politely. "I'm pleased to meet you."

The blonde gave her an icy stare. "I know who you are."

The woman's gaze slid to mine. "So, are you still operating as a private detective, or are you now on the LeDoux payroll?" The cynical thread in her voice suggested that Char's presence indicated I'd lowered my standards. Tired or not, I knew Char wouldn't let the veiled insults stand but I had no intention of letting her get involved.

"Just so you know, Peter and Will share an office," Maddie burst out before Char, or I could respond to the question. "They've each got their own firm, but they work together."

Peter refrained from commenting at all as he watched the scene play out. The cagey expression on his face indicated he wanted nothing to do with this conversation. Or this woman.

The waiter appeared with our check. I stood to leave.

"Oh, not yet," our unwanted guest said to the waiter, pushing his check tray away. "We'll have another round of whatever everyone is drinking, and I'll take a glass of your best champagne."

Not if I could help it. My tab was closed. I shook my head.

She gave me an innocent smile. "But, darling, we must celebrate your birthday properly since this is an important year. You've been waiting a long time to get your hands on your trust fund."

Char's jaw dropped. Her eyes widened as they searched mine, clearly upset to learn about my inheritance from a total stranger instead of from me. Given the family turmoil surrounding it, Maddie and I had agreed years ago to keep it to ourselves, but in a moment of weakness caused by too much to drink, I had confided my secret to someone else. I lost her because of it and now I had damaged Char's trust in me because of it.

Heat spread under my collar. Slipping two fingers behind my bowtie, I yanked it loose before I choked on it. I needed to explain the situation to Char, but not here.

Suddenly, the jazz band began playing a waltz. Seizing the opportunity to make a quick exit, I gripped Char by the upper arms, practically lifting her off the chair. "Come on, darling. I promised you one dance before we took our leave—"

"What?" Char looked absolutely flummoxed. "Will!"

Ignoring her protest, I clasped her hand. "Take care of the check, will you Peter? We'll settle up later." I snatched the wooden tip tray containing the bill from our waiter and dropped it in the center of the table then led Char through the room and onto the crowded dance floor, moving as far into the center as I could get. Sliding my arm around her, we began to sway gently to the music.

She glared up at me. The top of her head measured level with the bottom of my chin. "All right, mister," she snapped, "you've got some explaining to do!"

My jaw tensed. Where would I start?

"Who is she?"

I pulled her close. "No one important."

"For someone with no importance, you sure got nervous when she arrived. Who. Is. *She.*"

I sighed, wishing just once we could have an evening out without fanfare. "Someone I used to know."

Char stomped on my instep. Not hard enough to hurt, but firm enough to let me know she wanted answers, not excuses.

I jerked back in surprise. "Hey!" Loosening my grip on her, I spun her around. "Okay, her name is Eva."

"Does Eva have a last name?" Char persisted.

"Eva Baumann," I replied hating the mere sound of it. "We used to be engaged. That is until she found out about the delay in getting my old man's treasure chest. Then she went looking for a better meal ticket."

"Oh," Char said softly. "Maddie told me about her. She said you were 'dizzy in love with that dame and wanted to marry her but after you got engaged, she dumped you for a guy with a fancy car and a ticket to the big-time life in New York City.' Those were Maddie's exact words. From the way that *dame* acted just now, she wants you back."

I laughed. "You're imagining things. Besides, I'm taken." Angling my head, I kissed the tip of Char's nose. "I'm in love with *you.*" I slowly guided her around the dance floor, weaving deftly between the couples around us. The spiced tea had temporarily dulled the ache in my side, but

I had a feeling I would pay for it dearly tomorrow.

"Love needs to be grounded in reality to survive, Will." Her eyes suddenly reflected a look of sadness. "People only see me as Gus' widow. Are you sure you want to be shackled to the curse of his legacy like I am?"

"There's one way to fix that," I replied seriously. "When we get married and you take my name, people will forget about your connection to him."

"Oh, if it were only that easy..." she replied sounding discouraged. "Now, what's all this about a trust fund?" She looked hurt. "Why haven't you told me about it?"

I checked around, making sure no one was eavesdropping on us. "It's a long and uninteresting story," I said in a low voice as I slowed our pace, "but the short answer is that my father set up the trust so that if I didn't fulfill his expectations, I wouldn't receive the money until I turned thirty-five. He and Peter's father had a law office together and they wanted their sons to take it over when they retired. Peter did his father's bidding. In my case..." I let out a tense sigh to subdue old feelings of resentment. "I followed my own path."

She gave me a curious look. "Were you a rebellious kid? Causing him a lot of grief?"

"No, just the opposite," I replied matter-of-factly. "I didn't dare get out of line or I'd get a belt across my backside. As it was, I got it a lot anyway." I smacked my lips in disgust. "The older I got, the more I loathed him and everything he stood for. I hated the idea of going into partnership with him. When he died, his will specified that if I didn't attend law school, I'd wait years for the money, but I didn't care. I wasn't going to let that old goat dictate to me from the grave."

Char squeezed my hand. "After all this time, you must have quite a nest egg."

"Un-huh."

Her eyes widened with curiosity. "How much?"

I whispered the amount into her ear.

She stopped dancing and stared up at me. "Really? What are you planning to do with it?"

I shrugged. "Leave it in the bank. Let it continue to collect interest. I don't need his money. I like my life just the way it is."

She yawned heavily as she leaned into me, resting her cheek on my chest. "One day you'll change your mind."

I pushed the thought away as I glanced across the room to locate Maddie and Peter. They stood in the lobby, looking bored with each other as they waited for us. Burying my nose in the soft waves on the crown of Char's head I said, "Come on, kiddo. It's been a long and exhausting day. I'm taking you home."

Placing my arm around her waist for support, I guided her off the dance floor. From the moment we met, Char had captured my heart. Back then, however, she had been another man's wife, so I'd buried my feelings for her. But Gus LeDoux was dead; he'd been gone for over a year. Sadly, though Char had refused to carry on his illegal activities, his notorious reputation still overshadowed her.

As long as the woman I loved remained under his dark legacy, she wasn't truly free from him. Someone needed to break Gus' hold over her.

That someone was me.

Chapter Three

CHAR

"I'm sorry I wasn't able to make our meeting yesterday," I said to Sally Wentworth as I walked into the administrative office at Anna's House. Together, Sally and I established the shelter to help disadvantaged women. I had provided the operating funds and donated the building—the one that used to house La Coquette. After the Feds closed it down, it was overtaken by raccoons and skunks and would have gone into serious disrepair if it hadn't been repurposed. Sally, along with the women in her church, reopened it as Anna's House and now managed the daily operations.

"No need to apologize." Sally stood up from behind her desk. "You called me ahead of our meeting to let me know."

The buxom redhead was about twenty years older than me, more outspoken than me, and had a heart as big as the moon. She favored bright colors and today she wore a fuchsia dress that clashed with her coppery hair. Most women her age would have deemed such a bold statement to be inappropriate, but it blended quite naturally with Sally's forthright personality. "You look peaked," she stated in a motherly way. "Those dark circles under your eyes are concerning. How are you feeling today?"

"I've been unusually tired lately, but it's nothing serious," I confessed as I grabbed a chair and collapsed into it. "I've probably been pushing myself too hard."

Exhausted from that disastrous scene two nights ago at the Women's Friendship Club gala, I'd spent most of the following day in my room, reading an Agatha Christie novel and napping. Gretchen, the nanny to my eight-month-old son brought little Julien to my room to cuddle with me for a while. Then I dressed and went downstairs to eat dinner, but only because I didn't want my younger sister, Francie, to dine alone.

Sally walked around her desk and placed her palm on my forehead. "You're warm. Is it your sick time?"

"No," I replied candidly. "I haven't had one for several months, only spotting occasionally, but that's normal for me. I never know when it's going to come."

"I see." She leaned against the desk and folded her arms. "Have you been with Will?"

I looked at her, puzzled. "What do you mean?"

She didn't answer me, but the "you weren't born yesterday" expression on her face made me blush.

"Oh…that…" I shrugged. "Once, but it was a long time ago. Before Will was in the hospital." My mind spun back in time, recalling the night Will and I had spent together. We hadn't planned it—it just happened. Remembering the love and tenderness he'd shown me caused my heart to flutter as a sudden rush of déjà vu surged through me.

Sadly, a few days after that incident we disagreed over my reluctance to completely break away from Gus' attorney and Will broke off our relationship, shattering my heart. Not long after that, he was ambushed coming out of a restaurant and spent weeks in the hospital recovering from his injuries. The crisis brought us back together and made our relationship stronger, but we hadn't shared intimacy again and wouldn't until we were married. Will had been adamant that neither event would happen until he had fully recovered.

She stared at me. "How long ago was it?"

"About mid-April, I think." I was used to her bluntness, but I didn't see the point in this interrogation.

"Hmm…" She picked a small calendar off her desk and studied it. "That sounds about right."

Gee, it was warm in here. I grabbed a small catalog from a stack of papers to fan myself. "What are you talking about? I don't understand."

"You're pregnant, my dear. Two months by my calculation."

Wh—what did she say? I shook my head. "No, that's not right. I couldn't be..."

Her face softened with a wizened smile. "Trust me, honey. I've had a half-dozen little ones in my time and two that miscarried. I know the signs and you've got them all."

"But...but Sally..." I sputtered. "It was only one night! Gus and I were married for nine years before I had a pregnancy get this far. And what about the spotting?"

She stood up, patting me lightly on the shoulder. "I don't know why that happens, but sometimes it does. What I *do* know is those circles under your eyes tell me that you need to go home and get some rest. Take care of yourself so that baby is healthy when he arrives."

Stunned, I pressed my palm to my flat stomach. I'd been pregnant once before. How could I have missed the signs? Given the stress I'd gone through with Will's injury and all the events surrounding that time, perhaps I simply hadn't been paying attention. Perhaps I'd deliberately overlooked the obvious because I didn't believe that one stupid mistake could affect me.

I stood up. The swift rise made me dizzy. I sat down again and rubbed my forehead. "I...I need to go to the doctor to make sure."

"That's a good idea, but in the meantime, I want you to take it easy," Sally replied firmly as she poured me a glass of water. She set the pitcher down and held out the glass. "Don't worry. I won't tell anyone. Your life is your business."

I nodded and drank the cool water. "How are your new initiatives coming along?" I asked, changing the subject. "Did you get the new training program up and running yet?"

Sally and I had devised plans for a training and employment program for the residents. One of the problems we encountered with the women who found refuge at the shelter was that they often lacked sufficient skills to find employment to enable them to live independently once they left. They needed practical skills training and a basic wardrobe

26

to conduct a successful job search. I had set up a small apprentice program at my Ford dealership to teach receptionist skills, but that only addressed one woman at a time. Anna's House currently had thirty women in residence.

"I've made inquiries to several companies and the response has been positive," Sally said as we went downstairs to the main floor, "but so far only the telephone company has reached an agreement with us to hire and train our girls."

It was noon and the residents were gathered in the common area for lunch. Their chatter echoed through the wide, two-story room. The aromas of simmering soup and freshly baked bread should have sparked my appetite, but the sharp smell of peas and salt pork suddenly made me nauseous. I swallowed hard, struggling not to embarrass myself by losing my breakfast.

"Speaking of pregnant," Sally whispered, "there is our newest resident." She gestured toward a young woman sitting at a small table by herself staring down at her untouched bowl of soup. The woman wore a plain, light blue chambray shift, the standard uniform that all the women in the shelter were required to wear. She had twisted her fine, mousey-brown hair into a tight bun at her nape. The woman sat with her back toward the crowd, broadcasting that she wanted to be left alone. At the sound of our footsteps, she turned her head slightly and I got a glimpse of her delicate, fine-boned profile. Something about her seemed vaguely familiar.

"We didn't have room for one more, but her situation was so dire we couldn't refuse to take her," Sally whispered. "She's ready to give birth any day now. It's a sad case, really." Sally shook her head. "She lived with her mother, her sister, and her brother-in-law. From what I've been told, the sister's husband repeatedly molested her. When she became pregnant, her mother blamed her and disowned her. The family paid for her to stay with a relative, but now that she's ready to give birth, they've apparently abandoned her altogether."

How sad, I thought, *to be treated so cruelly by one's own family. She's all alone.*

"May I speak with her?" I asked as we stood at the bottom of the stairs.

"You can try, but she's not very friendly. Guess I don't blame her. She's been through a lot." Sally nodded in the woman's direction. "Tread carefully."

"I will," I vowed as I left Sally and made my way toward the woman. I had no idea what to say to her, but her situation had touched my heart.

"Hello," I said as I approached her. "May I sit down?"

"Go away," the woman snapped and turned away from me, facing the wall. "I have nothing to say to anyone here."

That voice...

Something about the bitterness in her reply struck a chord in my mind. I couldn't put my finger on why and it frustrated me. "I don't mean to intrude," I said softly as I approached the opposite side of the table. "I just want you to know that when your time comes, we will make sure you get good care. I understand you've gone through a difficult situation but you're safe here and you're surrounded by people who want to help you."

"How could you *possibly* know what I've gone through?" She twisted in her chair and stared up at me with defiance. "Why do you care?"

The moment our gazes met, I froze, stunned with disbelief. Her pale, angry face and cold eyes wafted through my mind like a ghost from the past. "Louisa..." I gasped as I collapsed into a chair. "Louisa Amundsen."

She used to be Will's secretary, a very smart and efficient worker, but also one of the most difficult people he'd ever had to deal with.

She glared at me. "Char LeDoux..." Her green eyes narrowed. "What are you doing here?"

"I own this building." The moment the words left my lips, I knew I'd made a huge mistake. "I—I mean, the building used to belong to my husband, Gus, but after he died, Mrs. Wentworth's church took possession of it." I was floundering badly, but her presence shocked me so much that I didn't know what to say.

She turned all the way around, revealing her swollen stomach. A derisive snarl curled her lips. "So, you're a rich widow now. Is that why you're here? To gloat over all of us poor souls who are begging for a handout?"

"No, of course not," I said, horrified, but realizing how my presence around the shelter must look to the women here. Faye Delacorte's condescending face flashed through my mind.

No…never, I thought stubbornly. *I will never become like her!*

"I grew up poor," I said gently, wondering if I should tell her that I had been born in Swede Hollow, a small, hidden neighborhood in St. Paul filled with dilapidated shanties that had no electricity, running water, or sewer. "My father was an alcoholic," I continued. "He would abandon us for weeks at a time and I had to work at a hotel after school to support my invalid mother and my little sister. So, I understand what it's like to suffer hardship."

She stared at me for a moment, absorbing my explanation. "How is Will?" she asked suddenly. The guarded look in her eyes indicated she still held deep feelings for him, even though he'd never made any amorous gestures toward her. "Do you still see him?" She looked away. "I suppose you do. He was madly in love with you from the day he met you."

After I left Gus and went into hiding, Will hired me to be his housekeeper, not knowing my real identity. Louisa and I got off on the wrong foot on the first day and our relationship never recovered. After Gus, died, Will and I remained friends, but I lost track of Louisa.

I weighed my words carefully. "We've stayed in contact with each other, yes."

"Please," she said gripping my forearm, digging her nails so deeply into my skin it hurt. "Don't tell him I'm here!" Her eyes filled with desperate tears. "He must never know. I couldn't bear for him to see how I've shamed myself and my family. Promise me you'll keep my secret!"

I gently pried her hand from my arm. "I won't tell him. I promise,

Louisa. I'd never do that to you." I stood up. "It's so good to see you again. I'm truly glad you're here. I'll speak with Sally, and she will see to it that you have everything you need."

"Thank you," Louisa replied in a bland voice, as though a wave of depression had overtaken her. "I need to lie down." Raising herself on shaky legs, she staggered away from the table, leaving me to stare after her with a grieving heart.

"Find the best midwife you can for Louisa," I said to Sally as she escorted me out of the building. "Don't worry about the cost. I'll cover everything. I'd like to buy her a layette as well and have it delivered here before the baby comes."

"She's not keeping the child, you know," Sally replied. "Given the situation, she really has no choice." Sally stood holding the door for me. "We're arranging for the baby to go into foster care right away. I'm sure whoever takes the infant will be grateful for the clothing."

"Consider it done then. Oh, and Sally…" I stopped in the doorway. "Order a uniform for me and have it sent to my home. I'll reimburse you for it."

She frowned. "What do you want that for?"

"I've had a few lessons in humility lately, and I'm taking them to heart." I signaled to Errol to bring the limousine around to the door. In the future, I planned to drive myself to the shelter and wear a uniform to look like everyone else. We hugged goodbye.

"Take care of yourself now," she lectured me. "And get that doctor appointment *now*."

"I will," I replied dutifully as I walked to the curb to wait for the car.

Once Errol seated me inside the limousine and shut the door, I stretched out on the seat and closed my eyes. The last couple of days had been tumultuous, to say the least. As I went over the incidents in my mind, I kept coming back to one thing—that I may be pregnant with Will's child.

I covered my face with my hands, upset at the thought. I wouldn't know for sure until I'd been to the doctor, but if what Sally said proved to be true, what would I say to Will? I thought about how difficult it would be to break the news to my small circle of female friends. Worse yet, I would have to confess what I had done to my fifteen-year-old sister. I'd promised my mother on her deathbed that I'd always be a good role model to Francie. The trouble was, I already found it difficult to reason with Francie most of the time. Would she lose all respect for me when she found out that I'd not only failed her but Mamma too?

My thoughts drifted back to what Sally said about needing to train the women at the shelter to enter the workforce. Anyone with a strong back could do housekeeping and factory work, but it was hard labor and often not in the best of conditions. Providing training opportunities would help the women to obtain better-paying jobs so they could support themselves.

I thought about the training position I'd set up at my Ford dealership. It was a busy shop, and the extra help would always be appreciated, but the opportunity only served one person at a time. If only I had the capacity to help more women! A crazy thought flashed through my mind.

What if I started a new business that catered exclusively to women? I'd establish it in my own name—without using Gus' money. I could get a bank loan to fund it and hire women from the shelter to staff it.

My eyes flew open. Why hadn't I thought of this before? Clinging to the back of the seat, I pulled myself to a sitting position as my mind swirled with possibilities. My fatigue melted away as I began formulating a plan in my head, spurred on by the anticipation of a new adventure. The more I thought about it, the more excited I became. If this new enterprise became successful it would be a good start to establishing my reputation as an honest businesswoman and at the same time, help other women rebuild their lives.

Oh! I couldn't wait to get started!

*   *   *

As soon as I arrived home from Anna's House, my English-born butler met me at the door. Gerard was a staunch, middle-aged man who rarely showed his emotions, but today he frantically relayed a message that Francie had been apprehended by the St. Paul police. I stared at him in shock.

Francie in trouble with the police? What in the world has she done now?

I instructed Errol to start up my Ford. The last thing I wanted was to roll into the police parking lot in a fancy limousine to pick up my delinquent sister. I drove my Ford Model T to my local police precinct and parked. When I walked in, I found Francie sitting at a small table next to the policeman's desk, projecting a resentful frown as she wrote: "I will act like a lady" on a tablet repeatedly.

"Hello, I'm Charlotte LeDoux," I said to the officer wearing a blue uniform. "I'm here to pick up Mary Francis Johnson. I'm her sister and her guardian."

"I'm Officer Mulvaney," said the short, portly man with bushy gray hair. He ripped a sheet from a book of paper tickets and handed it to me. "She was involved in an altercation at the Marshall Street Billiard Room. Since it's her first offense, she's getting off with a warning. Next time, she'll be sitting in juvenile detention for a few hours." He cast a hard look at Francie. "But there had better *not* be a next time, Miss Johnson. Do I make myself clear? Disorderly behavior is unbecoming to a young lady and will not be tolerated!"

Francie looked up. "Yes, officer," she replied demurely, but the moment he looked away, she made a rude hand gesture toward him.

I shot her a fierce look as I cleared my throat and turned toward the policeman, creating a buffer between him and Francie. "Thank you, officer. I'll make sure it doesn't happen again."

He placed a release form on the desk with a pen. "Then she's free to go. Sign here."

I signed the form as Francie ripped the page from her writing pad and crushed the paper into a ball. She pushed her chair away from the table and stood up, tossing the balled-up paper into the nearest wastebasket.

We didn't speak until we were sitting in the Ford with the motor running. I stared at the warning slip, struggling to keep my temper. "You were fighting? In a billiard hall of all places! Francie, what am I going to do with you?"

Francie folded her arms and stuck out her bottom lip as she pouted. Her flaxen hair had been styled in a short, wavy bob with a wide fringe of bangs. She had on my favorite drop earrings and one of my silk blouses, but I let it go for now. I found it so annoying the way my sister helped herself to my things without asking me, but I couldn't seem to stop her from doing it.

"Aren't you going to ask me why?" She glared at me looking hurt. "Or are you just going to side with the coppers and blame me for everything?"

"Why, then," I retorted, losing my patience. "Why did you get into a fight with another girl?"

"It wasn't a girl." She looked away, a smug grin pulling up the corners of her mouth. "I beat the tar out of a guy."

That surprised me. "What? What did he do to you?"

Francie set my handbag on her lap and sat sideways to face me, slinging her leg in a most unladylike manner over the seat. "He said some bad things about my friend, Maureen."

I waited, not sure where this conversation was going. "Who said some bad things?"

"Joe Crockett. He hangs out in the pool hall. That's where all my friends meet on Mondays." She shrugged. "Anyway, Maureen went all the way with him and…um…now she's…"

My breath caught in my throat. "She's going to have a baby?"

Francie blushed. "Um…yeah. She told my friend, Lucy, about it and asked her to keep it a secret but Lucy told everybody else. When Lucy told Joe, he laughed and said some pretty awful things about Maureen. It made me so mad I gave him a bloody nose."

I gasped, horrified. "Oh, my gosh! Francie! That's no way for a girl to behave."

"He deserved it!" she argued in her own defense. "I mean, Char, he's responsible too! It's not fair to place all the blame on Maureen. She isn't a bad person."

"No, it's not," I said as my own predicament lurked in the back of my mind. Regardless of the situation, if I was pregnant, people would look down on me as well. I would be the one who found myself in the middle of a juicy scandal, not the father. No—it wasn't fair, but I couldn't do anything about it. "Still," I said in an admonishing tone, "it doesn't help to go around beating up people you don't agree with."

Francie balled her hands into fists. "I hate the way everyone is treating Maureen! She's going to be expelled from school now and her parents are sending her away. It's not fair!"

I silently agreed with her as we drove the rest of the way home in silence. My staff greeted us at the door, visibly relieved that Francie was back home and unharmed. We entered the hundred-foot reception hall embellished with hand-carved oak woodwork and cut-glass chandeliers. The grand staircase, flanked by thick, Doric columns, led up to a wide landing where it divided into two staircases, one to the right and one to the left, both leading to the second floor. Multiple windows with etched glass spread across the back wall, filling the airy, two-story space with soft, natural light.

I explained the situation to Gerard as Francie made a beeline for the staircase and went up to her room. I had a notion she planned to use the telephone in Gus' study to call her friends to give them the juicy scoop on her little adventure in getting arrested. I wanted to listen at the door but resisted the temptation. I had never been that kind of sister and didn't plan to start now.

Adrienne Devereaux met me in the great hall. The tall, raven-haired beauty was my best friend, my confidant, and ironically, my late husband's ex-mistress. She was a talented performer with a beautiful voice who used to sing at La Coquette every weekend. Back then, she and I had been sworn enemies, but because of our mutual loneliness, we became close after Gus' death. Adrienne occupied the guest cottage on my property. I had hoped that she would eventually move into the main house so we could see each other more often, but she preferred the privacy of her little abode, so I didn't press her about it.

Her dark brows furrowed with worry. "I saw Errol driving your car into the garage, so I knew you'd come home," she said with a French accent. "Is Francie all right?"

"Yes, she's fine," I replied and pulled my yellow cloche hat off my head. My, word got around fast. I gave Adrienne a detailed account of my experience at the police station as we walked into the sunroom to chat.

She sat down on a yellow and white striped chair. "I have some wonderful news, ma chérie! I have finally secured employment. I am a professional singer once again!"

After Adrienne became Gus' mistress, he'd jealously forced her to give up her singing career and her independence. His death had devasted her and left her without any means of support, but her dire situation changed once I welcomed her into my home. For the past few months, she'd been practicing her singing and getting her voice back into shape.

I smiled and clasped her hands. "That's wonderful, Adrienne. I'm so happy for you! What club will you be performing at?"

"That's the most exciting part of my news," she exclaimed. "The Oasis! It's the newest club in St. Paul. You must come to my opening night! I'll secure a special table just for you and Will. Bring your friends along too!"

"Why, yes," I said slowly. "I'd love that."

Adrienne's smile faded. "Char, is something wrong?"

"Absolutely not," I said and forced myself to perk up. "I was just thinking that I need to go shopping and buy a new dress!"

I didn't mean to sound disappointed, but when she mentioned The Oasis, it swiftly reminded me of what a terrible evening I'd had the night Will and I had gone there with Maddie and Peter. What made it worse was finding out Will had kept an important secret from me. That, and his crossing paths with an old flame…

I just hoped my less-than-pleasant experience didn't bode ill for Adrienne's opening night as well.

Time would tell.

Chapter Four

WILL

I arrived at my office at eight o'clock sharp to begin my first full day back in the field as an investigator and learned that Astrid, my secretary, had already scheduled two appointments for me. Both men had insisted on seeing me this morning, so I assumed their issues were urgent. First, I had to pay a visit to Harv Katzenbaum, Char's attorney and a businessman who occasionally contracted my services. For my second interview, Cyrus Adley, the editor of a major newspaper summoned me to his office.

I grabbed my straw fedora from the hat tree and headed out to see what Harv had to say. His office was two floors below mine, so it took less than a minute to arrive by the stairs. Harv's balding, gray-haired brother, Marv Katzenbaum sat hunched over his desk, chomping on chewing gum as he worked on the Katzenbaum accounts. He looked up. The weathered creases in his wizened face deepened when he smiled. "Mornin', Will!" He gestured to a chair next to his desk. "Have a seat. Harv's with a client, but he'll be with you in a few minutes." I removed my hat and sat down. Marv pushed a wooden bowl toward me. "Help yourself."

I peered into the bowl. Marv had a collection of Teaberry, Clove, Beemans, and Black Jack gum. Issues with his throat had forced him to kick the smoking habit and he'd traded it for this one instead. The Black Jack gum looked tempting, but since I had another appointment after this, I didn't want to smell like licorice. I pushed the bowl aside. "I'll settle for a cup of coffee instead."

I drank my coffee while I waited for Harv. I had just finished the last drop when the door to Harv's office opened, and he appeared with his client. He escorted the man out of the office and then helped himself to a cup of coffee from his new electric percolator. I followed him into his office and sat down in a leather armchair.

"We have an interesting situation here," Harv said getting right to the point. He adjusted the rimless glasses on his nose and shoved his gold pocket watch on a thick chain back into the front pocket of his dark vest. "I received a telephone call this morning from Dewey Kingman, the owner of that new speakeasy in the caves on the river, King's Cave Royale. Antoine LeDoux has racked up a gambling debt there to the tune of five thousand dollars and he's claiming that Char is obligated to pay it for him because he's the rightful heir to Gus' estate." Harv grunted as he sipped his coffee. "Obviously, he's desperate for cash to come up with a story like that. LeDoux has seven days to cough up the dough or Dewey will be forced to take *other measures.*"

I gripped the arms of my chair, irritated that Gus' younger brother, Antoine, was trying to make his gambling issues Char's dilemma. My first thought was to do nothing, let the deadline run out, and allow the owner to mete out his own remedy. That, however, wasn't Harv's solution to the problem or he wouldn't have summoned me.

"Look into LeDoux's private affairs," Harv said. "Find out everything you can about his finances, his friends, and his lifestyle. I want to know what other messes he's gotten himself into and whether he's pulling the same stunt with other speakeasies. He may be testing the waters to see how I'll respond before he tries it again."

"I'll get right on it." I stood up and began to leave but stopped at the doorway and looked back. "Does Char know about this?"

"No," Harv replied gruffly, "and I don't see any point in telling her until we have all the facts." To Harv, "all the facts" meant "after" the fact where Char was concerned.

"It's her money and her brother-in-law," I argued. "She needs to know."

"I'll be the judge of when to inform her," he replied crisply. "Knowing Char, she'd take the situation into her own hands and confront LeDoux head-on. We can't risk her tipping our hand until we know the full extent of his situation. Agreed?"

I nodded reluctantly and took my leave. I didn't agree with Harv's decision to withhold information from Char, but I had no choice in the matter. Harv had handled the LeDoux family affairs since back before prohibition when Gus' father operated the family brewery. Char trusted him implicitly. The problem was that she also trusted me completely— and that included being truthful with her. If she found out I'd held this back, it could damage our relationship.

On the other hand, LeDoux was trying to get his hands on her money. I had to find out what her brother-in-law had up his sleeve—and fast.

*   *   *

I arrived ten minutes late for my second appointment.

Oak filing cabinets covered with stacks of newspapers lined the yellowed walls of Cyrus Adley's dingy office. "It's about time you got here, Van Elsberg," he bellowed at me as I hurried through the door and stopped in front of his large oak desk piled high with files. The elderly white-haired newspaper editor sat in his squeaky leather chair, reviewing pages of copy. "Sit down."

"Sorry I'm late, Cyrus," I replied apologetically as I removed my hat. I sat on one of the chairs squeezed in front of his battered desk. A wisp of smoke curled from his cigar in a large glass ashtray. The sharp twang assaulted my nostrils. "What can I do for you?" Cyrus hired me occasionally to verify sensitive information on a story usually concerning someone in the public eye. I wondered what he had for me this time.

He pushed the ashtray aside. Adjusting his round, goggle-style glasses with celluloid frames, he sifted through the material in front of him and pulled out a sheet of paper. "Here," he said as he brushed away cigar ashes. "This is going to be in the gossip column of tomorrow's newspaper."

I took the document and scanned it. The columnist had included a catty piece about Char's unceremonious ejection from the St. Paul Women's Friendship Club Ball and the unladylike outburst she displayed on her way out. From the way she had written it, I could almost hear the columnist snickering over the emotionally charged scene.

I tossed it on the desk. "This portrays not only Char but the ladies of the Friendship Club in a very unflattering light."

Cyrus' bushy brows lifted. "The reporter was there to write a story on the ball. She witnessed the entire incident."

I stared at him, wondering what this meeting was really about. Cyrus wouldn't ask me to his office just to shove the article in my face and gloat. He wanted something from me. Badly.

"All right," I said and let out a tense breath. "How do we settle this?"

"I need a favor." He pulled out another sheet of paper and offered it to me. "This is a sensitive matter that's best investigated by an unnamed third party."

In other words, I thought wryly, *you need an anonymous source to blame it on when the subject accuses you of printing lies.*

I let out a low whistle as I studied the handwritten information on the sheet. Cyrus wanted surveillance conducted on Dwight Wroebel, a prominent "pro-temperance" representative in the Minnesota state legislature who was alleged to be spending his evenings in his favorite speakeasy drinking and gambling—everything he'd railed against in his last campaign for office. Rumor had it that he'd taken a payoff from the gangster who owned the joint and it came with fringe benefits, including beautiful call girls and private, reserved seating in a corner that could be closed off to the public.

"I want names, dates, amounts, photographs—the works," Cyrus said gruffly. "When this story blows, it's gonna create a firestorm." He pulled off his glasses and pointed them at me. "Your reputation makes you just the man for this job. In exchange, I'll scrap the Friendship Club story."

He thought he had me over a barrel by dangling his damaging narrative about the woman I loved in front of my nose, but I knew an opportunity when I saw one.

"I want more than that," I demanded as I laid the paper on the desk, grabbed his pen, and wrote a figure on the blank side. I shoved it toward him. "This is my fee. I'll take cash."

He crossed it out and listed a smaller figure. He pushed it forward. "Take it or leave it."

I sat forward, glaring at him. "Fine, I'll take it, but instead of the lesser fee, I want something else, too. An in-depth article about Char's charity, Anna's House. I want you to give full credit to Char and Sally Wentworth for all the work they've done to help unfortunate women. And I want to read it before you publish it."

He squinted at me. "Okay. A quarter of the cash now. The rest when I get the information."

I stared back. "Half now, half upon receipt of the goods."

He pulled open a desk drawer, retrieved a leather pouch, and counted out the money.

Since I had Harv's case to work on, I planned to make my partner, Daniel Blythe, the lead investigator on this one and I would assist him. My former security guard and a good friend, Daniel had begun working with me about ten months ago. His face wasn't as well-known as mine around town yet and he could slip in and out of public places without attracting attention. Knowing Daniel as I did, he would jump at the chance to get this job.

I just wanted to spare Char from more embarrassment and humiliation.

Chapter Five

CHAR

"For the last time, Mrs. LeDoux," the elderly bank manager said sharply as he tapped the capped end of his fountain pen on the blotter on his desk. "The only way you will qualify for a business loan through this institution is if you produce a guarantor such as your father or your husband."

I didn't know what hurt more, sitting on a hard wooden chair that made my back ache worse than being kicked by a horse or being turned down again for a loan *because I was a woman*. Never mind that I didn't even need the money because my late husband had left me a fortune. I didn't want to use Gus' wealth to start my new business. I wanted to do this on my own.

"We've already been through this," I argued. "I told you—my father doesn't have any assets. I'm a widow. I have complete control of my husband's estate and I have the means to pay the money back. Why should I be required to have another person agree in writing to be responsible for the payment of my debt?"

"Because *that's* the rule." The glare in his eyes silently told me to take it or leave it.

I glared back. "Then I'll go to another bank!"

He gave me a thin smile. "That is your prerogative. Good day, Mrs. LeDoux."

I stood up and marched out of his office, seething with disappointment. This was the third bank I'd approached in downtown St. Paul for a loan to start my new business and the third time I'd been unceremoniously shown the door. Even the institution where I did all my

41

banking had turned me down. I walked through the lobby tired and discouraged but determined to keep trying until I found an entity to lend me the funds I needed. Once outside, I walked down the busy street toward the last place on my list. If that bank denied me, I'd go to Minneapolis tomorrow and try to get a loan from one of the downtown banks there. No matter how many times I suffered defeat, I would not give up.

I crossed the street and went into the bank on the corner. I requested to speak to a loan officer, gave my name to the young man sitting behind the information desk, and took a seat, prepared to wait as long as necessary. After twenty minutes, the young man approached me. "Come with me, please."

Finally, I complained silently to myself as I followed him into a large corner office. The room had a window facing the street, wall-to-wall bookcases, and a heavy, ornate desk situated in the center. I took a seat on one of the two chairs positioned in front of the desk, placed my clutch on the desktop, and waited.

Another ten minutes passed. I sat tapping the toe of my shoe on the floor and trying to ignore the ache in my back when a man walked through the door. "Good afternoon," he said as I anxiously stood to greet him. "I'm—"

As our gazes connected, we both froze.

"Antoine," I said, speaking first. The surprise in my voice left no doubt that I hadn't expected to encounter Gus' younger brother. I wasn't aware he worked in the banking industry. Though I hadn't seen Antoine since Gus' funeral, he hadn't changed much. He mirrored the spitting image of his older brother—tall and muscular with sandy-colored hair and grayish-green eyes. Like Gus, he favored expensive suits. Antoine and I were the same age—twenty-six.

"Hello, Charlotte," Antoine said, his voice deep and smooth. "I trust you've been well." He kept his expression neutral, but I detected a note of caution in his voice as we both took our seats. "What brings you to the bank today? Are you looking to start an account with us?"

"No," I replied and cleared my throat. "Actually, I'm interested in acquiring a business loan for twenty-five hundred dollars." I smiled, encouraged by the fact that he knew me to be a sensible individual. Someone worth taking a chance on...

The moment I mentioned the word "loan" his polished demeanor began to fade. He regarded me warily. "Why do you need a loan? Gus was worth a fortune when he died." His eyes narrowed. "What happened to his money?" The sudden tone of distrust in his voice indicated he suspected I'd blown through it already and needed the loan to survive.

"Gus' estate is intact," I said with a wave of my hand. "In fact, most of it is in a trust for Julien. I let go of the bootlegging piece and La Coquette is closed, but the rest of Gus' financial interests are doing well. I still own his auto dealership, his rental properties, and the soda shops."

The skepticism in Antoine's eyes grew. "Bootlegging and the nightclub were the entities where Gus made the lion's share of his money. Without them...are you sure you want the loan for a *business*?"

I resented being treated like a beggar with my hand out. "Yes, of course, I do."

He placed his palms on his desk and leaned forward. "Why? If what you say is true, you don't need it."

I stood up and placed *my* palms on the desk, leaning toward him. "I don't want to use Gus' money. This is something I want to do *all* on my own."

His face hardened. "Why should I believe you?"

I recoiled, shocked by his sudden antagonism toward me. "Because it's the truth!"

He sat back in his chair. "Go to the bank that holds your money. They'll lend it to you." He sounded cold, impersonal. The same attitude I'd been subjected to all day.

"I've already been there," I replied, shaking my head. "They turned me down."

My answer drew a smug smile from him in response. "I see."

"No, you don't! They said I had to have a guarantor—specifically my father or my husband—because they don't give loans to women. Which is ridiculous!" I let out an exasperated sigh. "My father has no assets to use for collateral and my husband is dead. That puts me back where I started."

He stood up and walked to the door, signaling to me that our discussion had ended. "We have the same policy."

I countered with a sardonic laugh. "You require a guarantor?"

No," he replied smoothly. "We don't give loans to women."

My next breath came out in a huff. This had been such a waste of time. *Again.* Only this time I'd been given the bum's rush by someone I knew. I grabbed my handbag and charged toward the door.

"Then again," he said with a tantalizing lilt in his voice, "perhaps I can offer you an alternative path."

I stopped and turned toward him. I didn't believe him or trust him, but I asked anyway. "What are you talking about?"

His gaze held mine. "For ten thousand dollars, I'll set you up with an open line of credit. I'll set the limit as high as you want."

I wanted to slap him. "That's a bribe! How dare you suggest I grease your palm to give me a loan! That would have been Gus' way, but it's not mine."

His eyes narrowed. "Do you want the money or not? Think about it. When you change your fickle mind, as I'm sure you will if you want the loan bad enough, you'll be back."

"I'll never be that desperate. Good day, Antoine." Turning away from him, I held my head high and walked out.

*   *   *

I left my car inside the carriage porch for Errol to park in the garage and hurried into the house, anxious to spend time with little Julien before he took his afternoon nap. I needed one too! My futile attempts to convince a bank to give me a business loan had left me tired and frustrated. Dealing with Antoine had made me so *mad* that I'd used up every bit of energy I had left.

Gerard opened the door and greeted me with his customary bow. "You have a telephone call, My Lady."

I had been expecting Sally to ring me and let me know when the layette arrived. I had ordered it right away from a sewing circle at her church. The ladies indicated it would take a couple of days to put it together, but they would deliver it to the shelter as soon as they finished.

I handed him my cloche hat. "Thank you, Gerard."

Most people didn't thank their servants or even acknowledge their existence, but I always treated my staff in the same manner I expected to be treated. I would never forget that I had grown up in a humble shanty town housing some of the poorest people in St. Paul and had been taunted in school by my classmates because of it. My late mother had taught me to live by the Golden Rule of "Do unto others as you would have them do unto you."

I hurried through the library and into the den, a small, but ornate room that I used for my office, and picked up the candlestick telephone. "Hello," I said breathlessly.

"The baby has arrived," Sally announced in a hoarse voice tinged with weariness. She sounded like she'd been up all night. "About an hour ago."

The large clock on the wall indicated it was nearly one o'clock. I sat on the edge of the desk, absorbing the news. "How are Louisa and her little one?"

Sally sighed. "She struggled all night in labor, but mother and baby are doing well. She had a girl."

Hearing that Louisa *struggled* evoked deep sadness in me. A lump formed in my throat, and I swallowed hard, wishing I could have been by her side to hold her hand during the contractions. I knew her well enough, though, to know that she would have requested it the day we met at the shelter if she had wanted me there.

I cleared my throat. "What did she name the child?"

"She didn't," Sally stated flatly. "That's for the adoptive parents to decide. She didn't even want to see the little one after it was born."

I understood why Louisa didn't want to see the baby. Holding the little girl would have made it much more difficult to part with her.

"It's for the best," Sally offered in a caring tone as if reading my thoughts. "It's tragic, I know, but she had no way to provide for the child and no prospects for a husband, so allowing the little girl to be adopted was the best thing Louisa could do for her. She really had no alternative."

I closed my eyes, wishing there was some way Louisa could keep her child. "When will I be able to see her?"

"Give her a few days to gain her strength back," Sally replied. "Having a baby takes a toll on a woman, both physically and mentally. She's been through a lot and needs time to adjust to the situation. The women here have been very supportive of her. They'll help her get through this."

I suddenly needed to hold my own child. I said goodbye to Sally and went upstairs to the nursery. Julien sat on the floor, playing with a rattle. He laughed when he saw me and threw down the jingling toy then he began to crawl toward me. A stream of drool dripped from his mouth and soaked the front of his bib. At eight months old, he had four teeth—two on the top and two on the bottom. He chewed on everything he could grab.

"Come to Mamma," I cooed as I walked into the room and gathered him into my arms. "My goodness, but you're growing fast. You're heavier every time I pick you up." I sat on the small sofa and placed him on my lap. His sandy hair had begun to curl around his ears and his eyes were turning grayish-green, just like his daddy's.

Gretchen, my eighteen-year-old nanny, began to pick up his toys. She was petite, like me, and had thick red hair, but the color was natural, not a product of the brassy dyes and rinses a person could buy at the drugstore. "He just had lunch a little while ago and had his diaper changed," she informed me. "He's ready for his nap."

I spent a while playing with him until he fell asleep on my lap. I placed him in his bed, covering him with a thin blanket. He looked so peaceful and sweet that my heart swelled with love for my little man. I kissed the soft curls covering his temple and left the nursery, heading for my room to take a much-needed nap myself.

But as I lay on my bed in the quiet of my bedroom, I couldn't relax much less sleep. Too many thoughts plagued my mind. Four banks—including the one holding my money—turned me down for a business loan today. Would I encounter the same resistance from Minneapolis banks as well? It was a discouraging thought, to say the least. The loan officers who turned me down were all men and though they didn't say so, they all believed my idea of starting a business that catered specifically to women was a waste of time.

I thought about that as I stared at the ceiling. Women needed services as much as men did so why was it so difficult to convince someone to lend me the money? And what kind of business did I want to establish? A dressmaking shop or an appliance store? A florist shop? I didn't know a thing about any of those businesses or where to look for information. Suddenly, the prospect of launching out into the unknown—by myself—became overwhelming. I needed to give the idea more thought. I rose from my bed and headed to Gus' study to grab a pen and paper to make a list.

Though Gus had been dead a year, I still referred to the second-floor study as his room because everything in it had belonged to him when he was alive, and I had put off redecorating it. Originally built as a bedroom, Gus had taken it over as soon as we moved into the house. I always found it odd that he chose that room as his office, but a couple of months ago, I found out why.

The room had a large mahogany desk positioned in the center with a candlestick telephone, brown leather upholstered chairs, and one solid wall of bookcases. Nothing spectacular or out of the ordinary there. No—it was the closet that had initially caught my eye causing me to further investigate. The walls in the long, walk-in closet contained ornately carved wainscoting like in the dining room downstairs, and, like the dining room, buried deep in the wood paneling was a small metal medallion about the size of a shirt button. It contained a hidden latch that opened the up wall—to a secret room.

In the dining room, the closet-sized space served as a silver vault for serving pieces, candlesticks, and flatware. In the upstairs bedroom, however, the closet wall opened to a vault-like door that sealed off an eight-foot-by-ten-foot room filled with Gus' greatest secrets.

Secrets he'd kept even from me.

Locking the study door, I went straight to the closet and parted the thick collection of hanging coats that concealed the wall. Leaning down, I found the metal button. It clicked and the wall popped open, revealing a heavy metal door. I dialed the combination, opened the door, and walked in, turning on the table lamp in the inky black, windowless chamber.

The simply furnished room held a small burgundy sofa, a drum table with a Tiffany lamp, a large steamer trunk, and a coffee table positioned in front of the sofa. A thick oriental rug covered the floor to absorb footfalls. Guns of every size and brand hung on the outside wall. Boxes of ammunition were stacked on a long, waist-high bookshelf on the floor that stretched from corner to corner. I didn't realize until I'd discovered this room that this was where Gus went to mull over his business decisions and strategize his next steps. I knew it for certain because I'd found a thick journal stored with his ledgers in the bookcase where he'd written down all of his thoughts, ideas, and lists of tasks. Now that I'd discovered his hideaway, I often came here myself when I needed to think something through.

This room was also where Gus hid the unspent cash he'd amassed from bootlegging. The wide coffee table didn't have legs. Instead, the inlaid walnut tabletop sat upon a solid two-foot-high block of bundled currency—counted, banded, and tightly stacked. The steamer trunk contained the same thing, and it was so full the heavy cover couldn't shut correctly. The Feds could never prove he'd laundered money through his businesses, and now I knew why. This cash belonged to me now, and I was certain no one knew about it but me. I had no idea how much I had stored in this room, but I didn't have any plans to count it or spend it—or tell anyone about it. Eventually, I'd use it for something, but for the time being, Gus' secret was safe right here.

I relaxed on the sofa with the notepad in my hands. Ten minutes later, the pad was still blank. I couldn't decide what kind of business I wanted to create. I only knew I wanted it to be something that served women. What service or product did women need that I could provide? One by one, as ideas formulated in my mind, I dismissed them as too impractical, too low-paying, or too complicated. Bored and frustrated, I picked at a little bit of leftover hand moisturizer from under my thumbnail. It smelled like gardenia, my favorite fragrance.

I could try to partner with the woman who makes this cream and get it into local stores, I thought as I worked it into my hand.

I chuckled at the silliness of the idea. How could women in the shelter make a living by mixing batches of hand cream? Maybe if a person rented a stall at a local market...

"What if I had a shop that sold all kinds of creams," I said thinking aloud. "Or perfumes or makeup?" I stared at the guns hanging on the wall, but my eyes didn't see them. My mind was focused instead on a vacant storefront I'd seen at the intersection of Selby Avenue and Dale Street, close to Will's house. What if I had a shop that specialized in cosmetics? Everything a woman could want all in one place. *A business for women and run by women...*

I stood up. "That's it! That's what I'm going to do."

I sighed and sat back down. I had the concept all figured out, but I still didn't have the money. Ironically, I sat in a room literally filled with cash, but I couldn't borrow a dollar from a bank. "I don't care if I have to open up a lemonade stand on the corner," I mumbled stubbornly to myself. "I'm going to get the money—somehow—and it won't be tainted by Gus!"

Given the way things stood, however, that lemonade stand appeared to be my only option.

Chapter Six

WILL

On the night of Adrienne Devereaux's opening performance at The Oasis, I arrived at Char's house hoping we could have a frank discussion about our relationship on the way to the nightclub. For the past week, I'd been busy gathering information on Antoine LeDoux while also working on an unrelated infidelity case. Regardless of my schedule, I'd made a point to call Char on the telephone every day to keep in touch. I asked her to attend the opening event with me and she agreed, but to my disappointment, the passage of time hadn't cooled the tension that developed between us the night she found out I'd kept my trust fund a secret. If anything, it had created an awkwardness that only made things worse.

Errol had parked Char's limousine inside the carriage porch. He lounged against the front fender smoking a cigarette, waiting for us to board. I pulled my car into a spot in the back of the house, grabbed a small box off the seat, and walked to the front door. I preferred to ride to the event in the limousine because it provided more security than my rag-top Ford and by not driving, I could focus my full attention on making sure Char was safe. Since she hadn't hired a team of bodyguards yet, I took it upon myself to provide security for her when she went out at night.

She met me at the front door, emerging down the steps in a sparkling silver gown, a matching cloche hat, and plenty of glittering diamonds. Her smiling face radiated with a glow I'd never noticed before. I couldn't help staring at her, taking in how beautiful she looked tonight. I greeted her with a kiss.

We didn't speak until we were inside the car and Errol had shut the door. The spacious cabin, covered in black leather and gold velvet, had a generous amount of legroom and a built-in beverage compartment. A glass partition separated us from the driver.

Char sat back and covered her mouth with both hands, overtaken by a huge yawn.

I made a mental note to myself to bring her home early.

"You look wonderful tonight," I said softly and held out the box. "This is for you."

The limousine began to slowly roll down the driveway.

She thanked me with a smile and accepted the gift—an orchid corsage. I carefully pinned it to the shoulder of her dress. "How are you feeling?"

"I didn't get a chance to take a nap today," she replied and yawned again. "I've been busy working on something." She looked away. "I'm starting a new business."

Our temporary truce suddenly shattered.

"Another business? Why?" I shot back, irritated. "You already have too many businesses to keep track of now. "You don't want Gus overshadowing your life, but you still think like him."

She let out a huff. "I knew you'd say that. This is different."

"How?"

"I'm going to rent a space on Selby Avenue and open a cosmetics shop. Most of the employees will be women from Anna's House. It's a way to help them learn new skills and one day start their own businesses or manage someone else's."

I silently fumed. *Calm down,* I told myself. *You're not going to get anywhere by upsetting her.* "What about Julien? You're always telling me you don't spend enough time with him. Won't this new business make that problem even worse?"

"I realize that my son comes first," she snapped. "The shop is only in the planning stages. It won't progress beyond that until I secure the funds and hire a manager to help me." She yawned again. "I have plenty of other things to keep me busy now."

"Your main priority should be hiring a security team," I argued, suddenly unable to keep my attitude under control. "You agreed over two months ago to get the process started and yet here you are, finding one thing after another to keep you from taking care of the most pressing *business* you have."

"I don't want to argue with you," she said and turned toward the window. "This is supposed to be a fun night out."

We'd barely been in each other's company for five minutes and we were already quarreling. We could tell Errol to turn the car around and take us back home or we could settle things now.

"You're right." I slid forward and took her hands in mine. "We shouldn't argue. Tonight is about Adrienne, not us. Let's put our differences aside and enjoy this evening, all right?"

She moved close and snuggled under my arm, resting her cheek against my chest as she let out a deep sigh. "Yes, I'd like that."

At the club, the host led us to a large table in a premium spot situated at the edge of the dance floor and very close to the stage. Maddie and Peter were already seated with my partner, Daniel, drinking their special iced tea and snacking on a cheese plate as they waited for us to join them. I guided Char through the heavy, wall-to-wall crowd with my palm on the small of her back and my gaze working the room. A lot of powerful people had gathered here to watch Adrienne Devereaux perform tonight—politicians, coppers, leaders of the underworld, and the idle rich—many of whom I knew. A few of whom I didn't. In either case, I didn't trust most of them.

We greeted everyone—me with handshakes and Char with hugs. I seated Char and took the empty chair on her right, sitting close to Daniel. He looked rather dapper tonight in a new dark suit. He'd had his coppery hair and thick mustache trimmed for the occasion.

The vacant chair between Daniel and me had been specially designated for Adrienne to occupy during intermission. A year ago, she and Daniel barely knew each other. Now they were sweethearts and he escorted her everywhere. Needless to say, he planned to spend the night making sure no one got "overly friendly" with her.

He leaned toward me. "This crowd makes me nervous. There are too many people here." He surreptitiously cased the joint, cataloging the exits. "Anything happens tonight, I'll get Adrienne and meet you outside the back stage entrance."

I nodded, not surprised by his precautionary measure. Whether we were working a case or simply out for an evening of pleasure, in a place like this, we always had a backup plan.

"I see our favorite politician is here tonight with his latest squeeze," I whispered. "Did you get good pictures of them together for Cyrus?"

Daniel patted his pocket. "Yep. Got the finished roll with me. Got 'em arriving and kissing before they got out of the car. He walked her into the joint with his hand resting down low on her backside."

I glanced around to see if I could locate him. To my irritation, Eva Baumann and her friends occupied the table to my right. Antoine LeDoux and his party sat at the table to my left. I wasn't sure if Char had noticed him yet, but the annoyed look in her eyes indicated that she had.

Something about her reaction set me on edge. "What's wrong," I murmured in her ear. "You look upset."

Her gaze rose to meet mine. "Gus' brother, Antoine is sitting at the table next to us. The last time he and I spoke, we had a difference of opinion."

"Is that so?" From the unhappy tone of her voice, I gathered it wasn't a friendly, agree-to-disagree discourse. I gazed over the top of her head and perused Gus' younger brother. Antoine noticed me studying him and responded with a bold stare of his own. His "tough guy" attitude didn't impress me in the least. "What was it about?" I asked Char.

"He's a loan officer at a bank downtown," Char said, pulling my attention away from Antoine. "Of all the places I approached for a business loan, he was the only person who agreed to give me the money, but it came with a catch." She stared at me. "A ten-thousand-dollar bribe for an open line of credit. I could decide the limit."

Antoine tried to bribe Char? I had the urge to get up and confront him about it with my fists. Instead, I drummed my fingers on the table, giving myself a moment to cool my temper. "What did you say to that?"

She folded her arms. "I told him what he could do with his offer and then I walked out!"

We had ninety minutes to spare before the show began. We enjoyed a leisurely dinner with lively conversation and plenty of drinks to go around. I enjoyed the revelry but kept track of the people around me, particularly Antoine LeDoux. As I observed him, I didn't care for the way his eyes narrowed whenever his attention focused on Char. I didn't have any idea what he was thinking, but I intended to find out.

My chance came a few minutes before the show was about to begin.

"Ladies and gentlemen," a loud, deep voice echoed, "the show will begin in ten minutes."

Antoine rose from his table and wove his way across the room. I guessed where he was going and excused myself to follow him, ending up in a line outside the door to the men's room. With all the people coming and going from the lavatories, I didn't have to fake an opportunity to bump into him. The first rotund fella that squeezed his way out of the doorway practically crashed into us trying to avoid the traffic milling about the narrow hallway.

"Excuse me," I said to Antoine.

"Yeah, sure," he murmured, turning his back to me.

"Aren't you sitting at the table next to me?" I asked jovially.

He turned around again, eyeing me suspiciously.

I smiled and stuck my hand out. "Will Van Elsberg."

He reluctantly shook my hand. "Antoine LeDoux." He gave me a curious look. "You're a private investigator. I've heard of you."

"I've heard of you as well. You're related to Gus," I said boldly, "and Char."

His eyes hardened like flint. "She uses his name, but I don't consider her good enough to be a member of my family. Her or her *brat*."

"You don't say." My muscles tensed. I stared into his cold grayish-green eyes. "Gus did. When she disappeared after the raid on La Coquette, he was desperate to find her. He hired me to track her down."

A muscle in Antoine's jaw twitched. "Did he also tell you she was a cheap doxy from that slum over by Phalen Creek called Swede Hollow? She knew his weakness for women, and she tricked him into marrying her."

I shook my head. "Gus was nobody's fool. He knew what he was getting into."

Antoine countered with a wry laugh. "Gus was a sucker for every pretty face with a sob story. He thought he was her protector, but he needed protection from her greedy little hands on his money. Now that he's dead, she's going through it like water through a sieve. Money that rightfully should be mine!"

My expression didn't change but my hand automatically tightened into a fist. I wanted to slam this guy in the gut for spreading lies about the woman I loved. Instead, the trained investigator in me purposely kept my voice even to come across as mildly curious. "What makes you say that?"

His face darkened. "She was married to him for nine years and never gave him a kid. Nine years! Then suddenly, she disappears and," he waved his hand, "boom! She's in the family way." He sniffed arrogantly. "It's not his."

The line began to move, ending our conversation, but on the way out of the men's room, I saw him again and he stuck his finger in my face. "Tell Char for me that the house she lives in is rightfully *mine*. One day soon, I'm going to be the one living in it!"

Knowing I would lose my temper if I opened my mouth, I didn't answer him. Instead, I turned and walked away with my heart pounding in my ears and my hands jammed in my pockets. I went back to my table and sat down just as the lights dimmed.

A hush fell over the crowd. A spotlight shined a bright column of light on the stage as a drumroll began Adrienne's introduction.

"Ladies and gentlemen," a deep voice boomed across the room, "please take your seats. It's time for the show to begin. Let's give a warm welcome to the one and only, Adrienne Devereaux!"

Thundering applause greeted Adrienne as a small orchestra began to play. She swept across the stage, a tall, raven-haired beauty in a red, floor-length silk gown embellished with hundreds of sequins that sparkled under the lights. Diamonds glittered from her earlobes and around her neck. A diamond bracelet dangled from her wrist, a congratulatory gift from Daniel. When Adrienne began to sing, her deep, smoky voice mesmerized the audience. No one got up to dance. Everyone sat riveted to their seats, taking in the presence of one of the most enthralling performers in the Twin Cities.

I slid my hand over Char's and squeezed it lovingly. She looked into my eyes and smiled. All was well between us. For now, anyway.

After a few songs, Adrienne urged everyone to get up and dance when the orchestra began to play "Reaching for the Moon," a popular tune this year. I stood and offered Char my hand, making a slight bow. "May I have this dance?"

Smiling, she stood up, holding her beaded clutch purse. We slowly walked hand in hand into the crowd on the dance floor, her silver dress shimmering as she moved. The platinum and diamond Riviere necklace around her neck twinkled in the light. I placed the flat of my right hand just below her tiny waist on the hollow of her back. My left hand encircled hers as our fingers entwined. We began to sway under the starlit ceiling. Pulling her close, I buried my nose in the crown of her hair and inhaled the sweet scent of her floral shampoo, suddenly realizing why Gus had become so obsessed with her. Why he had been so frantic to find her when she left him without a trace. He'd lost part of himself to her…

For such a petite woman, she was far from delicate; she possessed the spunk and vitality of a dozen women. Feminine yet vivacious and strong-willed. Fiercely loyal. When I gazed into her face, the spark in her wide, green eyes lit up my world and set my heart on fire.

Oh, how I loved this woman.

I angled my head and kissed her deeply, not caring that we were on public display. "I love you so much," I murmured in her ear.

She gazed up at me through thick lashes. A loving smile spread across her lips as her eyes met mine, shining with happiness. "I love you too, Will. So much. I wish things could always be like this between us."

"They can, darling. I promise I'll always be there for you—"

"Attention, everybody," Adrienne said, laughing. "We're going to liven things up. On the count of three, switch partners with the couple on your right. One, two, three..."

Suddenly, someone pulled Char away from me and I found myself thrust into the arms of Eva Baumann.

*   *   *

Wearing an ice-blue dress that clung to her curves so tightly it looked like she'd been poured into it, Eva slid into my arms with a beguiling smile curving her bright red lips. "C'mon, Will, let's kick up some dust!"

I pulled away. "Let's not." I scanned the area for Char, but I couldn't find her in the colorful sea of bodies spinning in time to the music.

Long, slender fingers gripped my jaw, turning my head. "I don't bite, darling," Eva said woundedly, pursing her cupid's bow lips into an exaggerated pout. "All I want is a chance to talk to you without your bootlegging queen butting in. Is that so terrible?"

I was so distracted trying to locate Char, I didn't pay much attention to Eva pulling my arms around her and coaxing me to dance by swaying to the music. "No, it's not terrible," I said irascibly as I danced with her, "but it's not my idea of fun, either."

Anxious to get rid of this traitorous dame, I grabbed her by the arms, confronting her nose to nose. "So, you want to talk? Let's get right to the point, then, shall we? What do you want, Eva? To pick up where we left off?" I answered my own question with a harsh laugh. "If you think you can simply *waltz* back into my life and expect me to kiss and make up, forget it. Baby, that train left the station a long time ago."

She slid her arms around my neck, earnestly engaging me by batting the mascara-laden lashes of her kohl-lined eyes. "You know it wasn't my fault, Will. Father pressured me to break our engagement when he found out you weren't coming into your inheritance for a long time." She tried to look upset by furrowing her finely penciled brows, but I wasn't buying it. "It disappointed him when you refused to go to law school," she continued. "He wanted more for me than you could offer at the time, so he forced me to find someone who had a better future ahead of him." She sniffled. "I swear, it wasn't what I wanted for myself."

And here comes the part where she tells me she still loves me, I thought cynically, trying hard not to laugh again. I didn't believe a single word of her sob story. "What happened to your sure thing? Why didn't the better prospect work out?"

She wiped a non-existent tear from her eye. "It didn't work out because I've never gotten over you, Will. In the end, I couldn't marry someone I didn't love."

Suppressing an urge to applaud her cheesy attempt at melodrama, I gently, but firmly pulled her arms from my neck. "Yeah, well I've gotten over you and I'm in love with someone else now, so let's just leave things as they are."

"Are you sure it's love?" She placed a hand on my chest. "Snagging a skirt who is richer than sin is obviously quite a feather in your cap, but now that you've come into your own inheritance, you don't need hers."

I laughed at the absurdity of her reasoning. "The moment I fell in love with Char, I had no idea who she was or if she had a dime to her name. Our relationship has nothing to do with her dough."

"Well, it has nothing to do with good breeding either," Eva said arrogantly. "Or a respectable family name. Your father must be spinning in his grave over what you're doing with your life."

"I don't doubt it," I replied cynically. "Funny thing is, getting involved with you was the only decision I made that earned his approval. He figured I'd go to law school to save my engagement. He misjudged me and so did you."

"But—Will, we were so good together. I know things could be as great between us again," she argued. "If you'd just give us another chance—"

Why, I thought, resisting the urge to swear, *because I've got the old man's money now, and that somehow makes me more deserving of you?*

She tried to put her arms around me again, but I stepped back, slipping out of her reach. "Goodnight, Eva, and good luck. I hope you eventually find someone Daddy approves of."

She folded her arms, frowning at me as though she'd been the one who'd gotten jilted. "I'm not giving up on you, Will! I'll find a way to get you back."

Fed up with her theatrics, I spun away and walked through the crowd to see if Char had returned to our table.

To my dismay, her chair was empty.

Chapter Seven

CHAR

"On the count of three, switch partners with the couple on your right. One, two, three…"

Raucous cheers erupted around me as Adrienne's announcement energized everyone in the cavernous room. I had no desire to switch partners, but before I knew what had happened, someone pulled me away from Will and spun me around. I found myself captured in the arms of a man of medium height and dark hair. Leon Goldman was one of the most powerful men in the St. Paul underworld.

"Good evening, Charlotte," Leon said. His smooth, polished voice emanated an aura of confidence. "Care to dance?"

Since he already had one hand on my waist and the other gripping my fingers, I surmised I didn't have much choice. I gazed at his rounded, middle-aged face and decided to make the best of a bad situation. I smiled, hoping this dance didn't last long. "Why, I'd love to, Leon," I replied with an ironic twist in my voice.

He responded with a generous smile and whirled me around the dance floor.

Leon was a businessman involved in bootlegging, gambling, and a variety of lucrative illegal activities, earning him the reputation of a prominent "wheeler-dealer" in St. Paul. He also had quite a reputation as a womanizer, even though he had a wife and a couple of adorable kids. He and my late husband had been fierce enemies, but after Gus' death, Leon and I had come to a truce of sorts, and surprisingly, we'd developed a mutual degree of respect for one another.

"Are you enjoying yourself tonight?" he asked, keeping in perfect step with the music. "It can't be easy sitting between LeDoux's brother and Van Elsberg's ex-fiancée. The looks they've been giving you all evening are quite telling. Be careful, Charlotte. They both harbor a grudge against you."

His statement surprised me. "How do you know that?"

"I know everything that goes on in this town." He gave my hand a friendly tug. "Like the fact that you've become close friends with Adrienne Devereaux. You've taken her in, treating her like family."

I stared up at him, offended that he chose to make my personal business public. "So what if I have? Even though she had an affair with Gus, she's not the villain that everyone makes her out to be. Gus used her and destroyed her career. His death left her destitute. I gave her a place to stay to make up for the damage he caused. We have a lot in common—besides Gus, that is."

Leon's coffee-colored eyes softened, and I almost detected a heart beating underneath his tailored suit. "You're a good woman, Charlotte. Gus would be proud of you." He shook his head. "I regret that he found you first. You and I would have made a formidable team."

I laughed. "I don't think so, Leon. I'm a modern woman. My views and yours definitely run counter to each other."

His thick dark brows furrowed. "What does your detective think of your *views*? He's been ill at ease over something all evening."

Leon's remark pierced my heart. I was the cause of Will's distress. "He's unhappy because I've been putting plans together to start a new business," I said truthfully. That wasn't the only cause of the strife between us, but I wasn't about to divulge anything else. "I'm going to open a shop that caters to women and staff it with the residents at Anna's House."

"Of course, you are," Leon replied, chuckling as though opening a shop for women was exactly the sort of business that he expected of me. "How much money is this little adventure going to set you back?"

I sighed. "Well, that's the only thing presently holding up my plans. I need twenty-five hundred dollars and I can't find a bank to loan me the money."

He stopped dancing, staring at me in disbelief. "Don't you have the money to fund it yourself?"

"Yes, but that's not the point, Leon," I argued. "I don't want to use Gus' money—"

"It's your money now," he declared, interrupting me as we began dancing again.

"Technically, it is," I said stubbornly, "but I don't want Gus' help. I want to do this the right way and that means obtaining the financing myself."

He nodded, impressed with my ambition. "Want me to pull some strings for you? I can make a few inquiries, talk to a few people."

I shook my head, horrified at the thought. First, Antoine had the gall to hit me up for a bribe and now a powerful gangster wanted to twist some arms for me among his banking associates to give me the red-carpet treatment. Their interference would blacken my reputation even more than it was now! "Thanks for the offer, but no. I need to do this *on my own*."

"Ask Van Elsberg for a loan," he said, twirling me under his arm. "I hear he's rollin' in the dough now."

Leon was right, but I couldn't ask Will. I couldn't use my relationship with him to put him on the spot for a loan. It didn't seem right.

The music ended. Placing his hand on the small of my back, Leon escorted me back to Will.

"Watch yourself around that LeDoux kid," Leon said as he cast a sideways glance toward Antoine. He left the sentence hanging, but I knew he meant the words as a serious warning. He knew something about Antoine that I didn't and that bothered me. Unfortunately, with so many people around, this wasn't the best time to ask about it.

When we reached the table, Leon and Will made eye contact but didn't speak. Leon's eyes narrowed in a feral stare as he signaled to Will with a jerk of his head in Antoine's direction. Will responded with a slight nod.

"Thank you for the dance," Leon whispered politely in my ear as he pulled out my chair. "You ever need my help, Char, just ask. Anytime, anywhere, I'll be there."

Sure, with a few intimate strings attached...

I sat down, a tad out of breath, and grabbed my water glass. Something was going on right under my nose and no one had bothered to let me in on it. Why?

*   *   *

I sipped on cool water to clear my head and gather my strength. Fatigue had begun to seep into my limbs, but I wasn't ready to go home yet and snuggle in the comfort of my bed. Adrienne promised to join us during intermission, and I didn't want to miss her.

Daniel and Peter were deep in conversation about an automobile Peter wanted to buy, leaving Maddie to sip on her drink in boredom. She wore a purple satin dress tonight with a black fringed hemline. Though she favored red, I thought the purple hue looked terrific on her.

"How are your plans for Anna's House proceeding?" she asked, sounding only half interested.

"Quite well," I replied enthusiastically. "We're setting up a program to help the women get training for jobs so they can support themselves when they're ready to venture out on their own."

"That's nice," she said absent-mindedly. "You're so good at organizing things."

"Not always," I said with a sigh and told her I couldn't raise the capital for my project. "I need at least twenty-five hundred to buy the equipment and the stock and set aside some money for payroll. I want to have a large display of cosmetics on hand for customers."

She frowned. "Cosmetics? What kind of business are you talking about?"

"A salon," I said slowly, "where women can buy any kind of makeup or cream on the market, including a huge line of perfumes.

Eventually, I'd like to add hair products like henna rinses and waving lotion. Scarves and hair combs."

Her eyes grew wide. "Here? In St. Paul? Oh, my gosh, I love that idea! I'll be your best customer!" She began to press me for details, asking about specific brands and making suggestions. The longer we discussed it, the more animated she became, telling me how exciting the idea of a cosmetics salon sounded to her.

"What a wonderful idea! It's going to be a terrific success. I want to be involved, Char. Whatever amount you need, I can get the money— the entire sum—if you'll make me a partner," she declared suddenly, making a frame with her hands. "Madeline's Salon... it sounds perfect, don't you think?"

I opened my mouth to speak, but nothing came out. How did she go from being my best customer to co-owner of the business?

"Come on, Char," Maddie said as she reached across the table and placed her hand upon mine, "let's do this together! It's so much more fun when you have a partner." Her eyes shined wistfully. "I need an adventure like this to liven up my life. It's so dull!"

Her words made me blink with confusion. Madeline Van Elsberg, the flapper party queen of St. Paul describing her life as *dull*? What was this world coming to? But then, she probably knew more about the popular brands of cosmetics than I did. If she could get the money from her trust fund and help put it together, I would be able to put my plans in motion immediately.

"All right," I said, taking her seriously. "Partners, then, fifty-fifty. Deal?"

A red-lipped smile spread across her beautiful face. She held out her hand to shake. "Deal!"

We shook hands and laughed. We had become business partners. Take that, Antoine LeDoux and all the other loan officers who'd looked down their noses at me.

Look out world, I thought triumphantly, *Charlotte LeDoux is on the move!*

*   *   *

Adrienne joined us for a brief period during the intermission. With Daniel by her side, she hugged each one of us, but I barely had time to speak to her before a crowd of adoring fans clustered around our table.

Adrienne approached me first and hugged me. "Thank you for the beautiful roses, Char!" she whispered in my ear. I'd sent a congratulatory bouquet to her dressing room a couple of hours before her performance.

I hugged her back. "I'm so happy for you, Adrienne. I wanted your first night to be special."

"Thank you for all you've done for me," she replied sincerely. "If it weren't for you, I wouldn't be singing here tonight. I owe you so much."

"There's no need to thank me," I said, embarrassed by her frankness. "You got the job because you're a natural entertainer with a very beautiful voice."

She pulled away. "Now that I have a steady income, I plan to rent my own place. I'll always be grateful that you took me in when I needed it so badly, but now that I'm able to support myself, it's time to move out on my own."

I should have been exceedingly happy for her, but the thought of Adrienne vacating the cottage behind my house and moving away flooded my heart with loneliness. She was the closest thing I had to a truly close friend; someone who understood me and cared about me because we'd been through so much together. Whenever I needed someone to confide in, she always listened and gave me her opinion, never judging me.

I struggled to blink back tears as overwhelming sadness gripped my soul. "I'll miss you."

"*Mon ami*, please don't be sad," she said, becoming concerned at my reaction. "We'll always be good friends, n'est pas? You promised to teach me to drive a car, remember? I can't wait! We have many good times ahead of us."

I nodded in agreement but didn't get the chance to reply before the swelling mass of well-wishers encircled her, cutting me off.

Her news had blindsided me. I suddenly felt so alone.

* * *

I didn't have much time to dwell on it, however. The crowd surged around our table to get up close to Adrienne. Some people wanted her autograph. Others had brought their Kodak Brownie cameras to pose for a picture with her. The chaos left me overwhelmed, but at the same time, I couldn't have been happier for her.

Despite the commotion distracting me, I sensed someone approaching me from behind, and as the fine hairs on my neck raised, I knew instinctively it wasn't Will.

"You've only got one more day to consider my offer," Antoine's smooth, deep voice murmured in my ear, startling me so much that I knocked over my water glass. Thankfully, it was empty.

I righted the glass and shifted in my chair, recoiling as his stoic face loomed close to mine. "I've already made my decision clear," I said sharply, regretting my clumsiness. The last thing I wanted was for him to think he had the upper hand. "I won't be bribed."

His eyes went cold. "Take the loan, Char. If you don't, I'll fix it so that you never get a shred of credit in this town as long as you live."

He walked away without another word, but one thing he'd made clear; his deal was no longer an offer. It was a threat.

* * *

Two days later…

"This place is perfect," Maddie said to me, her voice echoing off the bare walls as we walked into the cavernous room in the building at the corner of Snelling and Dale. "After we hire someone to paint the walls, we can put up movable partitions to divide the space. That way we can rearrange the floor plan to make more room as we add new products."

"I like that idea," I replied and stood in the center of the room to get a better sense of the layout. "We can use Oriental room dividers to partition off the showroom from the back of the house."

"Yes! In black lacquer and gold." Maddie spun around, taking in the scene. "We need to get the measurements so we can draw up a floor plan."

"Ladies," a deep masculine voice echoed behind us, "may I help you?"

We both turned at the same time and encountered a tall, slim man with thinning brown hair wearing dark brown trousers and a white shirt with sleeves rolled to his elbows. His lean face bore a curious expression. A thick mustache covered his upper lip.

"We have an appointment to view this space," Maddie said boldly. "We're interested in leasing it. Are you the owner?"

His curiosity turned to confusion. "I'm the manager, Tom Stevens." He glanced around. "Is your husband with you?"

"This is Madeline Van Elsberg and I'm Charlotte LeDoux," I replied, ignoring his question as I extended my hand. "We're looking to rent this property ourselves."

His eyes widened in surprise as he uttered an embarrassed chuckle. He reluctantly shook my hand. "This place is a might expensive for charity work. What church do you represent?"

Heat crept up the back of my neck. *Here it comes*, I thought angrily. *It's like walking into a brick wall...* "We're not a charity. Madeline and I plan to open a cosmetics salon," I said proudly.

"This isn't a good location for you," he interrupted dismissively. His mouth broadened into a derisive smile. "Besides, don't we already have enough stores pushing that silly stuff?"

Maddie stiffened beside me. "It's not silly," she snapped, "and yes, there are other shops that sell cosmetics, but we plan to create a unique, personalized experience for women."

He folded his arms, giving me the impression that he'd already made up his mind not to rent the property to us. "You ladies got experience in running a business?"

Maddie rolled her eyes. "We know what we're doing."

His skeptical gaze skimmed her from head to toe. "Yeah, well, you ain't no Elizabeth Quinlan."

"What difference does that make?" I demanded, irritated by his condescending attitude.

"She's famous," he replied with a sneer. "I ain't never heard of you two."

"Look," Maddie said in a crisp tone, "are you going to rent the property to us, or do we have to go over your head and speak with your boss?"

He laughed out loud. "I *am* the boss around here. Come back with your husband and we'll talk. I want him to guarantee the rent in writing. I ain't making any deals with *you*."

"We'll be in touch, Mr. Stevens," I said. Grabbing Maddie by the arm, I pulled her out of the building before she informed him that she didn't have a husband—and didn't need one. That would have ended the deal right then and there.

Once we were on the street, I let go of her arm. "Let's get out of this heat and go someplace where we can talk," I said above the roar of cars and trucks passing us along Dale Street.

"All right," Maddie conceded as she straightened her gold outfit and readjusted her matching cloche hat. "My house isn't far from here. I could use a nice stiff drink."

The thought of consuming bootlegged liquor made my stomach queasy. "I'm hungry," I said placing my hand on my stomach. "Why don't we go somewhere for an afternoon snack?"

We ended up at one of the soda shops I owned, Big Louie's, for ice cream and coffee.

"The *nerve* of that manager," Maddie spouted as we sat in a wooden booth drowning our sorrows in hot fudge sundaes. She scooped a spoonful of ice cream from her sundae dish. "Insisting I needed a husband to guarantee the rent!" Her spoon halted mid-air. "Who does he think he is?"

I swallowed a mouthful of cold, creamy ice cream covered with thick, warm fudge. "Now you know what *I've* been going through." I picked up my coffee mug with both hands, blowing on the strong, steamy liquid. "It's an uphill battle because men control everything."

Maddie's spoon clattered as she dropped it into her bowl. "Well, that's going to change!" She picked up a small bottle of cream and poured a generous dollop into her coffee. "Elizabeth Quinlan! Hmph!"

I set down my mug. "How does a two-bit sap like him even know who she is?"

"He probably read about her in the paper," Maddie said wryly. "The Minneapolis Tribune ran a lengthy piece on her when she moved her business into her new building. It's like a palace. Her merchandise is top-drawer and *very* expensive."

I'd read the article myself and had planned to visit the Young-Quinlan store in downtown Minneapolis to browse the fur shop after the grand opening crowds had settled down.

"She's rich now, but she started as a salesgirl at Goodfellow's," I stated matter-of-factly. "She and her manager, David Young, left the store and started their own shop. Now she has a huge state-of-the-art building on the corner of Ninth and Nicollet."

Maddie pointed her index finger at me. "See what we can become if we work hard and refuse to give up? The sky is the limit!"

I sighed and rested my chin on the heel of my hand. "Yeah, as soon as we find someone to lend us the money."

Maddie smiled proudly. "I already have it."

I laughed with glee until I realized where the cash came from. "You didn't—"

"Why not? It's just sitting in his bank account, getting moldy anyway." She picked a whipped cream-covered cherry off the top of her Sunday and popped it into her mouth. "Why shouldn't I ask my brother for the money? He inherited a lot more than I did!" She formed an invisible frame with her hands. "I can see the marquis now. *Madeline's Salon.*"

I let out a tense sigh. "I hope he doesn't think I put you up to it!"

"No, this is between him and me," Maddie replied emphatically. "Oh, and by the way, I got five thousand out of him." She waved my protest away with her hand. "Look, if we're going to do this, we're going to do it right!"

I stared into Maddie's sparkling blue eyes and realized that her enthusiasm had gone beyond mere excitement over our new adventure. She'd become obsessed. I didn't care for how she'd begun making decisions without consulting me first, but if I chose to object, it might damage our friendship. Then again, I'd never known her to take an interest in anything beyond shopping and partying. Perhaps she needed this success to prove her capabilities more than I did.

I had a choice to make: Dissolve our partnership and go my own way or swallow my pride and let her take the lead.

"Absolutely!" I said, deciding that Maddie's friendship meant more to me than having the last word.

Chapter Eight

Early July

WILL

The gray-haired woman sitting opposite me wore a black, custom-made suit and expensive Egyptian Revival jewelry. Though she obviously possessed much wealth, the heavy lines in her face made her look hard-bitten, as though she'd been through a great deal of strife in her lifetime. Unfortunately, I was about to add more fuel to the fire.

A thick manilla folder sat in the center of my desk. I pushed it toward her. "It's all here, Mrs. Rogers, with my report. The photos, the staff interviews, and the witness statements."

Mrs. Rogers sat like a marble statue; her white-knuckled hands clasped together as she stoically regarded the cataloged evidence of her husband's infidelity packaged neatly in front of her. "What is her name," she demanded flatly.

I cleared my throat and capped my fountain pen. My report contained in-depth background information on the woman in question, but obviously, Mrs. Rogers didn't want to look through it. I didn't blame her. "The woman's name is Roberta Fairchild. She's your husband's—"

"I know who she is," Mrs. Rogers said in a low, lethal tone. She reached into her handbag and pulled out a stack of cash bound with a rubber band. "Here's what I owe you." She slapped the bundle on the desk. "It's all there. Count it if you want. I'll wait."

I stared at the money and shook my head. "That won't be necessary. I trust the amount is what we agreed upon."

She slowly stood up and walked out, leaving the file behind.

Some days, I really regretted taking on infidelity cases. Today proved to be one of those occasions.

I waited until she had exited the office then I took the money and the folder and walked into the reception area to hand them over to my secretary. "Put this file in the 'closed case' cabinet and take this cash to the bank before the end of the day."

Astrid Anderson, my blonde, blue-eyed secretary, batted her long pale lashes at me. "Yes, Mr. Van Elsberg. Is there anything else I can get for you? Any other errands you need me to take care of before I leave?"

I turned away. "No, Astrid. That will be all for now."

I went into my office to study my notes on Antoine LeDoux's case. So far, I'd learned that he had inherited his parents' home and their bank accounts, but over the last year had gone through much of the money indulging his addictions. Besides his penchant for beautiful call girls and bootlegged booze, he was a regular customer at several gambling clubs and left a lot of his money at the tables. He'd exhausted his credit at several of them. No wonder he needed to get his hands on Char's money. The gambling clubs were breathing down his neck.

I was about to shut the door when Astrid suddenly approached me from behind. "May I have a moment of your time?" Her feminine voice trembled with nervousness.

Astrid was a sweet girl and an excellent secretary, but she was as transparent as my office window. She had romantic feelings for me, and she wasn't very good at hiding her emotions. I took great care to keep our relationship on a strict business level and kept my office door open during sessions where she sat with her stenographer pad and took down the words in shorthand as I dictated client letters to her. Even so, her constant eyelash batting and the beckoning lilt in her voice let me know she wanted us to be more than friends.

Now what, I thought tiredly. *Is she about to hit me up for dinner at her place?*

I turned around, keeping my expression neutral. "Of course, Astrid. What's on your mind?"

She bit her bottom lip as tears pooled in her eyes. "My mother is having a major operation tomorrow. She needs someone to care for her afterward so..." she swallowed hard. "I need to take some time off."

I never expected *this*. "I'm very sorry to hear that," I said sincerely. She didn't offer information as to what kind of operation the woman needed and I decided not to ask, figuring it was none of my business. "Please give my kindest regards to your mother. I wish her a speedy recovery. Of course, you may have time off. How long do you need?"

She drew in a deep breath. "About a month…"

Her answer took me by surprise. I had expected her to ask for a day or two, the rest of the week at best, but…a month? Our three-man office couldn't exist for that long without a secretary. I rubbed the back of my neck, at a loss as to how we would manage without her.

"I know it's a long time," Astrid said tearfully, "but I'm the only person Mother has to care for her. I don't want to lose my job!"

She threw her arms around me, and I suddenly found myself embracing her as she sobbed loud tears into the front of my starched white shirt. "It's all right," I said gently as I patted between her shoulder blades, hoping no one walked into the office at this moment and saw us with our arms around each other. Daniel was on surveillance for his political corruption case and Peter was in court today, but either one could show up at any moment and find me hugging my pretty young secretary. I'd never hear the end of it. "Don't worry about your job. Your mother's recovery is more important. We'll get by somehow," I said trying to sound sympathetic as I gently pried her arms from my body.

Peter, Daniel, and I had never talked about a backup plan should we lose our only employee. We should have anticipated this would happen to us sooner or later. Though it was too little, too late, we needed to get one together *now*. I didn't have any idea where to look for another secretary on such short notice.

I wondered if Char would help me out and try her hand at secretarial work for a few days. I had no idea if she'd ever touched a typewriter in her life much less knew how to use one, but I was desperate.

* * *

Later that day…

"Astrid will be gone for a month," I said anxiously as I paced the length of Char's library. "Dan and I can get by writing our reports by hand, but Peter's workload is huge. And who is going to answer the telephone or speak with walk-in clients when we're all out of the office?"

Char opened a hidden compartment in the paneled wall and pulled out a crystal decanter. She poured two fingers of whiskey into a lowball glass and handed it to me. "I can't do it, Will. I don't have time. Even if I made the time, I'm the worst two-fingered typist you've ever seen."

I let out a loud sigh. "I'm sorry. I don't mean to unload my problem on you. I'm just worrying out loud. Dan's working on a big case right now and so am I. Peter will be in court all week. We simply don't have time to look for another secretary."

I took the glass and sipped the whiskey. It was good stuff. Very smooth. I took another sip hoping it would settle my nerves. "I'm going to put an ad in the newspaper for a temporary replacement. She's got to be fast and accurate, and she needs to be able to step right into the job without any training. Do you know if any of the women at the shelter have office experience?"

Char shook her head. "Sally uses her church secretary to type her letters. Unless…" Her eyes widened as she mulled over something.

My day suddenly improved. "Sally has a secretary? Do you think she'd be willing to lend her out for a month?"

"I can ask," Char replied. "But first, I need some information."

The whisky had softened the edges of my nerves, settling me down. I sat in one of the easy chairs and relaxed. "Well, the job entails typing briefs for Peter and investigative reports for me and Dan, taking dictation, answering the telephone—"

"Not about that." She folded her arms and stared pointedly into my eyes. She had that determined look about her that usually spelled trouble. "I want to know why you and Leon were secretly communicating about Antoine at The Oasis."

"Char," I argued, "why do you keep asking about that? I've told you before, what goes on between me and Leon is confidential."

"Because I know it's something that concerns me," she shot back

74

stubbornly. "I saw how you two looked at Antoine."

I drained my whiskey and set the glass on the table. She had me in a bind. "He threatened you."

Her eyes grew wide. "What exactly did he say?"

"Antoine doesn't recognize you as a member of his family. He's convinced that Julien isn't Gus' son, and he believes he's entitled to Gus' estate. He swears he's going to get it."

She smacked her lips together in disgust. "That's no surprise. Gus' parents disapproved of him marrying a dirt-poor kid from Swede Hollow and they refused to accept me into the family. Like father, like son."

"There's more," I said hesitantly. "Antoine thinks you're blowing through Gus' money. I'm worried he might make good on his threat and do something to retaliate against you."

She shrugged it off. "Antoine is a mamma's boy who grew up pampered and spoiled. He's not like Gus. He's all talk and no action."

The cautious investigator in me didn't believe that. Not for a minute. Her lack of concern upset me. "People like that usually pay someone else to do their dirty work. Look, this wouldn't be happening if you were my wife, Char. He wouldn't dare say a thing against you—"

"Why, because he thinks I'm a helpless widow?" she snapped. "Honestly, Will, I'm not afraid of him! And I don't need a husband to hide behind every time someone says something negative about me!"

I stood and slid my arms around her. Her temerity was infuriating, but it was also one of the reasons I loved her so much. My sweet and sassy spitfire. "But I need *you*, darling. I don't know what I'd do if anything happened to you."

Resting my cheek on the soft crown of her head, I pulled her close and closed my eyes, trying not to worry about Antoine's threat toward her, but at the same time, telling myself we couldn't go on like this much longer.

Chapter Nine

The next day…

CHAR

It was a long shot, but I had to try.

The next morning, I donned my new light blue dress, the official uniform of Anna's House, and drove over there to ask Louisa to join me for lunch. According to Sally, Louisa hadn't made much effort to make friends in the shelter and spent much of her free time alone in her room. So, when I approached her about going to a soda shop for sandwiches and ice cream, her immediate refusal came as a disappointment, but not a surprise.

As a last resort, I planned to speak to her alone in Sally's office. Sally, however, had a different idea. She stepped in and encouraged Louisa to go, suggesting it would be good for her to take a break from the shelter and get some fresh air. I could tell Sally thought it might help Louisa to pull out of her depressed state. Though she clearly didn't want to, Louisa finally relented and got into the car with me.

On the way to the soda shop, she sat rigidly on the seat staring straight ahead with her hands clasped tightly in her lap. The last time we were together alone—a year ago at Will's home—our conversation had been laced with anger and bitterness. Then she betrayed me. I had every right to hate her, but I knew she'd been through a lot since then, suffering abuse at the hands of her brother-in-law and the eventual abandonment by her family, so I let it go. That was then, this was now, and it didn't do either of us any good to dredge up the past.

At Big Louie's Soda Shop, we sat in a wooden booth munching on egg salad sandwiches and chicken noodle soup. When I brought up the subject of a temporary secretarial job, Louisa resisted the idea right away.

"I realize it's only been about a month since your delivery, Louisa, but this is a terrific opportunity," I implored. "It'll provide you with some income and recent experience to fall back on while you're looking for something permanent. That's what you want, isn't it? A way to make a new life for yourself?"

Louisa put down her sandwich, frowning at my insistence. The dark circles under her eyes and pale skin indicated she hadn't recovered as much as I'd hoped she would have by this time. She was thinner now than before she got pregnant.

"You know it is. I never thought I'd wind up in a home for wayward women," Louisa said sadly and sipped her cherry phosphate. "I really need that job, but, Char, I don't have the right clothes to wear in an office setting."

That surprised me. Was that an excuse or did that statement mean she would consider it if she *had* the right clothes for an office setting? Louisa had always been very old-fashioned in how she dressed and styled her hair. She favored long, drab dresses in dark colors and wore her mousey-brown hair in a tight bun. I'd never seen her wear even a hint of makeup or jewelry.

"I want to help you get back on your feet, Louisa." I picked up my spoon and sipped my soup. "I'll buy you the right clothes."

"No," Louisa argued, shaking her head. "I can't allow you to spend money on me that I can't repay. An Amundsen doesn't take charity."

My spoon halted in mid-air. That refusal didn't sound like her. It must have been something she'd heard many, many times growing up. Maybe that was also why her cheeks had suddenly flushed. She compared getting help from someone to accepting charity that she didn't deserve.

"All right," I replied softly, wracking my brain over how I could phrase it differently. I suddenly thought of something else that might work. "What if someone I knew was cleaning out her closets and stuffing bags full of clothes to give away? The clothes will eventually go to someone. Why not you?"

Louisa's brows deepened pessimistically. "I don't believe in coincidences. Or begging people for things."

"Hey, it's not a crime or shameful to get someone else's last-season clothing." I ate the last bite of my sandwich and sipped my ginger ale. "Besides, my friend, the one with all the clothes, won't mind giving away a few dresses. She's a chronic shopper and has literally an entire bedroom turned into a walk-in closet. She's always trying to give me brand-new stuff! That way, she doesn't have to haul it to the donation bin at her church."

Louisa sighed. "I don't know…"

Our waitress, a young girl wearing bright red lipstick stopped at our table and gathered up our empty dishes. "Ready for ice cream?"

"Absolutely!" I looked up at the chalkboard on the wall showing the daily specials. "I'll take the Turtle-Myrtle sundae."

"Make that two," Louisa said.

"We'd both like coffee, as well," I chimed in.

The waitress smiled. "Coming up!"

"You didn't mention the name of the company that has the vacancy," Louisa said in a flat, disinterested voice. "Not that it matters. They probably wouldn't hire me anyway."

Though she didn't come right out and say it, I heard the truth loud and clear. She believed that because she'd been raped and borne an illegitimate child she was somehow to blame and therefore was undeserving of finding happiness or any sort of success.

"It isn't a company," I said, wondering how to break the news to her. "It's a small office downtown that three men share—two private investigators and an attorney."

We were temporarily interrupted by our waitress setting two steaming mugs of coffee in front of us, but that didn't stop Louisa from comprehending whom I was referring to. Her jaw dropped in slow motion as she stared at me. "Will's office?"

I nodded.

Her hands clenched into white-knuckled fists on the table. "You promised you wouldn't tell him about me!"

I raised my palms in a peacemaking gesture. "I swear to you, I haven't said a word to him. He has no idea whom I'm talking to about this job or what you've been doing since you left his employment. When you show up for work tomorrow, he'll be surprised to see you." Pushing my coffee mug aside, I folded my arms, resting my elbows on the table. "But he'll also be relieved. He knows you're an exceptional secretary. He said so himself, didn't he?"

She eyed me skeptically. "Why would you trust me around Will after how shamelessly I used to be so obsessive about him?"

"Because I trust *him*," I replied. He didn't take the bait then and I knew he wouldn't now.

Will's trustworthiness was one of the things that I loved most about him. He dealt with female clients regularly, and it was a relief to know that he didn't believe in mixing business with pleasure. When Louisa and I worked for him, he always treated both of us with respect by keeping his distance.

She gave me a curious look. "You said there were three men."

"Daniel Blythe and Peter Garrett are the other two. You know Daniel and you've heard Will talk about Peter Garrett many times." I leaned forward across the table. "You can do this, Louisa. You can do this job with your eyes closed and one hand tied behind your back."

"What about Mr. Garrett?" She gripped her coffee mug, staring at the wisp of steam rising from it. "I've never worked for an attorney before. I don't know how to type legal briefs."

I laughed. "Do you really think you, of all people, couldn't learn something new?" I paused for a moment to watch our waitress pull our sundaes from the serving window. My mouth watered at the thought of cold, creamy vanilla ice cream topped with pecans and warm caramel. "You can easily master it. You *know* you can."

Our sundaes were delivered. We both grabbed our spoons and dived into the best part of our lunch.

"I suppose so," Louisa replied, licking warm caramel off her spoon.

"But, why me?" Her eyes narrowed. "Why are you helping me after what I did to you?" She set down her spoon. "I told your husband you were hiding from him at Will's house and made him come after you. I probably got him killed." She winced. "I'm so sorry about that, Char. That day at Will's, I wanted Gus to come and get you, but I never meant for things to go *that far*. It's bothered me ever since."

A spoonful of ice cream stuck in my throat like an iceberg. I swallowed it down and sipped my coffee. "You had nothing to do with Gus' death, Louisa. He was murdered by one of his own men. For a long time, I blamed myself as well, but I'm convinced now that his execution had been planned long before that day by someone who wanted his position and power. So don't trouble yourself over that fact any longer."

We were silent for a while as we ate our sundaes.

"*If* I decide to take the job," Louisa said suddenly, "you can't tell *anybody* that I'm living at the women's shelter."

I kept my expression neutral, but Louisa's words made my heart leap for joy. She was slowly coming around. "Your private life is none of my business, Louisa. I'm just trying to help Will find a replacement secretary for a month."

"I'll need tokens for the streetcar," Louisa said thoughtfully as she chewed on a pecan.

I nodded. "Sally has a small fund for things like that. She'll give you as many as you need."

"About your friend," Louisa said tentatively, "are you sure she won't mind giving me her hand-me-downs?"

I laughed. "Wait until you see her closet. It looks like the overstock room of Dayton's Department store."

Her stern expression softened. "Sometimes I really miss working for Will. I suppose I could give it a try."

"All right," I said softly. My heart was dancing a jig.

I had started out doing a favor for Will, but once I talked to Louisa, the favor turned into a mission. The day that I saw her sitting alone at the shelter, pregnant and depressed, her unhappiness wrenched my soul.

I just hoped my good deed didn't backfire tomorrow when Will found out I had recruited her without asking him first.

* * *

The moment I turned my car onto Laurel Avenue, Louisa realized where we were going.

And she wasn't happy about it.

I pulled up to the huge, Victorian house Will and Maddie had inherited from their parents and turned off the car.

She glared at me as though I'd tricked her. "I'm not going into *that* house."

Leaving the key in the ignition, I grabbed my clutch and placed my hand on the door. "Why not? Maddie is a terrific person once you get to know her."

Louisa stayed put. "She hates me! I was terribly rude to her when I worked for Will."

I shook my head. "That was a long time ago and she's not one to hold a grudge." I opened the door. "I'll prove it to you. Come on."

She sat in the car until I reached the sidewalk. I stopped and turned around, waiting for her. After a few moments, she angrily slid off the seat and slammed the door. We walked up to the house and rang the bell. The front door stood open. "Maddie, it's me, Char!" I yelled through the screen door. The soft, relaxing whir of an oscillating fan in the parlor echoed through the house.

"Just a minute!" Maddie called from upstairs. Soft footsteps padded on the creaky wooden staircase, and before long she appeared on the other side of the screen. "Hi," she said with a bright smile as soon as she saw me. Then she saw Louisa and her friendly expression faded.

I ignored the sudden chill in the air and smiled happily as I grabbed the door handle. "Do you still have those clothes you wanted me to try on?"

"Yes," Maddie replied hesitantly. "I haven't gotten around to boxing them up yet so they're all still hanging in my closet."

"Great!" I jerked open the door and stood aside for Louisa to enter. She stood on the porch, looking mutinous and unwelcome. "My," I announced cheerily to break the ice, "it's been a long time since the three of us were together in this house, hasn't it?"

As Louisa entered the foyer, Maddie gawked as though she didn't know what to make of the situation. She was clearly flummoxed at seeing me and Louisa together. She wore a bright orange dress today with a rope of pearls around her neck. Her dark wavy hair looked freshly styled.

"What in the world are you wearing?" Maddie said, reaching out and grabbing the fabric of my simple blue chambray shift. "You two look like you just came from working in the laundry at the prison!" She turned around and went up the wide staircase to the second floor. "Come on. You're not leaving my house looking like that!"

"The prison laundry!" I mouthed to Louisa as I followed behind Maddie then laughed as though it was the funniest thing I'd ever heard. Louisa followed me, glowering.

Maddie's makeshift bedroom-turned-closet was the last room at the back of the house, the room that had a smaller one attached to it. I always assumed the smaller room was a nursery. Maddie had filled it with winter coats, boots, and sweaters.

I peered into the coat room. The walls were a soft cream. The window at the back of the room brightened the area with natural light. If I lived here, I would have used this room as a nursery. The happiness inside me dimmed, however, when I reminded myself that I hadn't made an appointment with my doctor. Why was I putting it off? Because—if I *was* pregnant, I'd have to tell my sister about the baby. I dreaded the thought. Did I secretly fear that she'd accuse me of practicing the opposite of what I preached or was it because deep down I knew I'd broken my promise to my mother to be a good influence on her?

Maddie turned around. "What's the matter, Char?"

"Nothing," I said and quickly looked away.

She glanced inside the coat room as though wondering what I had found so depressing. "For a moment, you looked so sad I thought you were going to cry." She frowned. "Are you sure you're all right?"

"Of course," I assured her and faked a smile. "I just was thinking about how much I've always loved this house."

The larger bedroom looked exactly as I had described it to Louisa. A room crammed full of racks of the latest fashions. All were purchased with the money Maddie received each month from her father's trust fund.

Louisa stood in the doorway, stunned by the sheer volume of garments.

"Come on in," Maddie said as she riffled through a rack of dresses. She pulled out a hanger holding a skirt and sweater ensemble in green and blue with a matching sky-blue silk blouse. She held it up to my body. "How about this one?"

I frowned at it. "The skirt is too long." I looked up. "It's made for someone taller."

Maddie held it up to Louisa. "You and I are about the same height. Here," she said as she draped it over Louisa's arm. "Try this on."

"It still has the price tag on it," Louisa replied in awe.

"So?" Maddie shrugged. "I probably got it on sale but it's not really my color, you know?" She bent at the waist and picked up a shoe box. "These go with it."

And so it went on for several hours. By the time we left Maddie's house, Maddie had given Louisa enough clothing and accessories to last her for a long time. We were hoarse from laughing and talking non-stop. Best of all, Maddie and Louisa had become friends, something I would never have believed until today. To my utter shock, Maddie had even convinced Louisa to let her trim Louisa's hair to make it look more fashionable! Louisa still kept her hair long in the back and wound it into a bun, as many girls opted to do, but she now had a fringe of bangs and enough chin-length hair covering her ears to make it look like she'd had her hair bobbed. Her transformation from the dowdy hen that she used to be to a modern woman amazed me. But then, she'd been through so many changes lately that perhaps it wasn't so difficult to make one more.

It was nearly dinnertime when I dropped Louisa off at the shelter and helped her bring in her new wardrobe. We locked the clothes in the closet in Sally's office for safekeeping. Back when the building used to house La Coquette, the office belonged to Gus. It included a private lavatory and a large closet to store his suits and shirts. Thanks to Gus, Louisa had a place to store everything and a private room to get ready for work each morning.

"Thank you, Char," Louisa said to me as we walked out of Sally's office. "For lunch today, for the job, and for taking me to Madeline's to get new clothes. I know I don't deserve it but—"

"Of course, you do!" I said, trying to encourage her. "You deserve to find happiness just as much as anyone else."

She looked down. "My mother says that no man will ever marry a woman who's done the things I have."

"You're not a bad person," I argued. "Don't look back. Keep going forward to get the life you want. No one has the right to pass judgment on you. Not even your mother!"

"I'll never go back to live with her," she said with determination. "Do you remember the week I took off when I worked for Will?"

"Yes, I do," I replied. "You never mentioned why, and I assumed you'd gone on a vacation."

She shook her head. "My brother-in-law struck me in the face because I fought against him, and it left a terrible bruise." Her hand went up to the fine bones in her cheek as though she could still feel the pain. "I couldn't allow Will to see me like that. I was so ashamed."

I slid my arm around her shoulder. "You don't have to go back to your mother's house ever again and subject yourself to his abuse. Sally and I will help you find a room once you get back on your feet."

"I'd like that, Char," she said, her eyes shining with emotion.

"I'll pick you up at seven-thirty tomorrow morning," I said enthusiastically as I left the building. "See you then!"

I drove home, wondering how Will would react when he found out whom I'd recruited to be his temporary secretary.

I couldn't wait.

Chapter Ten

The next morning...

WILL

Daniel and I were both in the office early, trying to get through a mountain of paperwork. Without a secretary to type our work we had to do all of it by hand, a task neither of us cared for because we were terrible at it. Writing long reports and trying to be neat at the same time caused a cramp in my hand. Daniel didn't mind writing reports, but his handwriting was so sloppy that sometimes even *he* couldn't decipher it.

At eight o'clock, the door opened, and Char appeared. Daniel and I were at Astrid's desk drinking fresh-brewed cups of coffee from the restaurant downstairs and discussing one of our cases. Our conversation ceased the moment we saw her. She had someone with her, but the person stood behind her.

"Gentlemen, as promised, I found a temporary replacement for Astrid," Char said as she stepped through the door and moved aside so her companion could enter.

I nearly swallowed my tongue when Louisa Amundsen stepped into view. I barely recognized her at first. My former secretary looked so different that I stared at her, not knowing what to say. The front of her hair had been cut short, framing her face in a most flattering way. She wore a pretty outfit—in colors and a style I'd never seen her wear before. "Louisa?" I set my empty coffee cup on Astrid's desk before I clumsily dropped it. "Louisa Amundsen?"

Louisa stepped forward, smiling timidly. "Hello, Will. It's—it's nice to see you again."

"It's nice to see you, too," I said slowly, still in shock.

Daniel stuck out his hand. "Welcome aboard, Miss Amundsen."

She reluctantly shook his hand. "Thank you."

She looked around, her gaze stopping at the pile of files sitting on Astrid's desk. "Is this my desk?" She pointed to the files. "Is this my work?"

Both Daniel and I started to talk at once.

"Wait, wait," she said quickly and held up her hand to silence us. "I appreciate all of your help, but I know what to do." She immediately picked up the top file, the notes on Representative Wroebel, and began looking at the first page.

"Here," Daniel said, eagerly pulling out her desk chair. "Have a seat."

Louisa sat down and began paging through the document. She began to ask him questions about what he wanted to be done and when he needed it. I stared at her in relief, yet at the same time, in unbelief.

It's as though she's never left my employment... I thought in awe.

"Would you like some fresh java?" I asked her as I grabbed my empty cup. "I need a refill and I'm sure Char wants a cup, too, so we'll go downstairs and let you get to work. You need anything, Dan?"

Daniel shook his head and went back to his conversation with Louisa.

* * *

I opened the door and waited for Char to exit first. Once we were out in the hallway, I pulled her aside. "What's *this* all about?" I pointed toward the closed office door.

Char's wide green eyes flashed with annoyance. "What does it look like? You said you needed a good secretary. She needed a job. What's the problem?"

"She needed a job, huh? You're always trying to fix everyone else," I argued. "When are you going to fix your own problems? Like hiring a team of bodyguards to keep you safe?"

She let out an angry sigh. "I did you a huuuge favor and this is the thanks I get? How dare you!" She stomped to the elevator.

I followed behind her, not ready to end this conversation yet. "That's not what I meant, and you know it. If I'd wanted to hire Louisa, I would have called her myself."

"Not so," Char snapped. "Louisa doesn't live with her mother anymore and if you had called there, her mother couldn't have given you Louisa's new telephone number anyway."

The elevator slowly stopped at our floor. "Look, I don't mean to act like a horse's behind, but you know what it was like when she worked for me," I said in my defense. "She became so possessive, she tried to run my life!"

Char turned her back to the elevator as the operator began to open the glass door and metal scissor gate. "She's changed. Lost her stiff upper lip. Or haven't you noticed?"

"I was stunned. I didn't know what to make of her at first," I said in puzzlement. "I saw this pretty, smiling woman enter my office and couldn't believe it was the same person who used to work for me." Our conversation ceased as we stepped into the crowded elevator.

At the restaurant, I bought two fresh cups of coffee for the women and a refill for me. By the time we arrived in the office, Daniel was in his office on the telephone and Louisa sat at her desk, busily typing up a storm. All seemed perfectly normal again. Still, I couldn't help my misgivings about employing Louisa. How long would it be before she started taking over the place?

Char and I had just stepped into my office when Peter arrived. I meant to spearhead introductions, but by the time I stood up from my desk, Peter had already dropped his briefcase and introduced himself.

"Hello," he said in a curious tone as his gaze locked with hers. "You must be the new secretary."

Louisa stopped typing. "Yes," she said cautiously. "I'm Louisa Amundsen."

He extended his hand. "I'm Peter Garrett. Pleased to meet you, Miss Amundsen."

The moment their hands joined, they both startled as though an invisible current had jolted through them. Their hands jerked apart, but they continued to stare into each other's eyes, looking completely spellbound.

"I'm...I'm p-pleased to meet you, too..." Louisa replied slowly, letting her sentence trail off as she flattened her palms on her desk, as though to steady herself.

Char and I stared at each other with incredulity. I leaned across my desk. "Am I imagining things," I whispered, "or did you see what I saw?"

She nodded quickly and focused her attention back on the scene unfolding in the other room.

Peter stood in front of Louisa's desk looking like a schoolboy dealing with his first female crush. His reserved, professional manner had dissolved into an insecure mess. "H-how are you getting along on your first day?"

Louisa still hadn't moved. "Quite well. Thank you."

"Wonderful," Peter said, sounding like he was struggling for something clever to say. "Would you like a cup of coffee, perhaps?"

She held up her cup. "I already have one."

Quit while you're ahead, old boy, I thought, amused. *That big foot of yours looks pretty silly sticking out of your mouth.*

"Oh...um...yes, of course." He laughed with embarrassment. "How silly of me. Well, I'll just be in my office if you need anything or have any questions, Miss...Miss..."

"Amundsen," she said. "Louisa Amundsen."

"Right!"

Then he tripped over his briefcase.

Char and I suddenly got interested in a file on my desk, but I couldn't manage more than a grunt. My eyes were watering from struggling to stifle the best laugh I'd had in a long time.

That poor stiff didn't know what hit him.

Chapter Eleven

Mid-July

CHAR

I sat on the examination table in a small, brightly lit room clutching a sheet around me, biting my nails as I waited for the doctor to arrive and examine me. I should have done this right after my conversation with Sally, but I'd put it off with one excuse after another: I was too busy. I didn't want Francie to overhear me make the appointment on the telephone and start asking questions. I didn't want my staff to worry about me.

I finally called this morning and, to my surprise, learned that I could come in at two o'clock this afternoon. Today was a busy day, but it was just as well that I got in so soon. I needed to get this over with so I could move on with my life.

The longer I waited, the more nervous I became. Thoughts swirled in my head, disclaiming what Sally had said. There was a good chance that I wasn't pregnant. After all, I reasoned, I hadn't been sick like the last time. No dizziness, no nausea, and no tenderness in certain areas. I tired easily, but that could be attributed to my non-stop activities and the fact that I'd had my share of disappointments lately. Constant troubles could wear a person down.

Fifteen minutes passed. I glanced at the clock on the wall, anxious to get this taken care of and be on my way. I had invited Will over for dinner tomorrow night and needed to get home to get ready for it. His last checkup had revealed that his wound had completely healed so we were celebrating.

The door suddenly opened. Doctor Daly entered, an older man in a white coat with short gray hair combed straight back and wire-rimmed glasses. "Good afternoon, Mrs. LeDoux." He paused to study the sheet containing the details of my routine preliminary examination on the clipboard that the nurse had left on his desk. "A pelvic exam. All right," he said and turned around, instructing me to lie down and put my feet up, knees apart.

I lay on the table staring at the ceiling, trying to distract myself from the discomfort that overtook me as he began the examination.

"Congratulations, Mrs. LeDoux," he said cheerfully. "You're going to have a baby."

*   *   *

I drove to Como Park and walked around the small lake in a daze, mulling over my predicament. Pregnant—me? Why? Yes, I wanted another baby—Will's baby—more than anything. Oh, how I wanted a baby girl. But not now. Not like *this*. Pregnant before marriage! Of course, my predicament would hasten our wedding plans. Will and I would get married right away in a small, private ceremony with only our closest friends in attendance.

Quietly tying the knot wouldn't be enough, however, to silence the gossip that was sure to spread once my tummy started to show. Francie's reputation concerned me the most. She knew firsthand how the kids at school could be thoughtless and cruel. If word got out that her sister had to get married because she'd gotten in the *family way*, Francie's character would be assassinated because of me.

That upset me more than anything. Francie had already been through enough grief in her brief lifetime. She didn't need my reckless behavior to cause more. Like me, she'd grown up being the caregiver of an invalid mother and had to cope with a drunken father who only came around when he had nowhere else to stay. I'd promised Mamma before she died that I'd take good care of Francie. I missed Anna dearly, but I was grateful that she'd never know what I'd done. She'd have been horrified over me being pregnant out of wedlock. And so disappointed in me.

I agonized over my dilemma as I drove home. It was after nine o'clock and getting dark by the time I reached the gates of my house, but the moment I drove up to the guard shack, I forgot about my maternity problems. Something was wrong. The big garage door stood open, all the lights were on and most of my staff stood in the driveway, gathered around Errol.

Hal, my nighttime security guard came running up the driveway to let me in when he saw my car waiting at the gate. I quickly drove through and sped down the driveway to the garage. Errol leaned against the limousine dressed in his mechanic overalls holding a bloody shop rag against his head.

"What's going on?" I cried as Gerard opened my car door. I jumped out. "Errol, what happened to you? Are you all right?"

"He was attacked!" Lillian, my maid, said in a shaking voice.

I looked around in shock. "Where? When?"

"There were two fellas," Errol said as he pulled the rag off his head. Blood soaked through his light brown hair on the right side of his skull. "They musta somehow got through the fence behind the garage. I was upstairs in my apartment making a sandwich when I heard Rory's dog barking up a storm," he said and nodded toward my new gardener, Rory Evers. "Captain sounded angry so I came downstairs and sure 'nuff—the dog had one of the men cornered. The other one jumped me from behind."

"When Captain heard the intruders prowling around, he started growling and took off like a shot," Rory said, backing up Errol's account of what happened. The short, middle-aged man wore blue jeans and a green plaid shirt. Captain, his two-year-old German shepherd leaned protectively against his legs. "I heard Errol shouting so I ran to the garage and found him in the fight of his life. When the attacker saw me holdin' a shovel, he took off. Captain got after the second guy and chased him right outta the back door. But not before he got his licks in." He patted the panting dog. "That man got bit up pretty bad."

"What did they want?" I asked Errol. "Were they after you?"

"They were going to burn down the garage," Errol said. "They had full gas cans with them. Luckily for us, Captain didn't allow them to spread it around."

I blinked with shock. "Burn down my garage? Why would anyone do that?"

"It's a diversion tactic," Hal said as he rejoined the group. He was out of breath from running back and forth. "They start the garage on fire. When everyone comes out to see the blaze and wait for the fire department to come, they slip into the house and rob the place."

Before I could get the question out, Gerard answered it.

"No one has breached the house, My Lady," he assured me in his deep, British voice. "We've locked all the doors."

"That's 'cause those fellas didn't count on running into this guy." Rory reached down and petted the panting dog. "He's a good boy."

Rory had been living in the gardener's cottage for a month, but his dog hadn't arrived until two days ago. He'd been boarding it at his sister's farm up north and had driven up there on his day off to get his furry sidekick. Until now, I hadn't been enthusiastic about having a barking dog on the premises, but Captain had already proven me wrong. His instincts were invaluable.

"Who would do such a thing," I asked myself aloud. "Why—"

I interrupted myself as a name popped into my mind. Antoine would do such a thing to get the ten thousand dollars he wanted. I glanced down the driveway wondering if he'd been waiting somewhere close by sitting behind the wheel of the getaway car.

Cook arrived with her first aid kit, a warm bucket of water, and a soft rag to take care of the cut on Errol's head.

"We'll get that break in the fence fixed tonight," Rory said to me as he adjusted his green bill cap, "and we'll walk the perimeter to make sure there are no other issues."

"Thank you," I said and looked down at the dog. "And thank you, Captain. You're the hero of the day." I bent down to pet him and got dog slobber all over my hand. "Cook will see to it that you get a nice fresh bone," I said as I scratched his ear.

"With your permission, My Lady," Gerard said to me, "I'll place the call to the police and handle the report."

"Since you were here when it happened, I agree," I replied with a nod.

I left the group and walked to the house, grateful that a rowdy German shepherd had saved the day, but I worried about what Antoine would try to pull next time. Hopefully, once the police were notified there wouldn't *be* a next time, but in my heart, I knew I couldn't depend upon them to solve my problem with my brother-in-law. I needed to take matters into my own hands. If Gus were alive today, that's what he would have done.

I decided to confront Antoine myself.

* * *

I walked into the house and headed for Gus' office upstairs to make a telephone call. Once I finished, I gathered up what I needed and returned to the den to secure it in my vault. Then I went into the sunroom to clear my head and wait for the police to arrive. I still needed to go over the menu with Cook for dinner tomorrow night, but that had to wait for now.

A soft breeze wafted through the open windows in the sunroom. I turned on a small light and pulled off my cloche hat, placing my handbag and hat on the table before toeing off my shoes. I collapsed on the chaise lounge, reeling with exhaustion from such a stressful day. Sinking my face into a soft pillow, I meant to merely rest my eyes for a few minutes…

The shrill ringing of the telephone awoke me.

That must be the police, I thought groggily. *I need to get up.*

But my body refused to move. Someone had tucked a blanket around me, and the soft cotton coverlet enveloped me like a cocoon. Fully relaxed, I pulled the blanket up to my ear and snuggled under it. Another minute of sleep wouldn't hurt. My eyelids, heavy with fatigue, slowly shuttered.

"I'm sorry to bother you, My Lady," Gerard said softly as he stood over me, disturbing my temporary bliss. "Hal says there is a car at the gate. A gentleman is demanding to see you."

Lifting my head, I squinted at him through sleepy eyes. "Who is it?"

"Mr. Antoine LeDoux," Gerald replied stoically as the melodious chimes of the wall clock struck ten times. "It's late. Shall I tell him to return tomorrow?"

What is he doing here at this ungodly hour? I wondered, struggling to raise myself on one elbow. I'd left a message with his answering service asking him to call me back. I figured he was out for the evening and would get back to me in the morning. I planned to arrange a meeting with him for tomorrow afternoon.

I clasped Gerard's outstretched hand. The blanket slid to the floor as I slowly sat up. My mind spun with fatigue, I hurt from head to toe and was not in the best mood to receive Antoine tonight. I needed to go upstairs and crawl into my bed to get more sleep and ease the pressure on my back. "Perhaps that would be best, Gerard. I—" Interrupting myself, I raised my hand. Truly, this couldn't wait. "No, if he's here, I might as well get this over with now. Tell Hal to let him in."

Expressing his disapproval with his customary deep frown, Gerard excused himself, went to the telephone in the front hall, and gave Hal my instructions. Soon after, Gerard reappeared in the doorway. His eyes were bloodshot with fatigue. "Mr. LeDoux has arrived."

I stood and straightened my dress. "I'll show him into the library myself. I won't be needing you anymore tonight, Gerard. Tell the rest of the staff they can retire as well."

"As you wish," he replied with a quick bow. He escorted me to the front hall and silently took his leave.

Antoine paced the hall with his hands in his pockets, impatiently waiting for me. He looked impeccable in a dark, pin-striped suit and starched light blue shirt. Tall with wide shoulders, my handsome, twenty-six-year-old brother-in-law reminded me a lot of Gus. He had Gus' sandy-colored hair, parted on the side, and grayish-green eyes that could quickly turn cold with anger. Tonight, they reflected wariness, as though approaching me on my turf put him at a disadvantage.

"Antoine," I said sounding more cautious than I had intended.

He stopped abruptly, dropping his hands to his sides. "You left a message with my service. You said wanted to talk…"

"Yes, I did. Let's go into the library," I said simply and led the way.

"Everything still looks the same as it did when Gus was alive," he remarked with surprise, staring at the built-in bookcases lining the walls filled with volumes of all sizes and shapes.

"I haven't changed anything," I replied as I walked toward the small fireplace and opened my liquor compartment in the wall. "Would you like a drink?" At his nod, I pulled out a decanter of Gus' private stock of bootlegged whiskey and poured the amber liquid into a glass.

His lean face registered surprise when I set the decanter down on the Queen Anne table in the center of the room and pulled out a chair. "Aren't you going to have one?"

I shook my head. "I don't drink."

"Suit yourself." He took a chair opposite of me and sipped his whiskey. "What happened to Gus' guns?"

I slowly folded my hands on the table. "I gave them all to Harv Katzenbaum." I shrugged as he stared at me in disappointment. "I had no use for them. Gus's collection of cars is sitting in the back lot of the Ford dealership. My staff there is going to auction them off later this month, but you're welcome to them."

His hand holding the crystal lowball glass halted midair. "I heard they're full of bullet holes."

I nodded.

He reached for the decanter to refill his drink. "About the money," he said changing the subject. "Char, I—"

"Why do you need it," I countered bluntly, interrupting him. Sitting back in my chair, I folded my arms. "I know you're desperate to get it. Otherwise, you wouldn't be here. So, what's the story? I want the truth."

He went silent, his eyes narrowing. "I have financial obligations."

"What kind of obligations?" Refusing to back down, I stared deep into his eyes. "Who are you indebted to?"

Antoine took a swig of his whiskey and cleared his throat. "I've had some bad luck at the tables at King's Cave Royale. Dewey Kingman wants five thousand dollars by Friday…or…"

"He'll take matters into his own hands?"

"Yes," he said, flinching slightly.

"How do I know you're telling me the truth?"

He pulled a folded piece of paper from the inside pocket of his suit jacket and slid it across the table to me. I unfolded it and found a hand-written IOU for five-thousand dollars on King's Cave Royale stationery signed by both Dewey Kingman and Antoine. The document was dated a month prior. The due date passed two weeks ago.

I stared at the IOU. "Why didn't you come directly to me about this instead of trying to bribe me to get a loan?"

"I thought Gus' mouthpiece would give me the money since he is still handling Gus' estate, but Katzenbaum refused to pay Kingman." Antoine shrugged. "I was out of options."

I glared at him. "Oh, but you had one more. You sent two men onto my property to start a fire in my garage and then break into my house to rob me! Thank God they were chased off before they could do any real harm."

"What?" He blinked with genuine surprise. "What are you talking about?" His face darkened with a scowl. "I don't know anything about that. Besides, I'd never stoop that low. I'm a businessman, not a thug. It sounds to me like Kingman was sending you a message."

"Why would Dewey Kingman threaten me?"

"Because I told him you'd give him the money," Antoine replied in a defiant tone. "Look, if Gus was still alive, he would have helped me out! I didn't have the money when it came due, so I begged Kingman to send a note to Katzenbaum as a last resort, but the old man turned him down. Sent his hired gumshoe, Van Elsberg to deliver the message to Kingman in person."

My mind churned with questions as my outrage grew. So, both Harv and Will knew about this, but neither thought it was important enough to discuss it with me? Or was it *me* they didn't consider important?

I folded the IOU and slid it back again across the table. "You're right, Antoine. Gus would have helped his brother out of a jam. *Once.* He loved you and he was loyal to you, but he was no fool. He wouldn't come to your rescue a second time for something as reckless and foolish as this."

Spreading my palms on the table, I leaned forward. "So, I'll do what Gus would have done and give you the money, but I don't want any misunderstanding between us. This is the only time I'm going to cough up the dough for you." I looked deeply into his eyes. "Don't *ever* ask me to cover your gambling debts again."

He stared at me in surprise, his eyes blinking rapidly as my words sunk in. "I promise, Char! I swear, after I settle with Kingman, I'll never set foot in that joint again." He picked up his glass and downed its contents. "What time tomorrow do you want to meet me at your bank to draw out the money? I'll clear my calendar."

"I'll give it to you now," I said as I pushed back my chair and stood.

"Cash?" His voice rose with astonishment.

"Yes, *cash*," I said boldly. "I'm going to take care of this tonight and be done with it, but I want to show you something first. Come with me."

I led Antoine upstairs to the nursery and placed my finger against my lips as I cautiously opened the door and turned on a small lamp. He followed me across the room to the wooden crib where Julien lay sleeping peacefully in a beige nightgown. I peeled back the soft blanket covering the child. "This is your nephew, Julien," I whispered. "Gus' son."

Antoine leaned over the side and stared in wonder. "My God... He looks just like Gus."

"He resembles his father in many ways," I replied as I touched the boy's soft curls. "Gus wanted a son so badly. I wish he would have lived long enough to meet Julien, but..."

The child stirred.

"We'd better go," I whispered and recovered Julien with the blanket. "If he wakes up and sees us, I'll never get him back to sleep."

I moved quietly toward the door and placed my hand on the lamp, but Antoine lingered at the crib. As he stared down at his nephew, the raw emotion gripping his face indicated that he missed his brother dearly.

We returned to the library and went into the adjoining den. I unlocked the closet door and opened the huge safe behind it, taking out a cloth money bag. "Here you are," I said as I opened the bag and dumped out ten thick bundles on the desk. "Each bundle contains a thousand dollars. That should be enough to pay Kingman back and hopefully cover any other outstanding debts."

Antoine stared at the money. "That's a lot of cash," he said in awe as he reached for the pile.

"I thought you should have these too," I added as I pulled several items from the top drawer of the desk and placed the pieces in his hand one at a time. "This is your father's pocket watch. Here are his diamond cufflinks too. This gold money clip belonged to Gus."

"Gee, Char, this is…" Antoine's eyes softened with humility. "More than I expected."

"Gus would want you to have them," I said gently. "I'll walk you out."

Antoine eagerly scooped up the money and stuffed it back into the bag. At the front door, he hesitated. "Say…ah…if it's all right with you, I'd like to stop by one of these days and visit my nephew again. Get to know him better."

"Anytime," I replied softly. "I'd like that, Antoine." I opened the door for him. "One more thing before you go. As far as I'm concerned, I never gave you this money. It's a private matter so it stays between me and you. Understand?"

He engulfed me in a hug. "Of course. Thank you, Char. As soon as I pay Kingman, I'm leaving town for a few days." He sighed. "I've got to get away for a while."

"Take care of yourself," I said as he walked out and descended the steps waving goodbye. Without regret, I closed the door and leaned against it, sighing with relief. I didn't want any more problems with Antoine. Or Dewey Kingman.

As for Harv and Will... I planned to have words with both—Will first. He, of all people, knew better than to keep something this important from me!

This latest issue was more than keeping me in the dark about a family matter. I expected this type of behavior from Harv, whose loyalty to my late husband guided his every decision concerning me, but not from Will. He knew how vehemently I'd always hated the way Gus had treated me more like a possession than an equal. Discovering that Will had deliberately concealed such serious information from me not only upset me, but it also hurt me deeply. Our marriage wouldn't survive without total honesty and equality.

I wanted to telephone him—tonight—to confront him about Antoine, but something as serious as this needed to be discussed in person. Our next conversation would determine whether we had a future together or if we went our separate ways. For our baby's sake, I hoped it was the former.

Chapter Twelve

July 21st

WILL

The heavy front door of Char's mansion slid open and Gerard's round, bearded face appeared. "Good evening, Mr. Van Elsberg," he said in a deep, melodious voice with his English accent. He opened the door and bowed slightly as I entered wearing my best tan suit and holding a bouquet of roses. "My Lady is anticipating your arrival."

I always found his reference to Char as "My Lady" to be amusing, but also endearing. Yes, she was quite a lady—and she was *my* lady too.

He placed my tan Panama fedora in the closet and led me into the sunroom, Char's favorite place to relax. I laid the paper cone filled with fresh-cut flowers on the table and made myself comfortable on the sofa. The fancy hinged box holding Char's engagement ring was buried deep in my trouser pocket. We'd had our differences lately, but I loved Char with all my heart, and she loved me. Months ago, in the hospital, I'd promised her that once my injury healed, I'd propose to her properly. Now that I'd been given a clean bill of health from my doctor, I planned to pop the question to her.

Ten minutes later, Char appeared in the doorway, smiling. She wore a green and tan print dress with a green satin sash tied around her hips. A fragrant cloud of floral perfume surrounded her as she moved toward me. My heart went into overdrive.

"Will, I'm sorry to keep you waiting. I was putting Julien to bed," she said as I took her in my arms and kissed her smooth red lips. Though she had a nanny to take care of the task, Char usually tucked her infant son into bed every night.

I grabbed the flowers off the table. "These are for you."

"Thank you, they're beautiful," she said with a smile, "but it's *your* celebration, Will! You've just received the greatest news from the doctor so I should be giving you something." An odd expression crossed her face as she took the roses from me and quickly set the bouquet back on the table for Gerard to put into a vase. I could have sworn she winced as she turned away and I wondered if she'd poked her finger on one of the thorns.

"A nice, quiet evening with you to myself is all I want," I replied as I pulled her into my arms and gazed into her eyes.

Gerard appeared in the doorway. "Dinner is served."

I was starving. I'd been saving my appetite all day for the meal prepared by Char's wonderful cook, and I couldn't wait to sink my teeth into it.

We followed Gerard to the dining room. She didn't let on that anything was amiss, but I sensed an uneasiness about her as we were seated at the large table. I wondered why.

For the meal, Char's cook had prepared Colbert breast of chicken, fresh green beans, and rissole potatoes with warm dinner rolls. Everything tasted delicious, but I especially liked the way Adeline, or "Cook," as she liked to be called, made those little herbed potatoes— crisp and buttery. They melted in my mouth.

For dessert, Cook had baked my favorite dish, the one that Minnie, my family's cook used to make for me as a young boy; a two-layer, dark chocolate cake with thick, finger-licking frosting. Cook served it herself, beaming with pride as she carried the cake plate into the dining room.

"That was a terrific meal," I said as I held up a small forkful of cake to Char's lips. "I'm looking forward to the leftovers." Whenever I came for dinner, Cook always made an extra portion of the food for me to take home and included a generous helping of dessert. I *never* turned it down.

Char nibbled on the cake and smiled at me, but I knew her mind was somewhere else. During dinner, the more I observed her, the more I noticed little things about her that didn't add up—her lack of appetite, the pallor of her skin, the slight tremble in her smile. What was she holding back? Was she still hurt about what happened at The Women's

Friendship Club ball? Or was she still upset with me over questioning her judgment concerning Louisa? I needed to find out more.

"Let's take our coffee out on the terrace," I suggested. "It's a beautiful evening."

The sun glowed like a crimson ball, slowly sinking behind the tall oaks lining the property as Gerard accompanied us out to the back terrace with the silver coffee service. A southerly breeze kept the evening temperature comfortably warm.

Gerard silently placed the tray on the table, poured the coffee, then left.

"Look at the sky," I said and dragged my chair close to hers. "The sunset is brilliant tonight." I slid my arm around her, expecting her to cuddle up to me, but she didn't seem to hear me as she stared across the yard at the twin cottages occupied by Adrienne and Rory, the new gardener with the frisky German shepherd.

"Dan's pretty proud of Adrienne getting the job performing at The Oasis. He wants us to join him there for dinner one of these days. Would you like to go?" I glanced at her, waiting for a reply, but she kept staring as though she was still so deep in thought she hadn't heard me. "We'll get Maddie and Peter to come along, too. I guarantee it'll be a lot of fun."

"Sure," she said as she looked away. "Sounds like a great idea."

She stood up and walked to the stone railing. I jumped up, following her. "What's wrong? You've been preoccupied with something all evening. What's going on—"

"I'm pregnant," she blurted out, placing her palms on the railing.

My jaw dropped in slow motion as I stood behind her, so stunned by her words it took me a moment to collect my thoughts. "You're— you're...*what*?"

"I'm in my third month." She turned and gazed into my eyes. "I didn't think it could happen so easily—after only one night together— but I was wrong."

I knew she'd been under the weather lately. That *one night* happened so long ago, I never suspected that was the reason. My mind churned in confusion. I'd never been in a situation like this before and didn't know the proper words to say, but her reaction puzzled me even more than my own. Wasn't she supposed to be indescribably happy? Crying tears of joy? Instead, she looked despondent. I took her hands in mine. They were cold and clammy. "Are you all right? I mean, is everything good with…with—" I glanced toward her stomach. I felt so awkward, I couldn't seem to get the rest of the words out.

"Everything is going well. So far, anyway," she said quietly, finishing the sentence for me. "What about you? How do you feel about this?"

"Surprised…" I replied slowly. But at the same time, I was mystified. Me…a father? Suddenly, the gravity of the situation began to sink in. "Once your condition becomes obvious, Char, people are going to talk. We need to get married." Slipping my hand into my pocket, I grabbed the ring box.

She pulled away from me. "Marriage is an equal partnership, Will. I'm disappointed that you don't take it seriously."

I found her answer confusing. "What are you talking about? Of course, I do."

She gave me a skeptical look. "I don't think so."

"We love each other," I argued. "You're going to have my baby. I'll raise your son as my own. We'll become a real family. It's what you've always wanted, isn't it?"

She leaned against the railing and folded her arms. "Yes, I do, and that's what makes this so difficult. I can't marry you unless you come clean with me, Will. About *everything*."

Leaving the ring in my pocket for now, I stepped in front of her, positioning myself between her and the windows to conceal our conversation from watchful eyes in the house. "You're not making sense, Char. I told you the story behind the money my old man left me and about my disastrous courtship with Eva. That's all there is to tell you about my past. What more do you want from me?"

Her eyes suddenly narrowed. "I want to know why you didn't tell me about Antoine's outstanding gambling debt at King's Castle Royale. And why I had to learn about it from Antoine instead of you—or Harv." She glared at me. "I'm angry at Harv for not telling me, but honestly, I never expected that you would conceal it from me, too!"

"Did Kingman approach you about it?" I asked, surprised.

"No, Antoine told me."

I shoved my hands into my pockets. I had plenty to say about the issue, but I needed to make her understand why I didn't tell her. It was crucial to get this right. Our future depended upon it.

"Antoine contacted Harv about paying his gambling debt," I began softly. "He told Kingman that you'd pay it. Harv refused to give in to Antoine's demands, so Kingman contacted him directly. And Harv still refused. Harv asked me to confirm Antoine's debt with Kingman otherwise I wouldn't have known about it, either. As your lawyer, it was Harv's call to keep the issue quiet for now, not mine. I could have refused to take the case, but I needed to know what was going on. Otherwise, how could I keep you safe? I know you're upset with me, but I had to agree to his terms, or he would have enlisted someone else. Harv was adamant that you be shielded from it in case the situation got ugly."

"We agreed there would be no more secrets between us!" she retorted icily, her cheeks darkening with anger. "You went back on your word almost as soon as you gave it! How can I ever trust you again?"

"Char, listen to me," I argued and placed my hands on her shoulders. "I kept this quiet because your safety is at stake. Kingman isn't asking for payment. He's demanding it—and he means business!"

She shoved my hands away. "So what?" Angry tears filled her eyes. "You think I can't handle Antoine or some fat old man who thinks I'm obligated to pay off my brother-in-law's bills? If that's true, you don't know me very well."

"The trouble is, my dear," I said losing my composure. "I *do* know you. I know how you react to threats and so does Harv. You're like a bomb with a short fuse. You'll storm Dewey Kingman's office and confront him with no thought of the consequences. A man like that doesn't take well to being called out by a woman."

"You're wrong, Will," she argued. "I'm not going to blow up at Kingman. I made peace with Antoine instead and gave him the money as a one-time gift."

I was aghast. "You paid him?"

"Yes, I did."

"Why—"

"Because I determined it was what Gus would have wanted me to do," she said cutting me off. "And because I'm capable of handling my own affairs. The real issue here is that I don't appreciate you and Harv making decisions for me behind my back!"

"You need to calm down," I said, keeping my voice low, hoping the servants hadn't overheard our exchange. "Getting so upset can't be good for your condition—"

"Don't tell me to calm down," she replied, seething, "and don't use that excuse on me! My condition isn't the issue here. Your deception is!" She pushed me away. "I put up with Gus' lies and disloyalty for nine years. I will not put up with it for one second from you!"

This made me angry. I gripped my hands on my hips, insulted at being ranked morally with her dead husband. "Don't ever place me in the same category as him ever again, lady! I'm not perfect, but I would *never* treat you like he did."

She glowered at me. "Then don't try to solve *my* problems without consulting me first, Will."

"You mean *our* problems, Char," I replied, growing exasperated. Desperate to bring down the temperature of this discussion, I pulled her close. "You know I love you with all my heart."

She looked up, her eyes stubborn and defiant. "Will, I love you more than I ever loved Gus and that's why we will work this out here and now or not at all. We can't be happy unless we trust each other implicitly."

Her stubborn refusal to listen to reason began to wear on my patience. "I won't compromise where your safety is concerned," I said with finality. She needed to know where I stood. "I don't apologize for my actions. I'll do whatever it takes to keep the woman I love safe."

She pushed me away. "How dare you suggest I'm not tough enough to fight my own battles!"

"Look," I said letting out a loud, exasperated sigh, "this conversation is going nowhere. You're becoming unreasonable—"

"Then go home, Will, before we start saying terrible things to each other we can't take back!" She wiped the tears of frustration from her cheeks with the back of her hands. "I'm not going to argue with you about this anymore. I may see things differently one day and change my mind, but for now, *I'll* decide what's best for me."

"Fine." I pointed a finger at her to put her on notice. "You get the last word tonight, but this conversation is *far* from over." I stormed toward the back door to get my hat and get out of there. I was so angry and disappointed I could barely hold my temper in check. I needed to find the closest speakeasy and drown my problems in a stiff drink to take the edge off my frustration while I figured out how to solve this argument. I had no intention of backing down.

Bad news traveled fast. Exceedingly fast in *this* household. By the time I reached the front door, Gerard stood in the entryway holding my hat. The concerned frown on his face indicated he'd heard everything. I grabbed my hat and kept going. The less I said right now, the better.

I slid into my car and realized I still had the ring box in my pocket. I gripped the steering wheel, disappointed that our argument had postponed our happy moment.

Two packages wrapped in brown paper and tied with string were lying on the seat. One of the servants had thoughtfully placed the extra dinner and the rest of my birthday cake from Cook in the car to make sure I took it with me. Char's servants were good, loyal people who cared about her deeply.

I cared about her deeply, too. And my unborn child.

Now that I knew about the baby, the situation made me more determined than ever. I planned to marry that woman, change her name, and erase the curse of Gus' legacy over her life.

Forever.

Chapter Thirteen

Saturday, July 22nd

CHAR

Saturday morning dawned sunny, hot, and miserably humid. I drank my first cup of coffee in bed, looking forward to a better day than I'd experienced yesterday.

Lillian, my maid laid out a yellow cotton shift for me to wear. After I dressed, I went down to the breakfast room to eat a light meal. Normally, I enjoyed drinking my coffee while watching the sun rise over the horizon, but the temperature had already climbed to an uncomfortable level, so the shades had been pulled to keep the room as cool as possible.

To keep my mind off my problems with Will, I planned to spend the morning working on a general floor plan for my new cosmetics salon and start an inventory list of items I wanted to stock but realized right away I couldn't concentrate. The argument with Will last night had shaken me. I hadn't expected him to dig in his heels and get so angry that he began shouting at me. That said, I knew he loved me and genuinely cared for my well-being. He believed he'd acted in my best interest and wouldn't back down even if it caused us to be at odds with each other.

Guilt pierced my heart. I had purposely dragged my feet on hiring bodyguards even though I knew he was adamant about getting it done. Using the telephone in my den, I called Will at home, hoping he could stop by for lunch, but no one answered. I called his office, but no one answered there, either. Disappointed, I set the earpiece back on the switch hook and slowly placed the candlestick telephone back on my desk.

The clock on the fireplace mantel in the library chimed nine times. I had only made it halfway through the morning before exhaustion had overtaken me. I had to go back to bed.

Lillian came into my bedroom just as I stretched out on my soft cotton bedspread. My energy had drained so low that I didn't even feel like taking my dress off to keep it from getting wrinkled. "What's wrong?" Her voice, though soft, echoed with deep concern. "Aren't you feeling well?"

"I'm just tired," I said as I sunk my cheek into my soft feather pillow. "It's already a scorcher today and the humidity is so uncomfortable I'm fading fast." I yawned as I curled up on my side. "I need to take a nap."

I hadn't said a word to my staff about my condition yet, but they most likely found out last night as Will and I argued on the terrace. I planned to speak with them about it, but I needed to tell Francie first. Unfortunately, I still didn't have any idea how to break the news to her.

Lillian made sure the drapes were tightly closed and turned on the oscillating fan. She quietly left the room but returned quickly with a thin sheet that she spread over me. "I'll bring you a fresh pitcher of ice water and make sure no one disturbs you."

"Hmmm…" I whispered as the methodical whirring of the fan relaxed me and lulled me into a deep, restful sleep.

By the time I awoke, the clock on my nightstand read noon. "Gosh, I've got to get up," I mumbled as I pulled the sheet away and sat up. My head swam with dizziness. My limbs felt sluggish. "Oh," I whispered to myself as I ran my fingers through my hair, yawning uncontrollably. "I can't believe how tired I've been."

The door opened and Lilian's tall, willowy silhouette appeared. She poured me a glass of water from the pitcher at my bedside. "You had a good nap. Are you ready for lunch?"

"Yes, I'm starved," I said and drained the glass. I yawned again as I set it on the nightstand. "I've got to get up and get moving or I won't get anything done today." The trouble was, I had plenty of ambition but not much energy. I just couldn't shake this lethargy overshadowing me.

I had just finished eating a chicken sandwich and a small dish of cucumber salad in the dining room when the telephone rang. Gerard appeared a few moments later. "You have a telephone call from Missus Wentworth."

Surprised yet curious, I drank the last of my iced tea then hurried into the library and picked up the candlestick telephone. "Hi, Sally," I said, happy to hear from her. "How are you?"

"I've got some good news," Sally replied quickly. "I got a call this morning from a woman who is interested in making a sizeable donation to Anna's House."

"Really?" I perked up. "Is she a friend of yours?"

"No," Sally replied. "I don't know who she is. Anyway, she wants to take a tour of the facility this afternoon."

Feeling lightheaded from the heat, I sat down. "Perhaps I'll join you."

"Goodness, no," Sally replied quickly. "Not in your condition. You don't need to drive over here in this heat. I'll handle it. I just wanted to keep you informed. I'll call you afterward and tell you how the meeting went."

She'd intended the words 'not in your condition' to mean that she was looking out for my health, but that wasn't what I wanted to hear. I wanted her to invite me to join her! The prospect of meeting a new donor had perked me up, giving me a surge of fresh energy.

After we ended the call, I went upstairs and grabbed my clutch then hurried back downstairs to get my cloche hat, deciding I didn't have time to change into business attire. Leaving by the back way, I hurried down the terrace steps and hustled across the yard, past the cottages to the garage. Inside, Errol stood leaning over my new limousine with a soft rag in his hands, polishing the shiny black surface of the car. Sweat covered his brow.

He started my Ford. I slid in behind the steering wheel and took off, waving goodbye to Errol and then to Chet, my daytime security guard as he opened the front gate. The wind cooled my face and neck as I drove to the shelter. I parked on the shady side of the building between a black limousine and Sally's gold Pontiac and turned off my car.

The place seemed unusually quiet for Saturday afternoon. I used my key to let myself in and walked through the common area then took the stairs to the second floor to Sally's office. I found the door shut but when I lightly rapped on it, she opened it.

Her face registered surprise. "What are you doing here, Char?" She had on a short-sleeved dress in a bright green print. Her cheeks looked flushed from the heat. The humidity had turned her coppery top knot to a ball of frizz. The buzz of an oscillating fan created a calming sound as it circulated the air around the office. "You should be home relaxing with your feet up."

"I needed to get out of the house," I said as I breezed past her. "I thought it would be great fun to accompany you on the tour."

"We just finished," Sally stated and turned to a woman resting in a chair with a glass of ice water.

Her visitor, a woman who looked to be in her sixties and wearing a black dress, sat in one of the blue wingback chairs that had been part of the original decorating back when this room had served as Gus' office. The stout woman's stone-gray hair framed her face with expertly styled finger waves. At the nape of her neck, a diamond and emerald comb held a thick chignon in place.

"Char, this is Mrs. Ethel Rogers," Sally said proudly. "Ethel, this is Charlotte LeDoux."

Ethel stood and extended her free hand to me. She shook my hand with a firm grip. "How nice to meet you, Charlotte. Sally has told me so much about you." Her deep, commanding voice gave her an air of authority. The sharp lines on her face deepened when she smiled. "It's wonderful what you and Sally have done here," she said, placing her empty glass on a small table. "I'm quite impressed with your leadership. I've decided to support your cause."

"Thank you, Mrs. Rogers," I replied gratefully. "Every dollar you contribute will go toward helping the women in our care to achieve independence."

"Just call me Ethel," she said kindly. She checked her diamond-encrusted wristwatch. "I'd like to stay longer but I'm afraid I must be going."

Sally's telephone rang.

"I'll see you out," I said to Ethel. We left Sally's office together.

"I understand you're starting a cosmetics salon with Madeline Van Elsberg to teach the women here business skills," Ethel stated frankly as we neared the stairway.

"Yes, we are," I replied. Gripping my hand on the railing, I slowly made my way down the wooden stairs while we talked. "Our plans haven't progressed as quickly as we had hoped, however. We're still looking for a suitable space."

"Yes, I know," Ethel said with a confident air as we reached the bottom of the stairs, "but that won't be a problem now."

Surprised, I turned to her. "How so?"

"My husband, Willard, owns the building at Selby and Dale," she replied, her voice hardening. "I overheard him and his manager discussing your interest in renting space." She shook her head as though their conversation angered her. "Your ideas intrigued me, so I made a few calls. My inquiries left me very impressed. That's how I found out about this place."

Really... I thought in surprise. "Thank you," I said softly. "I appreciate that."

"I admire what you're doing," she replied. "The good Lord knows how difficult it is for a woman to forge ahead with ambitions as big as yours. I give you credit for not giving up. There was only one acceptable path for a woman when I was your age," she said with a note of regret. "I'm glad that the young women of today are taking control over their lives."

Her answer convinced me that she'd heard about my humiliating ejection from the Friendship Club ball. "Forgive me if I'm speaking out of turn," I asked as we walked through the common area to the front door, "but how did you convince your husband to rent to us?"

111

She let out a tense sigh and squared her shoulders. "He's desperate to avoid the spectacle of divorce court. Willard won't oppose me on this."

I didn't know what she meant by that, and I didn't ask. Whatever Willard did, it must have made her exceedingly angry to threaten him with retaliation as drastic as divorce!

At the door, Ethel squeezed my arm. "You and Miss Van Elsberg are free to obtain the key from Tom Stevens whenever it suits you. There's no charge for the first month. After that, the rent is due on the first day of every month." Her brown eyes narrowed. "If he gives you any trouble, I'm sure you can handle it, but if he gets too ornery, let me know. *I'll* deal with him."

"Yes, Ma'am," I replied obediently and opened the front door to see her out.

She waved as she left the building. "Be sure to invite me to the grand opening!"

"Okay!" I shut the door and stared at the plate in the ceiling where the huge crystal chandelier used to hang, deep in thought. Ethel Rogers was an amazing woman. She had a big heart, but the hardness in her manner gave me the impression she'd seen her share of misery. Her husband sounded like a difficult man.

I folded my arms and let out a deep sigh. I'd managed to dodge that bullet, no pun intended, when my husband died of gunshot wounds at the hands of Leonard Murtaugh. Had Gus lived, I might have found myself in the same situation. Shuddering, I pushed myself away from the door and headed upstairs. I didn't want to think about Gus anymore or my failed marriage. Sally and I had something to celebrate!

* * *

My celebratory mood didn't last long.

I found Sally angrily pacing the floor of her office. Louisa sat in the chair that Ethel Rogers had occupied pressing a balled-up handkerchief to her scarlet face. Her eyes were swollen from crying. "What happened while I was gone?"

"That caller was Louisa's brother-in-law," Sally snapped. "He claims she needs to come home now that she's had her baby. He needs someone to take care of her mother and he's determined to make trouble for us if Louisa doesn't cooperate."

So…the brother-in-law was up to no good—the same man who had abused her.

"Well, that's *not* going to happen," I said emphatically as I folded my arms. "If this man thinks he's going to intimidate us with his threats, he's mistaken."

"I think we're going to let the police handle this one," Sally said firmly and smoothed a lock of stray red hair from her forehead. "From what Louisa tells me, he's got quite a temper."

"And when he gets upset, somebody has to pay," Louisa added tearfully.

I crossed the room and sat down in the other wingback chair. "I'm sorry this man continues to cause you problems, but I want you to know, Louisa, you're not alone. Not anymore. We won't let him touch you. What's his name?"

"Carl Brock," Louisa said, her voice thick with emotion. "He hates his job in the ticket office at the Union Depot and whenever he comes home from work in a bad mood, he starts to drink. He gets ugly and always takes his anger out on someone. It used to be me."

Well, he isn't going to take it out on anyone here, I thought grimly to myself.

Someone banged on the office door. "Mrs. Wentworth, open up, please! It's an emergency!" a feminine voice cried. "A man is pounding on the front door."

"Lordy, that was fast!" Sally opened the office door and one of the residents, a young woman, rushed in. "He's pounding hard. It's locked, but he's frightening some of the girls."

Someone else ran in behind her. "A man has kicked open the door!"

Louisa's face went deathly pale. Her eyes widened with fear.

Sally snatched her telephone and spoke to the operator, asking to be connected to the local police station.

We had to keep Louisa out of sight until we dealt with this man. I reached down and pulled the floor rug out of the way then stepped over to the bookcase and grabbed onto the shelf of the middle one. It slid out, revealing a steep, narrow staircase that led to the attic.

Both women stared at me, stunned to learn of my secret hiding place.

"This was Gus' hideout," I said to Louisa and gestured for her to ascend the stairs. "I found it a few months ago—back when this place was empty. There's a small room up there where you'll be safe." I showed her the handles on the back of the bookcase. "Pull it shut with these. When you're ready to come out, just push here and it'll open. We'll let you know when he's gone."

Sally put her hand over the mouthpiece. "Char, you need to go up there, too."

Heavy footsteps pounded on the stairway. Louisa quickly disappeared behind the door and pulled it shut.

I couldn't open it again. Time had run out. The man's footsteps echoed in the hallway. The women who'd come upstairs to warn us fled the room. Sally signaled to me to stand behind the door. She hung up the telephone just before a man of mid-height stepped into the doorway. I peered at him through the crack between the door and the woodwork and observed a middle-aged man wearing a brown suit. He had dark curly hair.

"How dare you break into this facility!" Sally said, facing off with him. "You're trespassing on private property. I order you to leave immediately!"

"A simple lock isn't going to keep me out of this lousy flophouse," he said to Sally in a steel-soft voice as he studied her.

"I beg your pardon," Sally shot back. "This is a *safe home for women*. I repeat, you aren't allowed here—*Carl Brock*. So, it's time for you to leave."

"Mister Brock to you," he said arrogantly. He glanced around, letting her know her demand meant nothing to him. "Where is she?"

"Where is whom?" Sally asked crisply. I held my breath; amazed she wasn't giving an inch.

"You know who I'm talking about." He stared into her eyes, his manner deadly calm. "I'm not leaving without Louisa."

"Well, as you can see, she's not here," Sally said firmly as she walked past him into the hallway. I didn't know if he realized it, but she was attempting to lead him away from this room. Though she didn't show it outwardly, I could tell by the elevated pitch of her voice that his bullying agitated her.

His condescending sneer projected a superior manner. "Now that her little predicament has been taken care of, she'll be coming home with me. Her welfare will be decided by her family."

"Where were you when she needed you?" Sally shook her head. "Louisa isn't going anywhere, *Mister* Brock."

"Yes, she is! Her mother is under a doctor's care, and she needs Louisa to care for her."

Why, I thought acidly as I watched the drama unfolding, *so you can continue to molest her and blame her for it?* Louisa didn't need her mother or her family. She needed a new life!

"I'm not turning her over to you," Sally argued as she walked away. "Louisa is in control of her own life and makes her own decisions."

"Oh, so that's the way you're going to play this, eh? You want me to come back with her sister and a couple of coppers?" Carl Brock's voice faded as they disappeared down the hallway. "I guarantee then you won't be so uppity!"

I scooted out from behind the door and followed them. When I reached the end of the hallway, Carl Brock and Sally stood at the bottom of the stairs.

"Get your hands off me!" Sally jerked her arm from his grasp. "Get out!"

The women began gathering in the common area, jeering at the intruder. One of them shouted, "Yeah! Get out!"

Suddenly all of them were shouting, "Get out! Get out! Get out!"

The militant mood spreading across the room frightened me. I ran downstairs just as one of the women threw a tin cup, hitting Carl Brock on the shoulder. At first, he turned toward the mob with his hands clenched. Then he charged into the crowd.

Sally ran after him and grabbed his arm. "Stop this! Now!"

He shoved Sally backward, causing her to slam into a drum table. The crowd gasped and crowded around Sally to protect her.

The drum table had a heavy lamp on it. While Sally and Carl Brock were arguing, I pulled the shade off the brass candlestick lamp and jerked the cord out of the light socket.

"*I've had enough of you,*" Sally said through clenched teeth and looked around for something to use as a deterrent.

Someone grabbed the lamp from my hand and swiftly moved toward him. *Thunk!* She smacked him on the head with it.

Everyone froze as he rubbed his fingers through his bloody hair and glared at her. "Why you stupid—"

Another woman suddenly kicked him—hard—distracting him. It gave Sally just enough time to move away as the woman with the lamp adjusted her hold on her weapon. This time, she swung and clubbed him harder on the side of his head with the heavy, round base.

Cheers mixed with the wail of sirens pierced the air as I stared at Carl Brock sprawled across the floor, groaning, and holding his bloody head with both hands. The women held him down and Sally leaned over him, poised to hit him again if he continued to resist. He didn't.

I slowly mounted the stairs to return to the office, my heart heavy with sadness over the entire episode. Louisa—and all the women in this building—were trying to turn their lives around and needed to be left alone. For most of the women, abusive men were the reason they'd landed here in the first place. They didn't need their problem relationships to follow them to the one place where they should be safe!

The police burst through the front door as I reached the top of the stairs. I kept going. Sally's husband, Bernard, was the Chief of Police in the St. Paul Police Department, and she knew every officer on the force. They would take over now.

* * *

The commotion downstairs gradually fused into distant, muffled sounds as I entered the office and pulled open the bookcase. "You can come down now," I said, my voice echoing up the stairway. After a few moments, Louisa appeared at the top of the stairs. "Come up here, Char. We've got a bird's eye view of the action."

I stepped through the doorway and climbed the steep stairway to a roughly hewn chamber. It was hot up there, but Louisa had opened the small windows that were camouflaged by slatted vents on each end of the long, narrow room allowing a much-needed breeze to flow through it. The room was sparsely furnished with wooden folding chairs, a small table, candles, and several bedrolls. Motheaten oriental rugs covered the floor. The place smelled musty.

Small clouds of fine dust billowed around me as I walked across the room, ducking the cobwebs hanging from the low, slanted ceiling. I peered through the slatted window. Several police cars and a Model T paddy wagon with its back doors open were parked in front of the building. We watched two officers drag Carl Brock outside and force him into the vehicle.

"I'm sorry, Louisa," I said quietly as I stared down at the ruckus below. "I don't know how he found out that you'd had the baby. Sally would never have informed your family unless you asked her to do it. I trust her completely."

Louisa's face hardened like a stone mask as she stared through the slats. "I don't know who told him, either, but I do know this—it's time for me to find a place of my own. If I don't get out of here soon, he's going to ruin *everything* for me."

That last sentence gave me the sense she had more going on than she was letting on. "What do you mean?"

She turned to me. "Peter and I…" Her face suddenly softened. "I've really enjoyed working with him. Truthfully, the past three weeks have been like heaven on earth. I know the job isn't going to last much longer, but it doesn't matter." Her lips parted slightly, and she drew in a deep breath as though she wanted to say more.

"Why doesn't it matter, Louisa?" I asked curiously and waited for her to continue.

"I stayed late at the office the first two days after I started, catching up on Peter's dictation. On the second day he asked me if he could buy my dinner to repay me for working so hard to get caught up," she said with a thread of happiness in her voice. "I knew he simply wanted to thank me for putting in extra hours, and I didn't expect him to go to a lot of trouble on my behalf, so I was surprised when he took me to a classy supper club. I've never been to one before! I had a wonderful time, but I didn't expect it to be repeated. To my surprise, though, the next night he asked me again." Her eyes began to shine. "We've been dining out together every night since then. Last night, he kissed me."

My jaw dropped. Louisa and Peter? I wanted to know more!

"When he brings you home," I asked curiously, "what explanation do you give to him about living here?"

She turned away from the window. "He doesn't know about this place. He drops me off at Sally's house and as soon as he drives away, I take the streetcar home."

This bothered me immensely. Louisa couldn't start a relationship with Peter based on deceit. Once he found out, that would be the end. And her heart would be broken.

"I've fallen in love with him," Louisa said as she leaned against the wall and smiled dreamily. "I know he feels the same way about me."

I stared in amazement at the change in her. She used to be sour, bitter, and critical of everything. Abandonment and being forced to fend for herself in a shelter were the equivalent of hitting rock bottom, but it hadn't been a disadvantage for her. Rather, it freed her by providing an opportunity to make her own decisions and create a new vision for her life.

"Then you need to be honest with him," I said seriously. "I'm so happy for you, Louisa. Peter is a good man and I hope your courtship works out, but at the same time, I'm worried for you, too. One day he's going to show up at Sally's to surprise you with a ride to work and then he'll learn the truth. You need to tell him everything. Lay all your cards on the table. If it's meant to be, he'll be understanding and supportive. If not, then it's over before your heart is broken." I took her hands in mine. "Don't wait. The longer you put it off, the harder it will be to tell him about it."

She stared at the ceiling, blinking away tears. "I know. It's been bothering me since the first time we had dinner together. I'm so afraid he'll be revolted by my past and turn away from me."

"That's a chance you'll have to take," I said gently. "You don't have any choice."

She wiped a tear from her cheek and nodded in agreement. "I'm so afraid! I don't want to lose him, Char. He's the only good thing that's ever happened to me."

I hugged her as tears smarted in my eyes and a lump in my throat prevented me from saying anything else.

We watched the cadre of police vehicles leave the premises then we shut the windows. We descended the stairs and pushed the bookcase back into place. Louisa went down to the common area to speak to Sally privately about Peter. I made a trip to the ladies' room and then went downstairs to say goodbye.

"I'm going home," I said to Sally. "I'll call you later."

I turned to Louisa and gave her another hug. "It will be all right," I whispered in her ear.

I left the building in better spirits than when I arrived. Louisa and Peter! How amazing was that? And wonderful, too. I had no way to know how things would turn out for them, but I hoped, for her sake, that it went in her favor.

I rounded the corner of the building to start my car and drive home. A black Model T hardtop with the motor running sat in the place where

Ethel Rogers' Packard limousine had been parked, and I wondered if it belonged to Carl Brock. I hadn't seen anyone else come into the building before I left, so I was curious.

But not for long.

The moment I stepped between the vehicles, someone came up behind me and smashed a gag over my mouth. Someone else grabbed my hands and tied them behind my back. A strong man with large hands jerked a musty gunny sack over my head and roughly shoved me into the trunk of the car.

It all happened so fast that I barely had time to think, but as the trunk slammed shut and someone shifted the car into reverse, I suddenly realized what had happened.

I had been kidnapped.

Chapter Fourteen

WILL

Where was Char?

I stood in my front parlor on the telephone, hoping to speak to Char, but Gerard indicated that she'd left the house in a hurry right after lunch to visit Sally Wentworth and hadn't returned yet. I spent the next hour idly wandering around my house, checking my timepiece, wondering why she hadn't called me back. I wanted to take her to The Oasis tonight for dinner. After the disastrous ending of our conversation last night, I wanted to make things right between us again. Tonight, after I brought her home, I *would* ask her to marry me and this time I wouldn't take no for an answer!

I'd made reservations at seven o'clock for five people. Peter and I were meeting Daniel there with Char and Peter's friend. He informed me he'd be bringing someone new as his guest for the evening and he couldn't wait to show her off.

I checked my timepiece again. It read four-thirty. If Char didn't return soon, she wouldn't have time to get ready.

Feeling rushed, I picked up the telephone and called her house again, hoping she'd already returned home and was busy getting ready. Gerard answered. "I need to speak to Char," I said cutting him off. "Is she back yet?"

"No, she hasn't returned, sir," Gerard replied, his deep voice threaded with English politeness. "Shall I take a message?"

I scratched my head in frustration and stared at the floor. "All right then. Tell her to call me as soon as she gets home."

"Very good, sir."

I hung up and called the shelter. The woman who answered indicated that Sally and Char were long gone. Char had left several hours ago, and she had no idea where Char had planned to go after that.

Something wasn't right. I knew it in my heart but the trained investigator in me warned me to stay rational. *Don't let your heart rule your head*, I thought to myself. *Follow the facts.*

I called Sally's house and grilled her over Char's whereabouts. She seemed puzzled that Char wasn't home yet because when Char left the shelter earlier that afternoon, she'd indicated that was where she was going.

"She said she'd call me later," Sally said sounding surprised. She paused as though thinking it over. "This isn't like her."

"Perhaps she went shopping and stopped at one of her soda shops for ice cream," I said evenly to avoid worrying her. "I'll drive over to Big Louie's and see if she's there." Not only was that her favorite soda shop but it also happened to be a stone's throw from my house.

"Ask her to call me when she gets home, would you?" Sally sounded worried.

"I'll certainly do that," I replied forcing myself to sound jovial even though I didn't feel that way.

I hung up, grabbed a black fedora off the coat tree, and left the house. I drove through the parking lot of the soda shop but didn't see Char's Ford. Disappointed, I headed to her Ford dealership on West Seventh to see if by chance she'd stopped there. No one at the dealership had seen her that day. Anna's House was only about a block away, so I drove up the hill and pulled into the parking lot.

I stared in astonishment at her Ford parked next to the building. I quickly pulled up alongside it and shut off my car, struggling to calm the alarm building inside my head. As I got out, I glanced around the grounds. The lot for this complex had been carved out of the side of one of the steep hills in this area. The parking area sat adjacent to a ravine covered in old-growth oaks. My chest tightened at the thought of what might be down there.

For now, I concentrated on looking for clues in the parking lot. What could this area tell me? I checked the inside of Char's car and found a plain piece of paper lying on the seat. My mind spun as I picked it up and saw that it contained only three short sentences.

Don't involve the cops. Or she dies. Wait for the call at her house.

Grabbing onto the car door for support, I gazed down at the note as the painful truth stared me in the face.

Char had been kidnapped.

*   *   *

Stepping carefully, I examined the ground and found fresh tire tracks in the dirt. And footsteps. Large and small. It looked like several people had been there. Some of the impressions looked disturbed as though there had been a scuffle.

Concentrating on the evidence, I shoved my worst fears aside and knelt to get a closer look. Something caught my eye. Bending down, my heart began to slam in my chest. Char's handbag lay under the car. I reached underneath it and retrieved her black beaded clutch.

I tossed Char's handbag onto the seat in my car and then quickly searched the parking lot for additional clues, but my efforts turned up nothing. I was on my way back to my car to head over to Char's house when I heard several female voices. I walked around to the back of the building and found two women in plain blue dresses sitting in a small gazebo sharing a cigarette.

"What's she doing in the office with the door locked, anyway?" the first woman asked her companion, unaware of my approach.

"Don't you know? She's getting herself all spiffy to go out with some fella tonight," the other woman remarked in a gossipy tone. "Marjorie overheard her ask Mrs. Wentworth for special permission to leave the premises."

"Who's the lucky guy?" the first woman asked.

"I don't know. She won't say," the other one said. "She's keeping him a secret."

I walked toward them. "Afternoon, ladies. Did you see Charlotte LeDoux today?"

"Yeah, but she ain't here now," one of the women said. "Left hours ago."

"Did either of you happen to see anything unusual going on around the time she left?"

They both jumped to their feet. The short one shook her head. "No, we were on lockdown. We had an incident with one of the girls. Why? Has something happened to Mrs. LeDoux?"

"Just tying up some loose ends." I pulled a pair of business cards from my shirt pocket and offered them to the women. "If you happen to come across anything out of the ordinary, I'd appreciate it if you'd call me. I'm a private investigator."

The tall one gingerly took a card and examined it.

"I need to make an important call right away," I said. "Mind if I use your telephone?"

"Are you going to call the police?" the tall one asked.

I glanced back at the parking lot. "That won't be necessary."

They led me into the building through the back door. In the common area, a woman sat on a gossip bench chatting on the telephone while a small group of women sat at the tables, each waiting impatiently for her turn. A woman standing next to the bench holding a clipboard looked to be the supervisor of the group. All of them wore the same plain dress style in light blue.

"Joyce," the supervisor said, "time's up!"

Everyone turned and stared at me as we joined the group.

"Marlene," the tall woman I'd been speaking to behind the building said as she crossed the room. "This here is…" she glanced at the card again. "Mr. Van Elsberg. He's a private investigator who's looking for Mrs. LeDoux and he needs to get on the line. It's an emergency!"

"Give him the telephone," the supervisor barked.

Joyce reluctantly ended her call and handed the telephone to me.

"Thank you," I said amid a flurry of excited chatter. "This won't take long." I quickly called Char's house. When Gerard answered I asked him to send someone to Adrienne's cottage to give Daniel a message for me. I relayed what I wanted Gerard to tell Daniel in general terms, being careful not to reveal too much. It was a party line and quite possibly the other occupants of this line were listening in. I told Gerard I'd be there soon and hung up.

"Thank you." I handed the telephone back to the supervisor and walked out.

I raced to Char's home and sped down the driveway to Adrienne's cottage. Daniel's car was gone. He and Errol were probably already at Anna's House retrieving Char's Ford.

In the main house, I went straight to the library to wait by the telephone. Within minutes, both cars rolled up the long drive. Hal waved them through.

"What's going on?" Daniel asked as he hurried into the library.

"Char left the house early this afternoon and never returned," I replied gravely as I shut the door. "I found her Ford parked at Anna's House—and this." I held out the note. "Everyone at the shelter said she left hours ago. Her handbag was lying under the car."

Daniel replied with a low whistle as he perused the note. "Do you think they'll call today?"

"Don't know but I'm not leaving this house until they do..." I could barely say the words.

"I'm supposed to drive Adrienne to the club. I'll get Errol to do it tonight," Daniel said hastily. "I'll be back in a couple of minutes."

While Daniel went to talk to Errol and Adrienne, I quickly called Peter to cancel my dinner plans. He wasn't happy about it until I said that Char wasn't feeling well. I ended the conversation as quickly as possible and helped myself to some whiskey. I needed something strong to quell my shaking. Not knowing where Char was or how she was faring was driving me crazy. I couldn't bear the thought of losing her—or my child.

Daniel walked into the library. "I'm sorry about this, Will," he said as he put a hand on my shoulder to reassure me. "There isn't much we can do now except wait for them to contact us. Are you going to call the police anyway?"

"No," I countered quickly and tossed back my whiskey, trying to hold myself together. "We've got to be very careful about this because we don't know who we're dealing with."

"Then what are you going to do?" Daniel asked seriously and shoved his hands into his pockets. "Do you have a plan?"

I poured myself another shot and capped the bottle. The alcohol had begun to settle my nerves, but at the same time, I needed to stay sharp. "I'm going to contact Harv. Besides you, he's the only person I trust to handle this with me."

Harv Katzenbaum, Gus' former attorney and mentor was the most ruthless and powerful man in the St. Paul underworld. Even more powerful than Gus had been. Harv had always treated Char like the daughter he never had and when he found out about her abduction, I had no doubt he would take it personally.

I was counting on that.

Chapter Fifteen

CHAR

For hours, I endured a grueling journey. Where were my captors taking me?

I lay on my side with my knees pulled to my chest on the hard surface of the hot trunk as the vehicle mercilessly bounced over one bump or pothole after another. The roar of traffic had ended long ago. Now, the crunch of gravel under the tires and the rumbling of the engine made me wonder how far into the countryside we'd traveled.

The gunny sack still covered my head. Every time I drew in a breath the dry, musty grain dust from the bag filled my lungs, adding to the agony of my pounding headache. I struggled to change position to relieve the awful ache in my lower back, but as my hands were still tied behind me, I could only shift slightly in the cramped space.

Why did they abduct me? Where were they taking me? Who were *they*?

The first possibility that popped into my mind upset me. Antoine LeDoux's shock over the cash I'd given him flashed through my mind. Did he suspect I had a lot more where that came from and wanted to get his hands on it? Was he the sole architect of this crime or did he have a partner? Were the men who abducted me agents of his? I'd read stories in the newspaper about kidnappings—some local—but I never imagined I'd find myself in the same predicament.

I wondered if anyone at the shelter had witnessed what happened. There weren't any windows facing the parking lot on that side of the building, but someone might have seen something. The women were always wandering outdoors to sit in the gazebo and smoke cigarettes. Surely, they suspected by now that I had met with foul play. Had someone at the shelter called my staff about my car sitting in the parking lot? Sometime during the scuffle, I'd dropped my clutch. I hoped it had been discovered by someone at the shelter instead of the men who'd committed this terrible crime against me.

The car suddenly swerved as though turning a sharp corner and the topography changed. The ride had become smoother, as though we were traveling over a sand-filled road—perhaps a private road or a driveway. Dust filled the trunk, making me cough.

Suddenly, the car stopped, and the doors banged in succession. The trunk lid creaked open, and two pairs of large hands lifted me out. The moment my feet touched the grass, my legs gave way and I nearly fell to the ground, but the hands caught me and dragged me through a doorway. One of my abductors placed me on the floor, and another one untied my hands. The door slammed shut. A lock clicked into place.

I pulled the burlap bag off my head and found myself sitting in pitch darkness. The place was as silent as a tomb and the stale air in this room had a damp, musty smell about it, making me wonder where they were keeping me. I crawled across the wood floor, searching out the room until I bumped into something covered in fabric.

"A sofa," I said aloud with a sigh of relief as my hand ran across a sagging, threadbare cushion. "Oh, thank God. At least I'm not stuck in someone's garden shed or garage."

If the place had a sofa, I hoped it had a lavatory as well. I stood up and spent the next five minutes groping in the dark looking for it. Once I found the wall, I guided myself along it, stumbling over boxes and chairs until I came to a crude restroom that reeked of urine and had barely enough room to turn around. I couldn't find a light switch, so I emptied my bladder as quickly as possible and rinsed my hands in a cold trickle of water in the small sink.

Following the wall once more, I retraced my steps to the threadbare sofa and collapsed upon it. Exhaustion had overtaken me and my back hurt like crazy but that was the least of my worries.

My fate rested in the hands of total strangers, miles away from home. I wondered if they had called my house yet and given instructions to Gerard to secure my release. Regardless, he must be frantic by now. I had no idea how much time has passed but I knew the sun had set a long time ago. I thought of my staff worrying about me because I hadn't come home. My sister was probably inconsolable. And Julien. I missed my baby so much!

Will...

My heart ached for him. He must be beside himself with worry. I missed him so much.

So stiff I could barely move, I slowly stretched out on the sofa and let out a depressed sigh. Tears flowed from my eyes, running over the bridge of my nose, and dripping onto the cushion.

"Go to sleep," I said to myself with a sob. "You can't figure out how to get out of here when you hurt everywhere and you're so tired you can barely think."

Tomorrow I'd size up my situation and try to get some answers out of my kidnappers but for now...

I said a prayer then closed my eyes and fell asleep.

Chapter Sixteen

WILL

I stood in the library and waited anxiously for Harv to answer his telephone. I hoped he hadn't gone out for the evening yet, but after a few rings the operator came back on the line to tell me there had been no answer. Where were his servants?

"He's not answering his telephone," I said grimly to Daniel. I hung up and rubbed the back of my neck. I needed to get ahold of Harv as soon as possible but my options were dwindling.

Daniel sat slumped in one of the chairs resting his head in his hands. He rubbed his face and stood up. "Then I'd better go find him. Where does a guy like Harv Katzenbaum spend his nights?"

"I know of a few places that he's recommended to me," I said. "Nice joints, all of them. No smoky back rooms for him. Ever since Ralph Dixon's men ambushed him, he's been pretty careful about the places he frequents."

"Right," Daniel said as he searched his pocket for his keys. "I'll get going then."

I told him the names of the places I knew of that Harv might patronize on a Saturday night. All of them were top-notch with food and entertainment but since The Oasis was the newest, Daniel said he'd go there first. I knew he wanted to check on Adrienne as well.

As soon as Daniel left, Gerard appeared.

"Dinner is served, sir," he said to me with his usual propriety, but I could tell by the questioning look in his eyes he found Char's absence concerning. "Will My Lady be joining you?" I wanted to address it with him, but I needed to hold off until I spoke with Harv.

"No, not tonight," I said and offered no more. It occurred to me that since the staff knew about Char's condition, perhaps they suspected that she had fallen ill and was in the hospital. I needed to set them straight as soon as I could. The grave looks on their faces indicated they knew something was wrong.

Food was the last thing on my mind, but I decided I needed a break to calm down and I obediently followed Gerard to the dining room. Francie was already there munching on a small plate of celery sticks stuffed with chopped olives and cream cheese.

"Hi, Will," she said, surprised by my solo appearance. "Where's Char?"

"I don't know," I replied as I sat down, acutely aware that Gerard was taking in every word I said. He spread my napkin on my lap and filled my water glass. I glanced at Francie. "Have you spoken with her today?"

"Uh-uh," she said with a mouthful of celery and cream cheese.

Gerard filled my wine glass and then set a dish of chilled shrimp cocktail in front of me. The shrimp and cocktail sauce bore excellent flavor, as usual, but I simply didn't have much of an appetite. I wanted to excuse myself, go back to the library, and walk the floor in front of the telephone, but I needed to put on a brave front until I had more information. Hopefully, no one would notice how badly my hand shook when I picked up my fork.

After dessert, I quickly excused myself and took my coffee to the library. I stared at the telephone feeling more helpless than I had ever felt in my life. Where had they taken Char? Why hadn't her abductors called?

I slung my suitcoat over a chair. Then I loosened the top buttons on my shirt and rolled up my sleeves. I walked the floor, my gaze alternating between the silent telephone and peering out the window at the darkness. Suddenly, a dark limousine pulled up to the guardhouse. The guard waved him through. I didn't see Daniel's car behind his, so I assumed Daniel had gone to pick up Adrienne after her performance.

The limousine stopped inside the carriage house and Gerard opened the front door. Harv jumped out of the car and bolted up the steps two at a time. He charged into the house, heading straight into the library. The balding, gray-haired man wore a three-piece suit and a gold shirt even though the temperature still hovered in the high seventies. "Dan told me what happened. Did they call?"

Shutting the door, I shook my head and told him everything I had discovered at the shelter. "Why *haven't* they called?" I demanded as I slammed my fist on the oval table in the center of the room. "This silence is driving me crazy!"

"That's exactly what they want. They're letting us wait to make us sweat," Harv said as he grabbed the whiskey bottle. "The longer we wait, the more desperate they think we'll be when they do call." He pulled off the cap and sniffed the whiskey, raising his brows in apparent approval.

If that's true, I thought as my chest tightened, *it's working.*

Harv poured a double shot into a crystal lowball glass. "This is what we're going to do," he said as he set the bottle on a small drum table. He paused to adjust his rimless glasses. "We push the furniture aside, put a leaf in the table and make this library our war room. We set up a schedule of one-hour rotating shifts, so someone stays by the telephone all the time. When the call comes, we listen to their demands and then plan our response."

How could he be so calm at a time like this? I pulled out my handkerchief and wiped the sweat from the back of my neck. "What about Char? How do we ensure that she's safe and not...not..." I couldn't finish. The thought of Char being raped or beaten at the hands of her captors terrified me.

Harv went suddenly still. "We make it plain during the negotiations that we want to see her physically before we hand over the money." His eyes narrowed. "Make no mistake," he said in a deadly soft voice, "if they harm one hair on her head, *they* will pay."

I collapsed into a wingback chair, knowing it was time I informed him of perhaps the most important fact of all. "Sit down, Harv. There's something else you need to know."

He had no way of knowing what I was about to say, but the fierceness with which his dark eyes pierced me indicated he suspected something was drastically wrong. He sat in the other wingback chair holding his whiskey glass with both hands.

I drew in a deep breath. "Char is pregnant."

He almost dropped his glass and for the first time since I'd met this man, his confident demeanor slipped. His shock quickly turned serious. "I assume it's *your* child."

I nodded, not knowing what else to say.

But he did. "You'd better be planning to marry her," he said in a dark, threatening tone. "You should have taken care of it as soon as you found out."

I sprang from my chair and pulled the ring box from my trouser pocket. "I've got the ring! Look, I wanted to propose even before I knew about her condition, but after she told me about the baby, she said she couldn't marry someone she couldn't trust. She knew all about Dewey Kingman's demands—Antoine told her—and she was upset that we'd kept it from her."

Harv grunted. "We were simply trying to protect her!"

"I tried to convince her of that, but she claimed I had deceived her," I said as I massaged the growing ache in the back of my neck. "You know how stubborn she can be."

Harv tossed back the whiskey. "You should have taken her over your knee. Sometimes she needs to be shown who's boss."

Take Char over my knee? The concept sounded so ridiculous I almost laughed. Even so, the idea was far from funny. I would never treat her in such a demeaning manner. Looking back, though, I wished I'd ended our argument and given her the ring anyway. For now, we needed to put the issue with Antoine aside and do what was best for her child. *Our* child. "I give you my word, Harv," I said earnestly. "As soon as I get her back, we *will* be married. I love her with all my heart."

He didn't reply, but we both knew that Char's pregnancy gave the situation even more urgency.

Prefaced with a sharp knock, Gerard suddenly entered the room. "Will you be needing anything else this evening, sir?" This was his roundabout way of allowing me to tell him what was going on.

I needed to address the servants. They knew something was terribly wrong and they deserved to be told the truth. They also needed to be warned not to talk about it to anyone. "Yes. Round up the staff and have them meet me in the dining room in ten minutes," I said to him as I glanced at Harv's frown.

"Very good, sir." Gerard gave a slight bow and quickly left the room.

"Be careful," Harv warned me.

"This house is full of telephones," I replied in my defense. "We can't guard them all. Someone might be listening in when the kidnappers call so we need to let the staff know precisely what's going on and why the telephone is off limits."

When I arrived in the dining room, everyone sat around the table— including Francie—staring at me with worried faces as though they were prepared for the worst.

Cook had provided coffee and frosted sugar cookies, but her goodhearted hospitality didn't do much to lighten the mood. I sat next to Francie and held her hand as I explained the situation to her. She stared at me with wide eyes, her face pale with worry. When I finished, I advised the group that the information I gave them needed to be kept confidential.

"You got our word on that," Hal spoke up. "Anything you need— just ask. We want to do our part to help."

Francie began to cry. Cook enveloped her with a loving hug, patting her back as she spoke to the girl in motherly tones.

I thanked everyone for their cooperation and went back to the library.

At ten o'clock, Peter's car pulled up to the guard shack.

"It's Peter Garrett," I said, surprised. "I swear—I didn't tell him anything."

Harv became concerned, worrying that the more people who knew about Char's disappearance, the greater chance it could get back to the kidnappers that the information had gone public.

"I trust him," I assured Harv as I stood at the window, waving at Hal to let him through the gate.

But then this happened…

"How is Char?" Peter asked as he burst into the house with Louisa on one arm and my sister, Madeline on the other. "Is she feeling better? We came to cheer her up."

"No. She's not here," I said as I stood in the entry, upset by their untimely presence. Was Louisa his mystery date? Or was she simply spending the night with Maddie?

"Why?" Peter looked confused. "Is Char in the hospital?"

"No, that's not—" I turned around. "Maddie, wait!"

Maddie had wandered into the library and saw the square note from the kidnappers stuck under the round base of the telephone. She snatched it up before Harv could take it away. She spun around and read it aloud. "What is this?"

"Char has been kidnapped," Harv said bluntly, "and that information doesn't leave this room. Understand?"

I stared at their shocked faces. "We're waiting for the call."

Louisa gasped. "Oh, dear God, no…"

Maddie tossed the note on the table and with tears in her eyes, hugged me tightly. "I'm so sorry, Will."

I didn't have much to say in return. I had too much on my mind.

At my suggestion, the women went to the dining room for some of Cook's refreshments. I glared at Peter. "Why did you bring them here?"

"I realize we should have called first, but we're here now and as Harv said, the information can't leave this room. Look, Will, you don't have to go through this alone," he said in a solemn voice. "Maddie and Louisa are both very worried about her. As am *I*."

Maddie appeared in the doorway of the library. "Will, I—"

At the same time, Francie suddenly appeared on the grand staircase. The moment she saw Maddie, she ran down the stairs and burst into tears as she called Maddie's name.

"Never mind. I'll get the details later," Maddie said and met her upon the landing, greeting Francie with a sisterly hug. "It will be all right, honey. Will and Harv will do everything they can to bring Char home. In the meantime, why don't you show me your room? I'll style your hair."

Francie brightened a little. "All right," she said with a sad smile. "We can use Char's dressing table. It has a lighted mirror and everything!"

Maddie took Francie by the hand and led her up the staircase to the second floor.

Peter and Louisa joined Harv and me in the library. I poured Peter a whiskey. Louisa had a cup of freshly brewed coffee and a cookie. They listened solemnly as I explained the situation.

Sometime after midnight, Daniel returned with Adrienne. They came straight to the house.

There were so many people crowded together in the library, I went into the sunroom, Char's favorite place, to be alone for a while. I soon realized Adrienne had followed me. The distinct fragrance of her French perfume preceded her as she came into the room.

"I'm so upset with myself," she said quietly as she stood behind me. "I let her down."

I spun around. "What do you mean?"

"At The Oasis," Adrienne said, her voice wavering, "on opening night. I told Char I had decided to move out of the cottage." She raised an embroidered handkerchief to her nose as she sniffled. "I thought it was time to go. I'd stayed so long I felt like I'd worn out my welcome, but when I saw the disappointment on her face, I realized I'd hurt her."

I gently rested my palms on her shoulders. "Are you unhappy living in the cottage? Is it too small?"

She shook her head. "I love it here. The people are wonderful, and for the first time in years, I feel safe. I'm grateful to Char for everything she has done for me."

"Then stay," I said simply. "If you were talking to her now, I'm confident that's what she'd say. The cottage is yours for as long as you want it."

"Thank you, Will." She dabbed the beautiful white cloth at the corner of her eye. "I do want to stay. I'd miss her terribly if I moved away."

After Adrienne left me, I sat on the edge of Char's favorite chaise lounge resting my head on my hands. I was tired and distraught, but I had to keep going. Not knowing where her captors had taken her or how she was faring upset me deeply, but until the call came, my hands were tied.

In the meantime, the waiting was killing me.

*   *   *

I lay on Char's chaise lounge for a long time, staring at the ceiling. I had no idea how long I'd been there but according to my watch, it was nearly two o'clock in the morning.

I stood up and slowly walked into the great hall, pausing to massage a deep ache between my shoulder blades. From where I stood, I could see Louisa and Peter standing close together in the dining room. They were having a serious conversation and given the way they looked into each other's eyes, their discussion didn't have anything to do with the office. Intrigued, I leaned against the doorframe and watched them. What were they talking about?

Louisa started to cry.

I stood with my gaze riveted to the scene as Peter gently took her in his arms and held her. Then he framed her face with his hands and kissed her. Raising on her toes, she hooked her arms around his neck and ardently kissed him back. My jaw dropped at the eagerness with which they came together. This was definitely *not* their first kiss!

I blinked—fully alert now. What was *my* secretary doing kissing my best friend? More importantly, how could I have failed to notice their relationship had gone beyond the professional realm to something much more personal?

As if sensing they were being watched, they suddenly pulled apart.

I quickly slipped back into the sunroom and leaned against the wall trying to process what I'd just witnessed. I couldn't help possessing a surge of protectiveness where Louisa was concerned. Despite her modernized appearance, she was still an old-fashioned girl at heart who knew very little about courtship and the ways of men. Peter, on the other hand, cycled women in and out of his life like they were going through a revolving door. The fast-approaching expiration date of Louisa's employment with us concerned me even more. Were Peter's intentions toward her genuine or was he entertaining himself with a temporary fling? My jaw clenched. He and I were lifelong friends and we got along well because we stayed out of each other's personal business. *But not where Louisa was concerned.* He had better not be playing with her heart—or her virtue—or he would answer to me!

I went back into the library to check in with Harv. A few minutes later Peter returned to the library alone. Louisa had gone upstairs to sleep in one of the guest rooms. Maddie and Francie had gone to bed, too. Daniel had escorted Adrienne to her cottage.

Harv pulled a gold watch from his vest pocket. "I'll take the first shift. Garrett, you take the second one. Blythe gets the third. The last one is yours, Will. We'll rotate every hour." He looked up at Peter and me. "You two get some rest."

Get some rest? How? By drugging myself with a half-dozen shots of whiskey? Sure, I could get sozzled and pass out for a few hours, but I needed to stay sharp. I needed to be ready when that call came.

Earlier, Gerard had offered to put me up for the night in one of the bedrooms on the second floor, but I declined, requesting instead to sleep in the men's quarters downstairs. I preferred the peace and quiet down there. And the comfortable temperature.

Even so, there was nowhere I could go to get away from my thoughts. I feared for Char's life. And it was tearing me apart.

Chapter Seventeen

Early the next morning…

CHAR

Slivers of Sunday morning light speared through the slats covering the windows of my makeshift prison. Someone had nailed weathered boards over them.

I awoke to find myself lying on a small, threadbare sofa covered with white dog hair. I slowly sat up and looked around. The small room appeared to have been used as living quarters at one time. Sparsely furnished, it contained an oil burner, a small, cast-iron cooking stove, a metal cupboard, and a sink. And a small, crudely partitioned area for the lavatory. A table and two chairs were pushed into one corner. A cot and a crumpled blanket had been shoved into another corner.

My head swam with dizziness. I flattened out on the sofa again, closing my eyes. I didn't feel well. My back ached and I had a queasy stomach. I wondered if I simply needed to eat something. Given the condition of this room, I knew I wouldn't find any food in the cupboard. Even if I did find something, it was probably littered with dead bugs and mouse droppings.

Sometime later, I awoke again to the sharp click of a lock being turned and the front door scraping along the floor as it opened about a foot or so. My body went rigid, my heart pounding as I lay still, watching. Large hands shoved a tray across the floor and slammed the door shut. The lock clicked again.

I slowly sat up and stared at the tray. It contained a small bowl of oatmeal, a chunk of bread, and a cup of coffee. I got up and retrieved it, suddenly ravenous with hunger. The oatmeal had turned cold, the dry bread had the texture of wool, and the lukewarm coffee tasted like someone has rinsed out their old socks in it, but I didn't care. I hadn't had anything to eat since lunch yesterday and I needed to put something in my stomach.

Afterward, I placed the tray back on the floor by the door and sat down again. Now that I had slept and eaten, I had the rest of the day to…to what? Plan my escape? Discouraged, I got up from the sofa and peered through a tiny crack between the boards. I saw green grass and a lot of mature trees but nothing else. Other than the leaves rustling in the breeze and the chirping of birds, I couldn't detect any other activity. Where had my captors taken me?

Looking around, I noticed the windows were only on the front and one side of the room. The cabin only had one door. The light fixture in the ceiling didn't contain a bulb. I found a small lamp on the countertop, but it didn't work either.

Looking up, I noticed a small area in the ceiling that had been sealed with a thin, flat sheet of wood. Water stains around it indicated that at one time there had been major leakage from the roof due to damage, perhaps from a severe storm. No wonder the air in this place smelled so musty.

Bored, I went back to the window and peered through the crack again hoping to find a clue as to my location or whom I was dealing with but like before, all I saw were trees and grass. Frustrated, I walked over to the sofa and sat down. A large black spider crawled up the wall and stopped as though it had decided to watch me. I didn't like spiders. I had always feared one would bite me and make me swell up like a balloon. Presently, however, this little guy happened to be the only friend I had. So, I watched him back.

"Hey, there, little fella," I said to him, "where are we? Who is holding me captive?" I chuckled. "Oh, I see. It's a secret. Thanks for all your help!"

The spider moved about an inch.

I let out a deep sigh, feeling guilty for not taking better precautions to protect myself from trouble. "I should have hired that security team that Will has been pestering me about, you know?" I said to the spider. "He was right. I was…" My eyes stung with tears of regret. "I was wrong," I squeaked out. "I shouldn't have been so stubborn about it. If I had listened to him, I probably wouldn't be in this awful place."

I missed him so much. And Francie.

And my baby. The thought of being separated from little Julien brought another rush of tears to my eyes. I wondered what my sweet little boy was doing now. Taking his morning nap? My heart ached to hold him in my arms again. Last night was the first time in months that I hadn't been home to check on him before I went to bed. What if something happened to me here and I didn't make it home alive—who would raise him? A tear dropped from my eye and cascaded down my cheek. My greatest fear was dying before my time and making my son an orphan. I couldn't allow that to happen!

I bolted off the sofa and paced the room. Crying did nothing to improve my situation. I could worry all day about things I couldn't control but it wouldn't change anything. Will, Francie, my staff— everyone was probably worried sick about me. I missed them terribly and knew I had to stay strong if I wanted to see them again.

I leaned against the boarded window. No wonder this room was so warm and stuffy. I found a small paring knife in a drawer and tried to jimmy the lock on the door, but I couldn't get it to work. Disgusted, I threw the rusty knife across the room. It bounced off the cot and skittered across the dirty floor.

By afternoon the room began to get uncomfortably warm. I stretched out on the sofa and spent the time trying to read an outdated newspaper that I'd found lying on the floor, but as the light waned, it became difficult to make out the small type. Tired of squinting, I gave up and took a nap.

Late that afternoon I heard the door unlock again. "Hey!" I shouted as I sat up. "Who are you? Why are you holding me prisoner?"

The person didn't answer me. Instead, he shoved the door open just enough to slide another tray into the room containing a bowl of soup, a glass milk bottle filled with water, and another hunk of bread.

"Wait!" I sprang from the sofa and stumbled toward the door. "Please, talk to me! When are you going to let me out of here?"

The door slammed in my face.

I fell against it and slid to the floor. Burying my face in my hands, I sobbed my heart out.

I didn't feel strong anymore. I just wanted this nightmare to end so I could go home.

Chapter Eighteen

WILL

On Sunday morning I awoke to complete silence. I yawned and rubbed my eyes then turned on the light next to my bed. Peter and I had come down together to the men's quarters to get some sleep. However, I found the rumpled bed next to me unoccupied.

Still tired, I flung my arm over my eyes and let out a deep sigh as I immersed my head into the softness of my feather pillow. As I lay quietly, a string of disjointed thoughts began to float through my head. Char's abandoned car...waiting for the kidnappers to call...Harv in the library. I pulled my arm away. My eyes flew open. I bolted upright. I needed to get up!

Throwing off the covers, I rolled out of bed, grabbed my clothes, and practically jumped into my suit. Voices echoed through the house as I mounted the stairs to the main floor. The sun had barely peaked over the horizon. I expected to find the house quiet and as solemn as a funeral parlor, but when I reached the great hall, I discovered the household staff bustling about serving breakfast to the guests and starting the day's chores.

I rushed into the library and found Daniel sitting at the table with his fist wrapped around a large mug of steaming coffee, staring out the window. I checked my watch. My shift had already started. "Why didn't you have someone rouse me?"

Daniel slowly turned his head. His thick rust-colored hair looked like it hadn't been combed in a while. His eyes were clouded with fatigue. "Harv said you looked pretty beat last night when he sent you to bed. I figured you could use the extra sleep so when my shift ended, I decided to stay on for a while." He lifted his mug and took a loud sip.

"Get some food into your stomach then you can take over. Gerard has had the dining room open for an hour. I'll get some shuteye at Adrienne's place and be back here in a few hours. Unless something happens. I want to know right away if they call." He stood and stretched his arms. "Oh, by the way, Harv's eating breakfast right now. His shift is after yours."

I left him and went straight to the dining room to check in with Harv, not caring that I looked like I'd just crawled out of a cave. No one said a word about my disheveled clothes and day-old stubble. Gerard picked up the napkin at a place set for breakfast and patiently waited for me to sit down. He spread the napkin across my lap while another servant poured my coffee. Then I was given ice water and a glass of orange juice. Everyone seemed, to me, to use busyness as a means to cope with the situation. I gave them a lot of credit for their steadfastness.

Harv and I had a brief conversation before he left to check on his personal security guards. They'd spent the night patrolling the grounds in shifts. The off-duty guys slept on cots in Errol's cottage with their guns once they were told about the break-in that had happened a few nights ago. We had no idea who had broken into the garage and tried to start it on fire or whether it was tied to the kidnapping, but we weren't taking any chances. If anyone came back for another shot at us, we planned to be ready for them.

After a quick breakfast, I shaved and relieved Daniel in the library. The windows in that room had a good view of the driveway and the guard shack so I could see if anyone arrived by car and wanted to enter or merely drop something off—like a ransom note.

By mid-morning, Maddie and Louisa had settled in the drawing room to wait for news about Char. They kept Francie busy with card games and "The Flower Girl," a Parker Brothers wooden jigsaw puzzle they'd spread out on a card table. Adrienne arrived, treating everyone to her favorite candy, a box of Maud Borop's fancy chocolates.

The men congregated in the library with mugs of strong coffee and the daily paper. I waited all morning, expecting a call "any minute now." None came. By lunchtime, I'd walked the floor so long, my feet ached. It had been nearly twenty-four hours since Char had been abducted and I had to fight to keep my spirits up. The longer we waited for the call, the worse the situation looked for her.

Daniel returned at about one o'clock. At one-thirty, the telephone rang. Everyone in the library froze. On the second ring, everyone dived for the telephone at the same time.

I reached it first, holding it an inch from my ear so my companions could hear as well. We huddled around the receiver; the looks on everyone's faces exuded anticipation and dread at the same time.

"Who is this?" a raspy voice demanded.

"It's Will," I said into the mouthpiece as a strange calm settled over me. This was it—the moment I'd waited for in what had seemed like a lifetime. "Will Van Elsberg."

"We want three hundred grand," the voice demanded. "Half in twenties and half in fifties. In a brown suitcase."

"What about Char?" I said, interrupting him. "I want to talk to her. I need to know she's all right."

"*Get the money, Van Elsberg.* Then we'll talk—tomorrow."

The line went dead.

At first, no one moved. I pulled the receiver away from my ear and stared at it, my mind processing the task of collecting three hundred thousand dollars in cash—in twenty-four hours.

"I'll handle this," Harv said as if reading my mind. "You can't walk into Char's bank and draw three hundred grand from her accounts unless you have a legal document giving you permission." As Char's attorney and accountant Harv and Marv, respectively, had the necessary credentials to pull the money from Char's accounts. They also had enough political clout to get the withdrawal started on a Sunday.

I let out a deep breath, only too happy to let Harv and his brother deal with that. "Right."

Harv pulled his gold watch from his vest pocket and checked the time. "I'd better get a move on. I've got a lot to do." His eyes narrowed. "Don't worry about the money. I've got a plan."

The women burst into the library all talking at once as they questioned us about the telephone call and Char's anticipated release. Harv grabbed his hat and left the house, delegating the task of placating them to the rest of us. I explained to the women in general terms—over their groans of protest—that a confidential amount had been set and instructions would be forthcoming.

"Is that all?" Maddie complained. "What can we do to help?"

I shoved my hands into my trouser pockets. "Stay out of sight in case they have people watching this house. Keep your mouth shut and wait." I glanced at Daniel and Peter. "That's all any of us can do."

"And pray," Francie said with her hands clasped together.

"Out of the mouths of babes," Maddie said softly as she slid her arm around Francie's shoulders. "And pray."

The women went back to the parlor to read the Bible aloud *and* pray.

Peter, Daniel, and I sat around the table and passed the whiskey bottle.

"I don't know why," Daniel said as he poured himself a shot, "but I get the feeling the kidnapper is someone who knows Char. Or you." He swirled the liquid in his glass. "The way that caller said, 'Get the money, Van Elsberg,' sounded like he was familiar with you."

I sat rigidly with my palms flat on the table. "That's interesting. I got the same feeling."

Peter lit a cigarette. "Given the way Antoine LeDoux threatened Char at The Oasis, I wouldn't put it past him to be behind this. He must be burning with jealousy that Char got Gus' wealth and he's forced to work at a bank for a living. His mother left him money, but he's squandered it. The trouble is, he still lives like a rich guy even though he isn't one anymore."

Daniel and I nodded in agreement.

"He talked his way into a line of credit at a fancy club," I remarked, "and dug himself a pretty deep hole before he got his golden shovel taken away."

Daniel tossed back his whiskey. "Oh-h-h-h that was good," he said with a grimace and pushed his chair away from the table. "But that's enough for me." He stood and pulled out his keys. "I think it's time I do a little digging myself. See what I can turn over on the whereabouts of Mr. LeDoux and who he's been associating with lately."

He waved goodbye and walked out whistling a tune off-key.

That left Peter and me alone. I stared into my untouched whiskey and pondered what to say to him about what I'd witnessed last night. I knew I couldn't let it go. Since I couldn't think of an easy way to broach the subject, I decided to get right to the point. "Hey," I said in a solemn voice, "what's going on between you and Louisa?"

He blinked at first, showing his surprise at my remark. Then he frowned. "What's it to you?"

I stared back with no intention of letting up. "She's a good woman, Garrett. I don't want her to get involved in something that will leave her heartbroken and damage her reputation."

He took a drag off his cigarette. "I'll be the judge of that."

His cavalier attitude angered me. "Just what are your intentions toward her?"

"That's between me and her," he replied with finality. "Stay out of my business, Will."

I smacked my hand on the table. "She is my business! Louisa worked as my private secretary for a year, and I never once took advantage of my authority over her. How long have you known her? Three weeks?"

Peter responded with a cynical laugh. "What gives you the right to pass judgment on a situation you know nothing about?"

"What gives you the right to kiss her?" I shot back.

The tension between us instantly crackled.

He crushed his cigarette in a glass ashtray and stood up. "Leave it alone, Will."

I jumped to my feet. "Why should I? She's my friend. I care about what happens to her."

Peter glared at me. "You think I don't? She told me what she's been through, and it's brought us closer together than ever."

I walked around the table and grabbed a fistful of his shirt. "What do you mean by that?"

Peter didn't flinch. "I'm in love with her."

My hand froze. "You haven't known her long enough to fall in love with her."

He placed his hand over mine and slowly loosened my grip on his shirt. "I knew the moment I saw her there was a connection between us," he said. "When I looked into her eyes, there was something about her... I had to know more."

"So, you've satisfied your curiosity," I retorted. "Now, what do you intend to do?"

"I'm going to marry her," he said boldly. "I haven't asked her yet, but I plan to as soon as we bring Char home." His eyes blazed. "And when I do, nobody is going to hurt her *ever again*."

I didn't know what he meant by that, but he didn't give me a chance to demand an explanation. Without another word, he pushed past me and stormed out of the library.

Peter and I didn't have much to say to each other for the rest of the day. He spent most of his time with Louisa, and I kept to myself in the library. I wanted to be close to the telephone, anyway, in case Harv or Daniel called. I didn't hear from Harv, but late in the day, Daniel came back with a report about Antoine. He confirmed that Antoine had paid off several gambling houses but was still under pressure to pay off the rest of his debts.

We now knew who had the motive to kidnap Char, but we didn't have any way to prove it.

Yet.

* * *

On Monday afternoon, Harv arrived at a quarter to one. "I've got the cash," he said as he walked into the library. "Half in twenties and half in fifties." He gestured toward his car, surrounded by his armed bodyguards. "It's locked in a brown suitcase."

Daniel whistled. "How did you manage to get so much so fast?"

"I have my ways," Harv said darkly.

The telephone rang at the exact time as the day before. I let it ring once then picked it up. I drew in a tense breath. "Van Elsberg here."

"You got the money?" I heard the same raspy voice as yesterday.

"Yes," I said evenly. "In twenties and fifties like you wanted. Locked in a brown case."

"All right. Listen up," the caller instructed.

My mind spun as I scribbled the rest of his instructions on a legal pad. When he finished, I said, "I want to speak to Char."

"Not until we get the money! Bring the coppers and you'll never see her alive again!"

As before, when he finished with me, the line went dead.

I slowly hung up, ignoring the fact that Peter, Daniel, and Harv were inundating me with questions. I held up my palms to silence them. "The exchange will be on tomorrow morning at seven o'clock." I paused. "In Pelican Township near Big Pelican Lake. We're to meet at a hunting shack in a clearing on the west side of the lake where County Eighteen intersects with County Four."

Daniel stared at me in disbelief. "That's a day's drive from here!"

We found a map of Minnesota in the den. Spreading it on the table in the library, we located the area and measured the distance. We were one hundred and fifty miles away.

"We'd better get going," Harv said as he checked his watch. "I've got a friend, Captain Billy Fawcett, who owns a lodge up there. It's not far from where we're supposed to make the exchange. We'll get a room there for the night."

"Errol will take the girls home," I said, "but someone needs to tell them we're leaving."

"What if we don't *want* to leave?" Maddie asked, standing in the doorway. "We want to be here when you bring Char home. Besides, Francie shouldn't be left alone. The poor kid's been through a lot this weekend. She needs us."

I convinced Maddie to take Louisa and Francie back to our house for a change of scenery. Now that the kidnappers were in northern Minnesota waiting for their money, the heat would be on me. I didn't think the girls were in any danger now.

Within the hour, Harv, Daniel, Peter, and I, along with a small but ruthless army of Harv's bodyguards, were on our way up north to exchange the ransom money for Char.

Chapter Nineteen

Monday afternoon, July 24th

CHAR

The waning light streaking through the boarded windows indicated it was mid-afternoon. I'd been locked up in this cabin for nearly forty-eight hours, waiting to be released. And it had taken its toll on me. My back ached worse than ever from sleeping on the hard sofa. Even though I'd had plenty of rest and food twice a day, fatigue overshadowed me. I blamed it on the dim light in the cabin and the bad air.

I stretched out on my side and tried to get comfortable, but no matter which way I turned, I couldn't get rid of the pain in my lower back. Sitting up, I wondered if the cot in the corner would be better. Until now, I hadn't touched it for fear of bed bugs, but I was desperate. I walked over to it and gingerly sat down. Immediately, I heard a loud crack as the wooden frame broke and the cot caved in. I scrambled off it before I landed on the floor. "Ugh," I said as I went back to the sofa and sat down, trying to get my mind off my discomfort.

My little spider friend had visited me off and on for the past two days. I didn't know where it went when darkness fell, but I was past caring. Bugsy—the name I'd given it—seemed to do a good job of staying out of my way.

"Hey, Bugsy," I said to him as he suddenly moved up the wall. "Where have you been?" I turned my body sideways and stretched my arm along the back of the sofa. "I'm so bored and you're the only person I have to talk to." Bugsy stopped for a few moments then moved up another inch. "And the best part is that you agree with everything I say!"

I laughed at my silly joke and then I sighed. How sad was it that talking to an insect ranked as the highlight of my day?

Sitting here alone had given me plenty of time to think about all aspects of my life; what had made a difference and what hadn't. Like how little my money and social status counted in the grand scheme of things. My family and my friends were dear to me, yet all the money in the world couldn't buy their love or respect.

"Who cares what people like Faye Delacorte think about me," I told Bugsy. "All that matters is what I think of myself."

I thought about how I'd spent most of my life dealing with a sick mother, an alcoholic father, and later, a lawless husband. Instead of caving under the pressure of so many issues I couldn't control, I'd directed all my energy toward achieving one success after another. No wonder I'd had so much trouble getting pregnant during my nine-year marriage to Gus. I'd worked too hard and stressed over details too much.

I sighed. When was the last time I'd taken a trip somewhere just for fun? Never! I had all of Gus' money—including a room literally filled with cash—and I had never paused long enough to enjoy it. What was wrong with me? In my teens, I'd worked every day after school to buy food for Mamma and Francie. Taking on my father's role of providing for my family. *That* was what was wrong with me. I had never moved beyond the sense that I had to keep working hard to make sure those whom I loved had enough.

In a crystal-clear moment, I realized I had so many truly good people in my life, but I'd taken them all for granted—with Will at the top of that list. He only wanted the best for me and yet I had treated him so badly the night I told him about my pregnancy. All I could think about was my own feelings. All he cared about was me and the baby. My heart ached over how deeply I had hurt and upset him. I loved him so much! I needed to set things right with him. That said, I needed to spend more time with Julien and Francie too. I had a wonderful family. It was about time I treated them like one!

I wanted to get out of this musty cabin so badly and go back to my home that I slid off the sofa and began walking around the small room, pushing against the windows to see if I could dislodge the nails that held them shut. My effort proved fruitless. Someone had done a good job of making sure they never opened again.

Other than the stove pipe and the pipe for the oil burner, I couldn't find any other openings except that square in the ceiling I had noticed yesterday. The trouble was, the opening looked very small, and I didn't have either a ladder to get up there or the tools to pull off the cover. The more I stared at it, however, the more curious I became. One side looked slightly warped.

I pushed the enamel-topped table across the floor until I had it positioned directly under the square. I climbed upon the table to get a better look at it, but I was too short to reach the ceiling, so I placed one of the chairs on the table and climbed up again. I was so close to the ceiling now that I had to get on my knees on the chair to examine it.

The wooden square over the attic opening had been nailed well, but time and moisture and probably heat, too, had warped one corner. Water stains indicated that over time the roof had repeatedly leaked and dripped on it. There was enough room to wedge a tool in between the wood and the ceiling. If I found something to use as a makeshift crowbar, could I pull it down?

The warm air hovering along the ceiling area overwhelmed me, and I gladly climbed down, but I wasn't finished yet. Though the effort might be for nothing, I had to try. Pulling open every cupboard door and drawer in the room, I searched for something strong enough to use to pry the wood off the ceiling. Nothing turned up except a small cast iron frying pan with a six-inch skillet. It had a small handle on it, and it was heavy for a tool, but it was strong.

I climbed upon the table and kneeled on the chair again gripping the little pan with my hands. Shoving the handle between the warped wood and the ceiling, I had enough room to slip my fingers around the skillet portion and pull down on it with all my might. The wood moved a quarter-inch. Dust, sawdust, and mouse droppings fell out of the opening, causing me to cough and brush debris from my face. Even so, I'd made some progress! Encouraged, I shoved the little handle into the opening again and pulled it down again. It gave way a little more. I kept going until I was able to slip my fingers in between the wood and the ceiling and use both hands to pull with all my might.

The underside of the wood piece and the area around it had rotted and as I tugged on it, the nails began to pull out of the ceiling. Taking small breaks in between to rest my arms, I tugged again and again. It suddenly gave way and fell to the floor with a clatter as more musty debris rained down on me. Coughing, I began to lose my balance and would have fallen off the chair if I had not stuck my hands into the hole and grabbed onto the edge with all my might.

After steadying myself, I slowly raised upon my toes, squeezing my shoulders through the narrow opening. The attic was extremely hot, musty-smelling, and dark. Directly above my head, I saw light seeping through the edges of a twelve-inch hole in the roof that had been patched with a heavy tarp. An odd sliver of light coming from another direction caught my eye. I looked toward the front of the attic and saw a narrow outline of light around the edges of a rough-hewn door. My heart began to flutter. I needed to crawl over there and see if I could open it.

You can do this, I thought, but I had to climb down once more to cool off. Given the suffocating heat, it didn't take me long. Collapsing on the sofa, I rested until my body cooled off and I felt well enough to continue. At the same time, however, I knew someone would be coming soon to deliver my dinner tray. Slipping on my flat, Mary Jane shoes, I climbed upon the chair again, managed to stand up inside the opening, and used my arms to push myself up enough to crawl across the boards toward the door.

Once there, I pushed against it. The door rattled slightly. It had a small piece of wood fastened with a nail to serve as a latch, and as I looked closer, I realized the door was merely a square that had been hastily cut out and put back on with small hinges.

The heat was getting to me, but I was determined to see if I could force it open. Turning around on my hands and knees, I thrust my foot against it, loosening the nail that held the latch. One more hard push forced the latch out of the wall. The door swung open, and a refreshing breeze flowed past me.

Oh, my gosh…

I began to breathe heavily as beads of sweat trickled down the small of my back. Reaching over, I pulled the little door back into place and scrambled back to the opening, hoping no one noticed that piece of wood, the latch, lying on the ground. I carefully slipped through the slimy hole again and placed my feet flat on the chair, shaking so hard I nearly lost my balance. I slowly climbed down and pushed the table back against the wall then collapsed upon the sofa. My back hurt worse than ever, and the musty attic heat made me sick to my stomach. At the same time, I had such a bad case of nerves my entire body quaked. But my heart thudded with excitement, too.

As soon as darkness fell, I planned to escape.

Chapter Twenty

Later that day...

WILL

It took all day to reach Pelican Township. Besides the four of us, Harv had included three of his best guards to drive the limousine and protect the money. By the time we reached the drop location, it was nearly dark, but we used flashlights to view the hunting shack.

My heart skittered as I flashed my light around the dilapidated hut. It had a dirt floor and no glass in the windows. In mere hours, we would make the exchange for Char here, and I would take her into my arms. I hadn't stopped worrying about her since she disappeared. I couldn't wait to see her again, but I wondered how such stressful conditions were affecting her. If they had mistreated her in any way...

I shoved the thought from my mind. It did no good to dwell on it. The most important thing to do was focus on getting her back.

We drove on to Breezy Point Lodge to get a room for the night. Harv's friend, Captain Billy Fawcett owned the resort. The grand lodge had a huge dining room that overlooked the lake, a bowling alley, a billiard parlor, a trading post, and a beauty shop. My friends had used words like "fabulous extravaganza" to describe the resort and claimed it wasn't unusual to see Hollywood celebrities on the golf course or in the casino.

We drove up the long drive to the sprawling lakeside resort on Pelican Bay and pulled up to the brightly lit lodge, a huge building constructed of large Norway pine logs. Cars of all makes, models and colors lined the road in front of both the lodge and the hotel. People milled about the open areas, enjoying the warm, balmy evening. Harv went into the lodge to book several rooms while the rest of our party stood next to the car, taking in our surroundings.

The first notion that came to my mind was, *are the kidnappers staying here? Is she being held here?* It seemed unlikely to hold a person captive in such a busy place as this, but the resort had dozens of cabins and the possibility of finding Char held captive in one of them tempted me to take a walk along the grounds after I got checked into my room.

Fifteen minutes later, Harv came out of the lodge with another man by his side, around forty, with brown hair and wearing a tan double-breasted suit. Both Harv and his friend were the same height, around five feet six inches. They laughed and talked like old friends.

"Will, come here," Harv said with a smile as he waved me over. "This is Captain Billy Fawcett." He turned to his friend. "Billy, this is Will Van Elsberg, an excellent private investigator."

"I've heard a lot about your investigative work, Will. All good," Captain Billy said with a hearty smile as he extended his palm.

"I'm pleased to meet you," I said to Captain Billy and shook his hand. "Nice place you've got here."

Harv went through introductions with the rest of our party. "Captain Billy says the resort is booked solid," he said, "but he's offered to put us up at his place." Harv pointed toward a huge log home across from the resort. "There's plenty of room to park around back."

Captain Billy waved goodbye as he started walking toward his home. "I'd better go on ahead and let the wife know you're coming. I'll see you there."

Harv waved back. "Thank you, Captain!"

As soon as Captain Billy walked away, Harv turned to us, his face solemn. "The story is, we're looking at land to buy for hunting. Not a word about Char or the exchange, understood?"

We agreed and the four of us decided to walk the short distance to the Fawcett House while Harv's guards drove the limousine up a slight hill and parked in the rear of the building.

"Come in," Captain Billy said, standing in the doorway as we reached the house. We walked into a huge living room constructed of pine logs with a cathedral ceiling, a wood floor, soft lighting, and a massive stone fireplace. At the opposite end, a curved stairway made of split logs led up to a wide loft. Hunting trophies of deer, elk, bear, and fish lined the walls. "We're all set," Captain Billy said. "I'll show you to your rooms. I'm having a table set up for your dinner at the lodge." He checked his watch. "In thirty minutes."

He led us to the lower level. I had a room with a private bathroom. I looked around, tested the softness of the bed, and then waited until Harv and Captain Billy went back upstairs before I knocked on Dan's door. He opened it a crack and peered out. He'd already taken off his suit coat. His suspenders hung at his sides. "I'm going to take a walk," I said. "Want to join me?"

Daniel opened the door wider and slipped his suspenders over his shoulders. "I was thinking the same thing. Yeah, let's go." He grabbed his shoulder holster laying on the bed and put it back on. Snatching his coat off the bed, he slipped it on and shut the door behind us.

We set out to cover as much ground as we could along the sandy road that took us deep into the residential area. Human banter and lively music gave way to a slow, methodical *whoosh… whoosh…* as the waves of Big Pelican Lake ebbed and flowed. Somewhere in the distance, a pair of owls hooted back and forth. Raccoons scurried across the road and deer watched from the bushes, but we didn't see or hear anything suspicious as we passed cabin after cabin.

Disappointed but refreshed by the invigorating lake air, we made it back to the lodge right on time. Captain Billy treated us to a lavish dinner on gold-rimmed plates in a private room where the liquor flowed like water. Obviously, no one cared about prohibition here. I tried to appear carefree and enjoy the meal, but my thoughts never strayed from Char.

After dinner, we met in Harv's room to finalize our plan for the exchange tomorrow. A half-hour later, we returned to our rooms to call it a night. As I lie on my bed with my hands behind my head, I wondered if I could sleep at all.

I couldn't stop worrying about Char and what would happen tomorrow.

Chapter Twenty-One

CHAR

Something was wrong.

As the last streaks of light slowly disappeared in the cabin I rested on the sofa, wondering why I hadn't received my dinner tray. My hunger had become so fierce that my stomach hurt. My captors only fed me twice a day. They had delivered my last meal early this morning. What was going on? Why hadn't someone delivered my dinner?

I stood at the window, peering through the slats until darkness had descended outside. Waiting. But no one came. Other than the soft, harmonious chorus of crickets and an occasional hoot of an owl, I couldn't hear any sounds to indicate the men were on the premises. I didn't know where my captors had gone, but the late hour indicated to me that they weren't going to bother feeding me tonight. Even if they suddenly showed up, they wouldn't be able to see me now.

The time had come to make my move.

My eyes had grown accustomed to the dark and I had little trouble repositioning the table next to the sofa where I'd moved it earlier. Placing the chair in the middle of the tabletop, I measured the distance with my hands to make sure it stood solidly in the center. I tucked my dress into my bloomers to prevent catching it on a nail or snagging it on the wood. With one hand on the chair, I raised up on my knees and used the other hand to grope for the opening. The moist wood felt slimy under my hands, but I ignored the uncomfortable feeling. Slowly, I stood up and climbed through the opening into the attic. It groaned under my weight. I grabbed onto the framework to keep from falling through in case the ceiling around the hole gave way.

Now that the sun had gone down, the temperature in the attic was almost bearable. I crawled through the narrow, slanted space on my hands and knees until my nose bumped into the door and slightly pushed it open. A welcome breeze wafted softly across my face. I pushed the door open all the way and stared out, listening. The night was strangely quiet. The moon shone brightly, casting silver streaks across the ground in between the trees.

Convinced I was alone, I carefully turned around in the small space, laying on my stomach, and slipped feet first out of the door, holding on to anything I could find as I slowly squeezed my body through the opening and lowered myself down along the side of the building. Eventually, I let go and fell a short distance, landing on my feet on the soft ground, but the momentum knocked me backward onto the grass. I scrambled to my feet and straightened my dress as I looked around. The little building I'd been confined to was attached to a larger structure made of cinderblock, a lodge of some kind, or a large home, but I didn't see any lights on in the building.

I took off running across the grounds until I came to the edge of an open field. On the other side of it, the woods extended as far as I could see. I ran through the field in the bright moonlight as fast as my feet could carry me until I reached the edge of the wood. Once there, I leaned against a pine tree to catch my breath as I looked back at the darkened buildings. As far as I could tell, no one was coming after me. I let out a sigh of relief.

I was free.

*   *   *

I slowed down, being mindful of where I stepped. The forest floor held many booby traps in the form of dead branches, fallen limbs, rocks, low spots, and thick brush. I didn't want to trip and fall. As I navigated the woods, my dress snagged on the brush and my feet stumbled occasionally, forcing me to tread carefully.

A branch snapped.

I stopped, my heartbeat pounding in my temples. Who was there? Slipping behind a tree, I stood in silence, then watched with fascination as a half-dozen deer passed by in single file. The *who-who-who* of an owl echoed overhead. A light breeze whispered through the trees.

I let out a deep breath. My shoulders relaxed. Amazingly, the forest sounds comforted me and calmed my soul, giving me strength. My newly found freedom fueled my determination with a surge of renewed energy. I had no idea where I was or where I was headed, I only knew I must keep going. And that was enough for me. For now, anyway.

Tiring, I stopped to lean against a tree and catch my breath, but my respite didn't last long. A swarm of mosquitoes buzzed around my head, forcing me to get moving again. Suddenly, in the distance, headlights flashed, moving toward me. I had no idea I was so close to a road. This was the first time I'd seen headlights since I'd escaped. Could it be my kidnappers? Who else would be out driving around this time of night?

I watched until the vehicle's headlights disappeared, then I began walking toward the road. The moon shone upon the gravel, illuminating it. I kept moving, knowing it would be an easier path to travel and it would ultimately lead me to a town or a resort—with people who could help me.

My feet suddenly sank ankle-deep in water. I'd walked into a shallow marsh! I backed out of the water and trudged along in squishy shoes until I came to a small meadow and crossed over it to get to the road. The pain in my back had extended to my thighs and now my stomach had begun to cramp as well. I hadn't eaten for so long that my limbs were shaky and weak.

Royal blue skies eventually faded into gold and crimson streaks of the morning sun poking above the horizon. I welcomed daylight, but I had to be careful now and stay vigilant in case my kidnappers were still searching for me. I walked past a sign with Pelican Lake Township painted on it. Okay… Though it was valuable information, I still had no idea where I was.

I came to a fork in the road. On the left side of the divide, a narrow driveway led up to a small, weathered farmhouse. I was so thirsty, so hungry, and in so much pain I could barely stand it. By the time I reached the edge of the yard, the cramping in my stomach hurt so much I couldn't go any further.

A gray-haired woman wearing a brown dress emerged from the house and cautiously approached me. "Miss, are you alright?"

"I—I'm dizzy," I whispered, clinging to a fencepost. "I don't feel well."

She looked around, baffled to find me alone, then she took my arm and started to slowly walk me to the house. "Where did you come from?"

I managed to point toward the road. "I've been walking all night. I had to get away."

She shook her head, not understanding my explanation as she slid her arm around my waist. "Let's get you inside and then we can talk some more."

A short, balding man appeared in the driveway wearing denim overalls and pushing a wheelbarrow carrying a gunny sack of grain.

"Ernie! Come here. I need help!"

He dropped his wheelbarrow and hurried toward us. "What's wrong? Who is this?"

"All I know is that she's ill," the woman said. "I found her clinging to the fencepost at the end of the driveway."

Ernie took me by the other arm and together they half-walked, half-dragged me into their home. They set me on the sofa and placed a small blanket across my lap. "Darla, fetch her some water," Ernie said as he lifted my feet onto a small ottoman.

"Thank you for helping me," I said to Darla and Ernie though the pain made it difficult to speak. I gratefully accepted a canning jar filled with chilled well water. "I'm Charlotte LeDoux. I've been walking for hours—all night—after I…" I winced with pain. "After I got away."

Darla and Ernie exchanged worried glances and I sensed I'd given them the impression I'd escaped an abusive husband. I certainly looked the part in a flowered yellow dress that used to be pretty but was now torn and dirty. Ugly bruising all over my arms from being dumped into a car trunk attested to gruesome treatment. Bloody scratches covered my entire body from stumbling through brambles in the woods.

I decided not to correct their first impression. Telling them I'd been kidnapped and that my aggressors were looking for me might frighten them and deter them from getting involved. All I needed was help contacting the police. The authorities could take it from there.

I gulped the water before another cramp overtook me. I doubled over, clutching my abdomen.

"Are you hungry?" Darla asked, misreading my actions. My stomach did hurt from hunger, and I hoped getting some food into my body would help, but the pain was much worse than that. At my nod, she went to her kitchen to make me something to eat. Ernie followed her. As dishes clattered and cabinet doors banged, I heard them whispering in earnest, but couldn't make out their conversation.

Darla returned with a small plate containing a sandwich of buttered bread and sliced ham. I thanked her profusely and gobbled my sandwich all the while thinking I'd never tasted anything so good in my life.

Ernie went back outdoors.

Darla sat down next to me. "Do you feel better now? Is the food helping your stomach?"

A deep contraction enveloped my lower back. I groaned in discomfort. "I need to contact my family so they can bring me home. I'm pregnant."

Darla frowned, her eyes reflecting new concern. "Where is the pain?"

I gestured toward the areas I hurt the most—my stomach, my lower back, and my upper thighs. "I hoped it would go away once I got off my feet, but it's persisting."

She placed her hand on my forehead and shook her head as though she feared the worst. "Have you lost any blood?"

"Yes," I replied and avoided her gaze. The last time I'd squatted in the brush to empty my bladder, I noticed the stickiness in my bloomers. Now that I'd spoken the truth out loud, I needed to come to grips with the obvious. When I finally looked up, I saw recognition in her grayish eyes. We both knew what the targeted pain and the blood meant.

I wasn't pregnant any longer. The child had miscarried.

*   *   *

Ernie pulled his car up to the house, a new Ford, and opened the door to the back seat. He and Darla helped me inside the vehicle.

"Are we going to the police station?" I asked curiously.

Darla leaned across the seat, covering me with the blanket. "You need medical attention first. Then we'll contact the police."

They slipped into the front seat and shut their doors. I curled up on the hard seat and closed my eyes as the car slowly ambled down the driveway.

I thought it a bit odd that a small-time farming couple could afford to own such a nice car, but if they were cooking moonshine on the side that would account for where they got the money to buy it. The low land and thick woods in this area provided the perfect cover for a still. People who were "making moon" needed reliable transportation to get supplies and transport the finished goods. If someone owned more than one vehicle, it was usually a dead giveaway of what they were *really* doing for a living.

I didn't give a darn where they got the money. They were kind people who cared enough to help me when I needed it the most.

I curled up on my side and closed my eyes, in so much pain I could barely think, but I also needed to stay out of sight in case my kidnappers passed us. I didn't realize I'd gone to sleep until the car pulled to a stop and the slamming of the front doors shook the vehicle. They opened the back door and helped me out.

"Where are we," I asked, groggy and confused as to why we were stopping in front of a small log house. A tall, slender woman in a dark green dress with wire-rimmed glasses and brown hair swept into a knot stood in the doorway, studying me with concern.

"We're at Ruth Hemsted's place," Darla said. "She's the local midwife."

Darla introduced me to Ruth and explained my condition. The woman immediately took charge and ordered them to take me into the

164

house. She held the door while they brought me inside and guided me into a small bedroom.

Darla helped me ease onto the bed. Once she got me settled, she patted my hand. "I've known Ruth all of my life. She'll take good care of you." She straightened, alerting me that she was about to leave me.

"Wait," I said struggling to raise up on my elbows. "I need to contact my family. They're probably very worried about me."

"There's a filling station a few miles from here," Darla said. "They have a telephone. We'll call the police and tell them where you are."

Of course. She and her husband didn't want to get involved in my personal issues—which they obviously considered a private matter. They thought it best to turn it over to the police and go on their way. I didn't say it out loud but given the fact that my *true* situation was far more serious than I had let on, I agreed with them. This was between me and the local coppers and the sooner I talked to them, the sooner I could get a message to Will about where I was and that I was safe.

"Thank you, Darla—you and Ernie—for all you've done for me," I said sincerely and lay back down. "I don't know what I would have done without your help."

Ruth came into the bedroom carrying a small tray. "I've brought you some raspberry leaf tea. It will help ease the pain."

She set the tray on the nightstand and turned to Darla. "I'll take it from here. There's nothing much we can do for her now except keep her comfortable until it's over."

My eyes filled with tears. I didn't want to lose this baby. In the beginning, I'd been disappointed by the news because the scandal would disgrace my family, but now it felt like a part of me was unjustly slipping away; a child that I would never know, never hold, never kiss. And I couldn't do anything to stop it. I'd been through this heartache before, this sense of utter helplessness, but this time it felt different, more devastating than ever because I was losing part of Will, too. Oh, how I wished he was here. I suddenly felt so lonely, so alone.

Covering my face with my hands, I began to sob.

Chapter Twenty-Two

Tuesday, July 25th

WILL

At six o'clock the next morning, we arrived a mile north of the hunting shack to regroup. Everyone climbed out of the limousine. I got into the driver's seat with the suitcase next to me.

"Be careful," Harv warned. "We don't know who we're dealing with."

Daniel held a Tommy gun. "We'll be in the woods watching from a distance, but we've got you covered, Will. Anything happens, grab Char and run. Leave the rest to us."

The men took off on foot through the woods. I waited until a few minutes before seven o'clock then started the car and drove to the hunting shack.

It looked deserted.

I stared at the ramshackle building as a sinking feeling formed in my heart. "Something isn't right," I muttered to myself. "I've got a bad feeling about this." I wrapped my fingers around the handle of the car door and opened it, listening for natural sounds—birds chirping and squirrels squawking—a sure sign to me there were no intruders in the woods beyond the shack. Stepping out, I looked around and then walked cautiously over to the place where I hoped to find Char.

I peered inside. The building sat empty. They were supposed to be here by now.

Trying hard to stay focused on my surroundings instead of Char, I quickly walked back to the car and opened the door to sit inside while I waited for the kidnappers to show up and conduct the exchange.

Suddenly, a hush fell over the area. I stood behind the open car door for cover and waited.

Two men brandishing Tommy guns emerged from the west side of the woods wearing dark clothing and cloth masks over their heads. They advanced toward me with their guns pointed at the car. I hoped my reinforcements from the north had also arrived and were watching every move of these men.

"We told you to come alone," the tall one hollered as they stopped in the center of the clearing.

"I am alone," I replied and stepped away from the limousine with my hands up. "See for yourself."

The man eyed the automobile suspiciously. "That's a pretty big car for one person."

"I needed a good-sized machine to carry all this dough," I shot back.

The spokesperson stepped forward, pointing his gun toward my chest. Though the mask covered his head, I noticed a scar running diagonally across his right eyebrow. "Get the suitcase."

I didn't flinch. "I want to see Char first. Then I'll hand it over."

"You don't have a choice," he bellowed. "If you want to see her alive give us the money! Now!"

I had all I could do to keep my anger from exploding. "This isn't what we agreed on. We're supposed to make a *trade*."

"The rules have changed," the leader said harshly. "Hand over the suitcase. Then we'll tell you where she is."

"It's on the front seat," I said angrily, knowing I had no other choice. "I need to reach in and get it."

"Don't try to pull anything on us you'll be dead before you hit the ground."

They kept their guns pointed at me as I slowly reached into the car and grabbed the handle of the large brown suitcase. It was heavy, but I managed to stand it up and pull it out in one deliberate move. Leaving the door open, I walked toward them carrying it with both hands.

The leader pointed his gun toward the ground. "Set it down and step back."

I didn't move. "*No*. I want to see Char first. Tell me where she is!"

They advanced toward me. "You'll find out when *we* decide to tell you!" the leader shouted as they surrounded me.

Suddenly, I knew they weren't going to turn her over to me. "Where *is* she?"

"She's in the woods," the leader replied as the other man grabbed the handle of the suitcase from me and dragged it away.

"Where in the woods?" I demanded. "They go on for miles around here!"

He shrugged. "Don't know. She escaped. With any luck, you'll find her before winter."

Both men laughed.

Suddenly, the air exploded with a rapid stream of bullets as one of the men fired his Tommy gun across the clearing to cover their retreat with firepower. I dove to the ground, watching them disappear into the woods.

I lay on my stomach breathing heavily, my mind spinning. Char had escaped? I didn't know whether to believe them or not. If she did, that meant we were looking for a needle in a haystack. For all I knew, she could be miles away, lost in the woods.

My men suddenly appeared, running toward me from another direction. Harv helped me to my feet. "What happened? Where's Charlotte?"

"I don't know," I replied gravely. "After they forced me to give them the money, they said she's escaped."

Everyone stared at me in shock.

"What do we do now, boss?" one of Harv's men asked. "She could be around the next bend or miles from here. There's no way to know where to look for her."

"We go to the nearest town and notify the police," Peter said with authority. "If what they said is true, she may have already turned up on her own. If not, we'll get a search party organized and start combing these woods on horseback. If she's still out here, we'll find her."

*   *   *

We decided to search the immediate area first. We spread out and moved in the direction the kidnappers had retreated. On the edge of the clearing, we found a narrow deer trail leading through the woods. With our guns out, we followed the trail until we came to a footpath that led us to a sprawling, one-story cinderblock house. After a thorough search of the grounds, we determined the place was deserted, but we found a full trash can, empty liquor bottles, and fresh tire tracks, all indicating that people had recently stayed there. Then we found a mask.

Daniel picked the black hood off the ground next to the garage and examined it. "They were here all right." He pointed toward a set of muddy tire tracks in the driveway. An unopened pack of smokes lay on the grass. "Looks like they left in a big hurry, too."

I saw the open attic door and went into the little cabin, figuring Char had been held there. In the center of the room, a rectangular table with a chair mounted upon it was positioned directly under a small hole in the ceiling. I let out a deep breath. So—that much of what the kidnappers said appeared to be true.

Daniel came into the cabin and saw Char's escape route. "Let's fan out and scour the area. Hopefully, we'll get a break and find something that indicates which direction Char went when she lit out of here."

That sounded like a good plan. Outside, I looked around, trying to determine which way she would have run once she'd slipped away. Turning to my right, I noticed a grassy field just beyond the yard. *That's where she went*, I thought. *I'd bet my life on it.*

We split up, each of us taking a section of the woods. I went straight across the field and began searching. It didn't take long before I found her small footprints on the wet ground. Then I found a cluster of dark hair clinging to a tall raspberry stem with sharp thorns. I went back to the clearing. "I found it! She went this way!"

We followed Char's trail until we came upon her footprints in the wet, spongy earth at a marshy area alongside the road.

"It looks like she came upon the road here," Peter said pointing to footprints in the gravel. "She might still be walking. Let's go back to the car."

We went back to the shack and got the car. After driving several miles, we came upon a small farmhouse, but no one answered our knock on the door.

"It feels like we lost her trail," I said, becoming discouraged. "If she ended up here, it's possible the people living here took her to the police station. Let's go back to our original plan. Let's find the nearest town and approach the police."

We got back into the car and checked our map. The closest town appeared to be about eight miles away. I sat in brooding silence as we drove to Nisswa.

If it takes the rest of my life, I'm going to hunt down the people who did this to Char and make them pay, I thought to myself. *But first, I must find her before anything else happens to her.*

"We'll find her, son," Harv said quietly as if reading my thoughts. "We're not giving up until we do." He leaned forward, his eyes narrowing. "In the meantime, I have a little surprise planned for the fools who made off with the money."

Daniel spoke up first. "You booby-trapped the suitcase?" He verbalized what we were all thinking.

Harv laughed. "In a way, yes. This one, however, won't blow up until they try to spend it. The suitcase is filled with counterfeit bills."

The group burst out laughing. This was no time for gallows humor, but for a few precious moments, our hilarity took the edge off the intense pressure that overshadowed us. I'd heard a skilled person could make realistic forgeries by bleaching the ink off genuine one-dollar bills and reprinting them as higher denominations. I wondered if Harv's money had been created that way or if they'd simply been printed on quality linen paper.

170

"Where did you find a green goods man to supply you with that much bad dough in the twin cities?" Peter asked, looking concerned. "And on such short notice?"

"I never divulge my sources." Harv sat back and folded his arms. "The less you boys know about that piece of it, the better. And for the record, we never had this conversation, right?"

Everyone agreed.

What a sly old dog you are, I thought to myself. *If LeDoux is behind the kidnapping, he'll probably squander his share of the take at the best clubs in town. If he thought his luck was bad before…*

Along the way to Nisswa, we stopped at a small filling station to quench our thirst. I stuck my hand into a barrel of ice water and pulled out an ice-cold bottle of Coca-Cola. I selected a maple-flavored cluster bar from a display and went to the cashier to pay for it.

"That'll be five cents for the soda and another five cents for the Nut Goodie," the female cashier said as she held out her hand. The stout, middle-aged woman wore men's overalls and had her brown hair cut in a "helmet" style with a thick fringe of bangs. The rest of her straight hair had been blunt cut level with her jawline.

I dug into my pocket and pulled out a couple of nickels.

"You fellas just passin' through," she asked in a friendly way, "or are you staying at one of the resorts?"

"We're on our way to Nisswa," I replied amicably as I placed the money on the counter. "Say, can you tell me where the police station is located in town?"

"Why?" She put the nickels in her till. "You got a problem?"

"I'm looking for a woman by the name of Charlotte LeDoux. She's about so high," I said, raising my hand to illustrate Char's height, "short dark hair, middle-twenties. She had on a yellow dress. Have you seen her?"

"No," the woman replied, "but I think I know someone who has. She dropped in this morning to use the telephone. She called the police to assist somebody."

"You don't say," I said becoming intensely interested. "Do you know her name?"

"Darla Erickson. She and Ernie drove over here just to make the call. I wasn't eavesdroppin' or nuthin, but I kind of overheard the conversation." The woman leaned across the counter. "Darla told the copper on duty that early this morning, she found a woman in her driveway who was on the verge of collapsing." She moved closer. "According to Darla, the woman had been roughed up pretty badly by someone. She was so ill she could barely stand up."

Though I tried not to show any reaction, my heart began to slam wildly at the details. Deep down I knew it could be Char, but the injuries, the call to the police—that worried me.

"What happened to the woman," I said, not caring how many people were waiting in line behind me. "Was she with them?"

"No," the cashier said. "They took her to Ruth Hemsted fer lookin' after until the police notified her relatives. Didn't get the lady's name, but I gather she wasn't local or Darla woulda known her."

She'd lost me now. "Who is Ruth Hemsted? Where does she live?"

The guy behind me impatiently cleared his throat. I moved aside but kept my attention on the cashier.

"She's the local midwife," the woman said. "Takes care of most everyone in this town. Her place is just down the road apiece. Small log home. If you came down County Four, you passed it on the way here."

She turned her attention to her next customer.

"Thanks," I said as I used the bottle opener attached to the side of the counter to pull the cap off my Coca-Cola. I grabbed my cluster bar and walked out. The trip to Nisswa could wait. We were going to pay a visit to the local midwife.

*   *   *

My anxiety mounted as I stood alone on the stoop of Ruth Hemsted's log home and knocked on the screen door. I had asked everyone to wait in the car until I'd confirmed that we'd found Char. If it was her, I wanted a minute alone with her first.

A tall, slender woman came into view. Through the screen, I noticed she wore wire-rimmed glasses and a plain dark-colored dress. "May I help you?" She sounded wary.

"Hello, I'm Will Van Elsberg. I'm a private investigator," I said and held up my business card so she could read it through the screen. "I'm looking for a woman by the name of Charlotte LeDoux. Is she in your care?"

"What do you want with her?" Ruth asked warily as she scrutinized my card.

"I'm here with Char's attorney, Harv Katzenbaum, on behalf of her family," I said politely. "Three days ago, Char was abducted in St. Paul and her kidnappers brought her to this area to hold her for ransom. We know she escaped and that she ended up here." I removed my hat. "I'd really like to speak with her ma'am if I may. If you need to verify my credentials and Mr. Katzenbaum's, he's waiting in the car. Char's family is very worried about her."

"Come in, Mister Van Elsberg," Ruth said as she unlatched the door. "I didn't mean to be rude. I had to make sure it was you and not one of those men who kidnapped her. Charlotte has been talking about you all morning. She told me the same thing, that you were a private detective and she insisted you'd come for her as soon as the police were able to locate you. My goodness, you certainly got here fast."

"Actually, I haven't spoken to the police yet," I said as she opened the screen door to let me in. "I found her through a combination of detective work and good old-fashioned luck." I stepped over the threshold. "How is she doing?"

"As good as can be expected given the situation," Ruth replied in hushed tones.

I hesitated. "Has she talked about her kidnappers?"

Ruth nodded. "She told me everything."

I hung my hat on the coat tree and turned back to her. "After I speak with Char, I'd like to ask you some questions, if I may."

"Certainly," she said. "She may not be able to talk much right now.

173

She's exhausted and needs her rest, but I'll leave it up to her to decide what she wants to share with you about her medical condition."

I wondered what she meant by that as I followed her through the modestly furnished house to a small bedroom in the back. She motioned for me to enter the room but didn't follow me.

Char lay in bed with her eyes closed wearing a sleeveless nightgown. Her face looked as white as my shirt. Dark circles underscored her eyes. Deep scratches and large bruises covered her neck and arms. A large yellow-green bruise spread across her jawline on the right side of her face.

I'd witnessed many gruesome situations in my line of work and considered myself a strong man, but nothing had prepared me for this. Seeing the woman that I loved lying in bed so frail and so battered filled me with feelings of utter helplessness. At the same time, though, it also made me murderously angry at the people who did this to her.

Finding it difficult to speak, I cleared my throat. "Char…" I whispered leaning over her. "Darling, it's me, Will."

She opened her eyes. "Will!" she cried and struggled to sit up, "Oh, I'm so glad you're here! I knew you'd find me!"

"Careful now." I gently slid my arms around her to help her sit up, but I was so worried I might cause her additional pain my hands were shaking. "You need to take it easy."

"I missed you so much! I thought about you the whole time they kept me locked up in that dark cabin," she whispered in my ear as she slid her arms around my neck. "You and Julien and Francie. I was so afraid I might never see any of you again."

"I'd never let that happen," I said as I held her close. "I've been trying to get you back ever since you disappeared. I nearly lost my mind when I discovered someone had taken you. When I found out you'd escaped I feared that you'd get lost in the woods and never be found. I don't know what I would have done if something had happened to you." I kissed her gently, so thankful she was still alive. "I love you so much, Char."

"I love you, too, Will. I'm so sorry that I—" She grimaced with pain.

I froze. "What's wrong? Did I hurt you?"

Slipping through my arms, she collapsed onto the bed with a labored gasp. "It's not you. I can't sit up very long. My back hurts too much and I have cramps."

I pulled up a chair and sat down. "Don't worry, Char. Once I get you home, you'll get better fast. Your staff will fuss over you like mother hens. All of us will."

That got a smile out of her for a moment, but it soon faded when another surge of pain caused her to writhe in discomfort. Her fingers gripped mine. "I can't go home yet. Ruth thinks I should stay here for a couple of days, at least until the bleeding has—"

"You're wounded?" My gaze quickly swept over her. "Where?"

"No, Will. It's not me." She went very still, her eyes glistening with a deep sadness that indicated something was terribly wrong. "It's the baby. It didn't survive."

At first, her words stunned me so much that I didn't know what to say. The baby—our baby—*died*? I'd barely had time to get used to the idea and now it was...over? Just like that? I saw the pain of loss on Char's face and realized this was no time for me to dwell on my own disappointment. She was taking it pretty hard.

"I'm so sorry, honey," I said and framed her face with my hands. A deep sense of loss gripped my heart, but I couldn't imagine what it must be like for her. "I'm not leaving your side until you're ready to come home. We'll get through this together."

"This isn't the first time I've had a miscarriage," she said as a tear seeped from the corner of her eye. "I had several when I was married to Gus." She looked away. "That doesn't make it any easier."

Her pain broke my heart. Two people had been taken against their will. One didn't survive. The other needed justice. "I don't care if it takes the rest of my life," I said angrily, "I'm going to find out who did this to you, and when I do—"

"Maybe it didn't have anything to do with being abducted, Will,"

175

she said as she placed her fingers across my lips. "Maybe it just wasn't meant to be."

I leaned over and kissed her cheek. "Whatever you say. I just want you to rest now and get well."

She didn't need to know we'd set a trap for the kidnappers with the money, and that it was only a matter of time before someone got caught spending it. She simply needed to concentrate on getting well. The rest was up to me, Harv, and the boys.

Justice was coming.

Chapter Twenty-Three

August 4th

CHAR

I stood at my bedroom window and stared at the huge, puffy clouds floating across the wide blue sky, wondering why I felt so tired, listless, and distraught. It had been ten days since my miscarriage happened. I'd returned home after the worst had passed, and though my body was slowly mending, my emotional wounds were still as tender as the day it happened. Overwhelmed by grief and a deep sense of loss, despondency had overtaken me, rendering me incapable of continuing with the life I'd had before that fateful day at Anna's House.

I didn't know why, but I couldn't make sense of my life now. Everything I had planned to do before I lost the baby ceased to interest me. I didn't want to see anybody. I didn't want to go anywhere. I wasn't good company for Will and that upset me more than anything. Sadly, I didn't know who I was anymore. I had fallen down a dark hole filled with emptiness and loneliness, and I didn't know how to climb out.

Though I'd given up on myself, Will refused to give up on me. He'd tried everything he could to cheer me up with flowers, candy, and pretty cards. He'd even given me a book of poems—which I thought was so sweet of him, but it still didn't help me deal with the deep melancholy permeating my soul.

My staff didn't know how to handle the change in me. They treated me with the utmost care, like a fragile piece of glass in danger of breaking.

Sadly, I was already broken.

Footsteps in the hallway interrupted my thoughts. I turned just as Francie appeared in the doorway to my room with Julien in her arms.

"Hi," she said cautiously, "Julien and I came to cheer you up." Her ears were adorned with a beautiful pair of drop earrings, and surprisingly, they weren't mine. I wondered where she'd gotten them.

The moment Julien saw me, he began to squirm in her arms. Pushing away my dark thoughts, I smiled as I crossed the room. "Come to Mamma," I said to my son and took him in my arms. "My sweet boy is getting so big." I kissed his cheek. He reached up and tried to put his fat little fingers in my mouth.

"He's heavy, too," Francie added. "Gretchen says he weighs twenty-two pounds."

"Golly," I cooed. "Somebody's eating too much of Cook's tapioca pudding." Julien was truly the only bright spot in my life and as I held him, I thanked God for my son. I had no idea why his little body grew and survived in my womb when all my other babies didn't, but if he turned out to be the only child I had, I would always be grateful to God for blessing me with him.

Francie was right—he was heavy—and it didn't help that he had so much youthful vitality that he couldn't be still. I placed his little stockinged feet on the floor, curling my fingers around his little hands as I helped him steady himself. It wouldn't be long before he started walking around the furniture. My little man was growing up so fast!

"Maddie is taking me to the pictures tonight," Francie said suddenly. "She's picking me up at three o'clock. We're stopping at her house to fix our hair and makeup. Then we're going out for dinner before the show. Do—do you want to come along?"

I paused at first, surprised that such an unlikely pair would hit it off so well. Will told me that Maddie had befriended Francie during my absence, slipping into the role of a big sister and helping her cope. By the looks of her sky-blue dress and jewelry, Maddie had made a positive impression on her. The blue matched Francie's eyes and contrasted nicely with her flaxen hair.

"I'm still not feeling up to going out," I replied softly. "Maybe next time." My heart ached with guilt as the corners of her mouth turned down with disappointment. I regretted refusing her request, but I just didn't have the energy for it. "I'm sure you and Maddie will have a good time together. She's a lot of fun."

"She's smart, too," Francie added. "She's organizing everything we need for the cosmetics salon and planning the grand opening. I'm helping her!" Francie smiled proudly. "Maddie says that when I turn sixteen, I can work there. After I graduate and start working steady hours, she's going to train me to be a manager!"

I blinked. *After I graduate...?* My goodness, Maddie had convinced her to finish school?

"But she says I have to get good grades and take business courses at the university if I want to take over the store someday," Francie proclaimed. "I can't wait!"

"I think you're going to love it," I said with a positive note in my voice, overjoyed that my sister had changed her primary focus from boys to business.

Francie stared down at the floor. "Um...Char...the other reason I came to see you is..."

The sudden change in her demeanor gave me pause. Something was deeply troubling her. I waited for her to continue.

She looked up. "I'm sorry about your illness. The...the baby."

My jaw dropped. "You know about that? Did Maddie explain what happened?" I cringed with regret for not telling her myself.

She shook her head. "Everybody knows. Somebody heard Will tell Maddie about it after he brought you home and so we understand why you're sad..."

Of course. I should have known that my staff would uncover the information. Nevertheless, now that the truth had found me out, I didn't need to keep it to myself any longer. I breathed a sigh of relief. "It's all right, Francie. I'm sorry too, but I'll get through this."

Her sadness turned to hopefulness. "Are you and Will going to get married now?"

I shrugged, truly not knowing the answer to that. Ever since the night

I turned him down, Will had avoided talking about it. "We'll see what the future brings."

Lillian's tall, thin form appeared at the door. "You have a visitor. Mrs. Wentworth. Shall I tell Gerard to send her away or do you feel up to receiving her?"

"Please, send her up," I said quickly. I didn't have the energy to receive anyone, but I could never turn Sally away.

"Yes, ma'am," Lillian replied. "Shall I serve coffee?"

Knowing Sally, she'd rather have a stiff drink, but I nodded to Lillian. "That would be fine."

Francie took Julien's hands. "I'll bring him back to Gretchen." Her nostrils flared. "Oh, boy… I think he just filled his diaper."

Grimacing, she picked him up and scurried back to his nursery.

I sat on the edge of my bed, waiting for Sally, the one person I knew who could help me navigate my way through the debilitating emotional fog that had settled over me.

*　　*　　*

Sally appeared in the doorway, wearing a teal dress, and carrying a large straw basket.

"Hi," I said apologetically as I slid off the bed. "I hope you don't mind that I insisted you come up here to see me. I just don't feel up—"

Sally's orange-red lips curved in a wise, empathetic smile as she waved the notion away. "It's all right, honey. The most important thing right now is to take care of yourself. Losing a child takes a lot out of a person, but what you're going through isn't permanent. This too shall pass."

The care in her tone reminded me of Anna. Oh, how I missed my mother! Oh, how I needed her now!

"How are you doing?" Sally asked frowning with concern. She set her basket on the floor next to an armchair by the fireplace and stretched out her arms for a hug. "Are you eating well? You look a little peaked."

I embraced her. "I'm tired all the time. I just can't seem to get my energy back."

"You need to get out of this room," Sally lectured boldly. "Get some fresh air. Find something to keep your mind off your troubles. You're never going to recover if you hide away up here and dwell on it."

The bundle in her basket moved. A small hand emerged from the swaddling blanket.

"Oh, my goodness," I said as I leaned over the basket and pulled back the flannel. "Is this a new grandchild?"

Sally laughed. "Not this time. She's a foster child."

How sad, I thought to myself, *that this little one had survived childbirth, only to be surrendered to a stranger.*

Sally lifted the bundle from the basket and cradled it lovingly in her arms. "She's probably my last one, too."

"What a darling little girl," I remarked as I brushed the infant's soft dark hair with the tip of my finger. "Why is she your last one? Are you going to adopt this sweet little thing?"

Sally's eyes misted with regret. "I want to keep her, but Bernie says we're too old to keep raising babies. We've raised all our kids and a fair number of foster kids too. He says it's time to pass the torch to the next generation." She held out the bundle. "Would you like to hold her?"

My arms were still tired from holding Julien, but I didn't have the heart to turn Sally down. Gingerly, I took the little one in my arms and as I gazed down at her, I beheld her sweetness. My heart suddenly melted...

"She's so tiny," I said marveling at the little girl's doll-like face with rounded cheeks and soft pink lips. "Such big eyes. Like a Kewpie doll." I looked up. "What's her name?"

"She doesn't have one yet," Sally replied soberly. "Her adoptive parents should be the ones to name her. For now, I'm calling her Missy."

So, the child had no name. No identity. That bothered me but I kept it to myself. Judging by the way Sally looked at Missy, she was quite attached to the child. Naming the little girl would make it even more difficult to part with her.

My arms were beginning to shake with fatigue. I sat in an armchair next to Sally's and held the bundle on my lap. "When is her adoption going through?"

Sally shook her head as her brows formed a troubled frown. "No takers yet. If she doesn't get spoken for soon, she'll go into the Catholic Charities adoption program and wait for placement at St. Joseph's orphanage."

I swallowed hard. Send this innocent little girl to the institution on Randolph Street? To grow up waiting for someone to give her love, a name, and a home? What if it never happened? The thought of relocating her to that overcrowded place struck a chord of sadness in me. How utterly tragic...

Sally must have read my thoughts. "It's going to break my heart to give her up," she said frankly. "I'd adopt her myself in a heartbeat if I could, but Bernie won't budge."

I clutched Missy tighter. "When are you turning her over to the orphanage?"

"I've got a few more weeks to find a place for her," Sally replied then leaned forward in her chair. "Would you consider taking her?"

I blinked, blind-sighted by her request. "Me? Sally, I'm not married. The welfare system would never permit me to raise a foster child alone." I didn't mean to sound pessimistic, but her suggestion took me completely by surprise. Me, the widow of a notorious bootlegger to foster a child? If the people in the welfare office were anything like Faye Delacorte and her cohorts in the Friendship Club, the effort would undoubtedly end in a swift, humiliating rejection.

"That's only one issue," Sally argued. "There are other factors to consider. You have the financial ability to care for the child and provide her with an excellent education. I'm on good terms with the people in the child welfare office. If I could get your application approved, would you take Missy?"

"I—I don't know," I said slowly as I pondered her proposal. Sally had always been good to me. This was important to her and turning her down didn't seem right, but what she was asking me to do was impossible. I didn't want to get my hopes up—or hers—only to have them dashed. "It's a serious responsibility, Sally. I want to help but I don't believe it's possible. Not with my reputation."

Lillian appeared with the coffee service. She saw me holding little Missy and halted in the doorway, her eyes widening. As she stared at the bundle in my arms, the grave expression crossing her face gave me the uncomfortable feeling she wanted to say something but was holding back. Feeling awkward, I stood immediately, placing the child on my bed. "Ah, just in time," I said to change the subject as the brisk aroma of fresh-brewed coffee filled the room. "I'll pour it, Lillian. That will be all."

I didn't realize how badly my hands shook until I lifted the silver coffee pot and poured a cup for Sally. The cup rattled in its saucer as I handed it to her. Then I quickly poured one for myself, sloshing coffee over the rim. Sitting down, I sipped too much of the hot liquid and burned my tongue. "How about a ginger cookie?" I put my cup down and grabbed the plate, hoping Sally hadn't noticed my discomfort. "They're Cook's specialty. Great for dunking."

Sally selected one and dipped it into her coffee. "How is Will coping? I imagine he's plenty concerned about you."

I grabbed a cookie and nibbled on it. She didn't know about the kidnapping. Will told her only that I'd taken ill with the miscarriage after I left the shelter and had sought out a midwife to help me through it. "I think he's still in shock. He barely had time to get adjusted to being a father before it was taken away from him."

I didn't have the heart to tell her I hadn't seen much of him in the past week. He and I chose to deal with my kidnapping and my miscarriage in different ways. He'd jumped back into his work, and I had retreated from the world.

Little Missy began to fuss. I jumped from my chair and picked her bundled form off the bed.

"She's probably hungry," Sally said as she pulled a small Pyrex baby bottle from the basket. "Would you like to feed her?"

I sat in my chair and fed the child her bottle as Sally filled me in on everything going on at the shelter. Little Missy eventually fell asleep in my arms and as I watched her slumber peacefully, I wondered if I'd ever have a little girl of my own. A wave of longing washed over me. *Maybe someday*, I thought hopefully, but given my past issues, my heart had doubts.

Sally drank the last of her coffee and stood. "I'd better get going. I need to get Bernie's supper on the table."

I stood and handed the child back to her. She tucked Missy into the basket and said goodbye with a quick hug. On her way out the door, she paused. "If you change your mind about little Missy, I'll do everything in my power to get you approved as a foster parent. Think about it, Char. You need her as much as she needs you."

After Sally left, I spent the rest of the day struggling *not* to think about the child's situation. That night, curled up in bed, I tried to clear my head by reading a book, but I couldn't concentrate. Little Missy's dire predicament haunted me. I couldn't stop seeing those innocent eyes and thinking about how she, so little and so helpless, would fare in an orphanage with hundreds of children.

The book dropped to the floor as I turned off the light and lay on my side, staring into the darkness. Tears suddenly filled my eyes. My problems were small compared to what that child was facing, and my heart ached for her. Yes, I'd had a rough childhood, but somehow it had made me strong. Though the odds had been against me, I survived. Would she?

I wondered why Sally brought along a newborn to visit me when she had a small army of women at the shelter to mind it for her. She made a point of handing it off to me as soon as she arrived. Did she do it purposely to get my mind off my own issues? If so...her ploy worked.

I fell asleep worrying about the fate of that little girl.

Chapter Twenty-Four

The next day...

WILL

Daniel and I hustled down the alley in the inky pre-dawn darkness past houses, garages, and towering trees that stood like sleeping giants as we made our way to a garage situated next to our intended target. Other than a few birds tweeting intermittently and the scream of a couple of cats embroiled in a turf war, the only other sounds we heard were the soft scuffing of our shoes on the pavement.

At the side door, Daniel pulled a tool from his pocket and unlocked it. We pulled flashlights from our knapsacks and quickly went inside.

"I saw a light on in the house," I said as I fanned my Winchester light across the floor. "Are you sure the occupants of this property are still away?"

"That's just the housekeeper. She's probably up early to let the dog out to do his business. The Andersons won't be back until next week," Daniel said and walked over to the opposite wall. He pointed to a spot at eye level. "Here's the hole I made. It's right in line with Wroebel's vegetable garden. He'll be out there tending his tomatoes at eight o'clock like he does every Friday."

"I just hope it doesn't start raining beforehand," I said as I peered through the one-inch hole he'd drilled in the wall facing Representative Wroebel's property. Thick clouds overhead made the night so dark I couldn't see a thing.

Daniel pulled up a heavy wooden crate and sat down. "If it does, Wroebel will probably wait for his weekly payoff on the porch. It'll make our job harder because he'll be farther away, but hopefully, we'll still be able to get the transaction on film."

I found another wooden crate and set it next to Daniel's. I sat down and placed my flashlight on the floor for now, leaving it on. My timepiece indicated it was five o'clock. We had a long wait. I grabbed a couple of roast beef sandwiches from my canvas knapsack and handed one to Daniel.

"How is Char doing," Daniel asked as he pulled back the waxed paper. "Is she feeling better?"

I shook my head. "Her progress is slow. It's been a tough road since she lost the...the baby." I nervously bit into my sandwich. Surveillance on a crooked politician I could handle. Char's female troubles were a different story. "I'd give anything to see that beautiful smile back on her face, but I don't know how to help her heal. I feel so useless."

"It can't be easy to deal with what she's been through, but she's a strong woman, Will," Daniel replied sympathetically. "Give her time. She'll get through this."

I ate my sandwich in silence, wishing I could drop everything right now and go to her, but I had to get this job done before the legislature went back into their session. If we got the information we were hoping for today, the case could be wrapped up quickly.

The morning dawned dreary and humid. We took turns peeping through the hole as we waited for Dwight Wroebel to venture out into his garden. At seven forty-five, a tall, gray-haired gentleman appeared in work clothes, wearing gloves, and carrying a bucket. He walked into his fenced garden and began picking tomatoes and beans.

I pulled two cameras that had been loaded with fresh film from my knapsack and handed one to Daniel. I peered through the hole in anticipation as the man worked silently at his task. At eight o'clock, a green and black Model T milk truck pulled to a stop in the alley. A man wearing dark trousers with suspenders, a white shirt with a bow tie, and a dark fedora climbed out. "There he is," I announced apprehensively. "Right on time."

The man walked around to the back of the truck and retrieved a wire basket containing two bottles of milk.

"Well, well," I exclaimed in a whisper. "It's Jimmy the Swede. I didn't know he did his own dirty work."

"Maybe Wroebel doesn't trust anyone else," Daniel replied.

I snapped a picture of Dwight Wroebel staring at the milkman walking by his garden. Daniel exchanged cameras with me. I snapped another one while he advanced the film on mine to the next picture. We exchanged cameras again.

The man crossed the porch and opened the small square "milk door" in the wall next to the back door, placing two glass milk bottles inside. He shut the door and pressed the buzzer to alert the occupants the product had been delivered. On his way back to the truck, he stopped at the garden for a conversation with Mr. Wroebel. He frowned with caution as his gaze darted around the yard. I squeezed off another camera shot with the milk truck in the background. "Here we go," I whispered and stepped back, giving Daniel room to take his turn peeping through the hole. We exchanged cameras again.

"Here comes the payoff," Daniel said and took a couple more shots of the men. "They're arguing," he said suddenly. "Something's wrong." He froze for a moment. "Jimmy's looking our way. Duck!"

We hit the floor as hot metal pumped into the wooden wall of the garage, whizzing over our heads. "Come on," I said crawling toward the door. "Let's get out of here!"

Daniel handed me his camera and I stuffed both into my knapsack as he jerked the door wide open. We burst out of the garage and bolted in the opposite direction, ducking behind a shed. Huge drops of rain began to splatter on us.

I looked at Dan. "Did you get it?"

"Sure did," Daniel said proudly as he peered around the corner of the shed. "Got pictures of him accepting an envelope of money, peering into it, and stuffing it into his trousers."

"Great!"

We took off running between houses like our tails were on fire until we reached our car parked a couple of blocks away.

"Don't think I'll trust my local milkman ever again," I said wryly as

I quickly cranked the engine. "He just might be packing heat."

We laughed but we both knew it really wasn't funny. If Jimmy the Swede got away with it once, he'd try it again, and possibly next time he'd use it as a cover to kill someone.

I couldn't wait to get back to the office and have this film developed. The faster I got this case wrapped up, the better. Dan and I would get paid, Cyrus Adley would have the information he wanted for his front-page bombshell and the article about Char would finally give her the public recognition she deserved.

It was about darned time.

*   *   *

Cyrus Adley stared at me intensely. "You got the goods for me, Van Elsberg?"

I nodded. "Everything you need to take down your favorite dirty politician," I replied as I sat in his dingy office, trying not to sneeze from the decade-old dust motes floating in the musty air around us.

I reached into my briefcase and pulled out a thick file. "We got him, lock, stock, and barrel. The girls, the gambling, and the gangster money to look the other way. He can refute your claims, but pictures don't lie. Wroebel is as corrupt as they come." I placed the file on his desk in front of him and waited as he paged through the evidence we'd collected.

Cyrus let out a long, low whistle of surprise at the photograph of Representative Wroebel accepting a thick envelope from Jimmy the Swede. "I knew I could count on you, Will. This is going to blow the lid off politics in Minnesota."

He opened his wall safe and counted out the balance of what he owed me. "Here you go," he said as he dropped the money on the desk. "This should do it."

"Not quite," I countered. "We agreed you'd write an article about Char's charity."

Cyrus frowned as though he'd forgotten all about it. "Ah...right. The last time we met, you did mention that..." He leaned back in his chair. "Fair enough. I'll assign a reporter to the story right away. I'll run it mid-week."

I grabbed the cash and shoved it into the inside pocket of my jacket. "I'll be watching for it."

I stood, eager to leave. This had been a tough case and I was relieved to wrap it up. I had a wad of cash in my pocket and the rest of the day to do whatever I wanted. I checked my timepiece. Yes, I had just enough time to make it to the florist shop for a bouquet of red roses. I couldn't wait to spend the evening with my gal.

Chapter Twenty-Five

Mid-August, grand opening day

CHAR

"Oh, my goodness." I stared through the oval glass door of Madeline's Salon at the line of anxious women waiting outside for the store to open. "Where did all of these ladies come from?" I turned to Maddie as she walked across the small lobby to stand next to me. "How did they find out about us?"

Maddie shoved her hands into the pockets of her smartly tailored red suit and smiled proudly. "I ran an ad yesterday in the Sunday paper to announce our grand opening." She darted a glance through the beveled glass. "Someone told me the line extends to the other end of the block."

We stared at each other for a heartbeat then triumphantly hugged each other. This shop represented a dream come true for both of us, and Maddie had made it happen. She'd designed and decorated the showroom with oriental dividers in black lacquer and covered the wood floor with large oriental rugs exactly as we'd planned to do. Crystal chandeliers sparkled from the ceiling. She'd divided the salon into five sections—makeup, creams, fragrance, bath, and body products.

The salon had twelve beauty assistants on duty today, all women from the shelter, outfitted in aqua broadcloth dresses with matching shoes, white aprons, and lace headpieces. They'd been trained to assist the customers with all our products. Two of the women stood behind the sales desk ready to ring up customer sales and bag the items. The looks on everyone's faces, as they stood patiently at their stations, broadcast a mix of nervous apprehension and unbridled excitement.

Unlike everyone else, I had to talk myself into showing up today. I didn't have the enthusiasm for the shop that I'd once had, and I knew I'd just be in the way. Maddie had supervised the entire operation by herself,

190

and it really didn't feel like my project any longer. I held no jealousy or resentment toward Maddie for continuing without me, I simply didn't feel a part of it anymore. Even so, failing to show up would disappoint both my business partner and my sister, so I had to stay at least for the morning. And pretend that I was enjoying myself.

I turned to Maddie and clasped her hands. "Thank you for all you've done to make the shop a success. It looks marvelous. I'm so sorry you had to put all of this together by yourself."

She shook her head kindly. "Look, don't worry about it, Char. You're here now and that's all that matters. I'm just glad you're feeling better. Besides," she said flashing a mischievous grin, "I got to organize everything just the way *I* wanted it!"

We burst out laughing and for the first time in a long time, my gloom began to lift. I'd never seen her so energized and enthusiastic. Her crazy sense of humor was just what I needed today.

Sally Wentworth and Ethel Rogers suddenly burst through the front door. Ethel wore a long emerald dress and sparkling diamonds, a major departure from her usual severe black attire. "Lordy," she said breathlessly, removing her matching cloche hat, "there's a mob out there. When ten o'clock rolls around, we're going to have a stampede on our hands!" Ethel had invited a lot of her friends to the grand opening. Many were stopping by later in the day and she planned to personally greet them and show them the newest project she had championed.

Sally greeted me with a hug. "How are you? I'm glad to see you getting out of the house and living your life again. You look terrific."

Sidestepping her question, I replied with one of my own. "How is little Missy?" I couldn't help asking. I desperately needed to know. Ever since the day I'd held the child in my arms, she had plagued my thoughts. When would she be transferred to the orphanage? Would she get any attention at all once she got there? Would she have a happy childhood? Deep down, I already knew the answers and it bothered me so much that my worries had become a nagging echo in my soul.

Sally's smile faded. She winced as though fighting back the urge to cry. "She's eating cereal now with a bit of mashed banana." Sally exhaled a slow, distraught sigh, her brows furrowing with unconcealed worry. "I'm going to miss my little peanut. Have you given any thought to what we talked about?"

My heart constricted. Yes, I'd thought about it. *A lot.* But I knew in my gut that no welfare committee would trust me, the widow of a dead criminal, with the responsibility of caring for an orphan child. I needed to let it go…

"I don't think it's possible, Sally," I replied softly. "I'm sorry."

Accepting my excuse, Sally nodded and stared past my shoulder at the enticing displays around the room. "Say, do you mind if I do some shopping before the doors open? I can't stay long. I've got to get back to the shelter."

"Be my guest," I said, my voice trailing off as she brushed past me and headed straight for a table filled with face creams. One of the beauty assistants stepped forward and began to speak with her. Grateful for the distraction, I left her to it and went back to the sales desk to wait with Francie for the shop to open.

At ten o'clock, our eager customers let out a Bronx cheer as Ethel held the door open. Francie and I stood on each side of the entrance with wicker baskets and handed out free samples to the women as they entered. The shop filled up quickly with laughter and the chatter of happy shoppers. Throughout the morning we sold so many products that Maddie had to help the staff restock the tables.

We were so busy the time flew by fast. By early afternoon, the line had disappeared, but customers were still steadily arriving. Francie and I had run out of samples and stood behind the sales desk assisting the clerks. I was so busy wrapping a bottle of perfume in tissue paper I didn't notice someone approaching us.

"Adrienne!" Francie called excitedly and ran to greet her.

Looking as beautiful and regal as ever, Adrienne hugged Francie and continued smiling as she made her way toward me. She wore a burgundy chiffon dress. Under her narrow hat, her short, raven hair glistened with perfect waves as though she had just left her stylist. "*Ma Cheri*! What a wonderful store you and Maddie have designed." She

192

clutched my hands as I came out from behind the counter to greet her. Matching her lips, the bright red of her manicured nails glistened under the dazzling lights. "Ever since you told me about this salon, I've been saving my money for a shopping spree!"

"Then I'll personally show you around," I said with a sudden burst of energy. "What would you like to see first?"

"Do you always focus on your friends and ignore everyone else?" The question, spoken loudly for everyone to hear, sounded more like an imperious demand than an inquiry.

Adrienne and I spun around at the same time and encountered Eva Baumann. Her sleek, calf-length dress and matching clutch glittered with the same blue intensity as her icy stare. She wore an exquisite asymmetrical hat embellished with a satin band and a diamond brooch. A matching ostrich plume, attached beneath the brooch, extended down the length of her swan-like neck and partly concealed her blonde hair.

"Eva, darling. You look *wonderful*. Welcome!" Maddie said breathlessly as she rushed toward us. "Come with me. I can't wait to get your opinion on the newest fragrances from Paris." Slipping her arm around Eva's, she smiled. "Your taste in perfume is *excellent*."

Ignoring us, Eva arrogantly lifted her chin at the compliments and walked away with Maddie.

"By all means serve the prima donna first..." Adrienne grumbled under her breath.

I stared at her in shock. I'd never seen Adrienne show a dislike for anyone *ever* and I wondered what Miss Baumann had done to garner such enmity with my friend.

"That woman is a witch," Adrienne replied as though reading my mind. "Utterly self-centered and cold-blooded."

I stared at her in disbelief. "Did something happen between you two?"

"She complained about me to my employer," Adrienne replied in a smoldering voice.

My jaw dropped. "What in the world..."

"*That woman* and her friends have a permanent VIP table in front of the stage at the club," Adrienne replied with unconcealed resentment. "Every night, they drink too much and become so loud they ruin my show. Last week, I told the leader of our security detail to ask them nicely to quiet down." She drew in a tense breath. "In retaliation, *that woman* went to my boss and demanded that he fire me for offending them." Her eyes narrowed. "I'm too popular to let go. Instead, to appease her, he reprimanded me in front of her and her friends. Then he forced me to apologize."

"Adrienne, I'm so sorry to hear that," I replied sincerely. How humiliating that incident must have been! "Perhaps you'd like a private showing."

"Thank you for the generous offer, but I'd rather come back later," she said and turned away. "When the atmosphere in here isn't so hostile."

"Adrienne, please, wait!" I called out after her, but she kept on walking and quickly left the shop. It broke my heart to see her so upset.

I stared at Eva Baumann, smoldering with anger. I didn't like the way she looked down on me, but her arrogance didn't intimidate me one bit. I simply ignored people like her. Going after a dear friend who didn't have a mean bone in her body, however, was a different matter. Eva's treatment of Adrienne was vindictive and inexcusable. Something had to be done to make that wicked, self-serving witch aware that it would not be tolerated. If she tried to make trouble for my friend again, I would be the one to do it.

*   *   *

I ended up staying at the salon until closing time.

Adrienne returned a couple of hours later—long after Eva had left—and we spent a wonderful time together sampling everything in the store. Adrienne concluded that her favorite section was our bath products line and bought one of every item on the bath table.

Louisa stopped by after work to chat with me while she shopped for face cream. She couldn't stay long. Peter had given her a ride and had parked in front of the shop, waiting for her. Her employment should have ended two weeks ago but Astrid had needed additional time off. Louisa had eagerly accepted the extension to work until the end of this week. She and I made a date next week to catch up over lunch. I was eager to hear all about how her relationship with Peter Garrett was progressing.

As soon as the last customer left, Maddie locked the front door. The beauty assistants set about busily restocking their stations and cleaning the showroom while Maddie tallied the day's receipts. I sat with Francie waiting for Maddie to finish counting the money. I was dead tired and anxious to take Francie home.

Someone tapped on the beveled glass of the front door.

Francie sprang to her feet. "It's Will! I'll let him in!" She dashed to the door and opened it wide. "Hi, Will! Come on in!"

Tall with broad muscular shoulders, Will stood in the doorway dressed in a dark tweed suit and a black fedora tipped to a slight angle. He stepped across the threshold and glanced around, but his gaze quickly rested on me. "Hi," he said softly as he approached. My heart skipped a beat at the devotion in his intense blue eyes. "How'd your day go? By the looks of things, you were busy."

"It was a madhouse," Maddie said with a wry grin, temporarily looking up. "I hope we do it all over again tomorrow."

"The ladies who came in today spent a lot of money," Francie announced excitedly. "One lady bought a lot of perfume and paid for her products with a fifty-dollar bill!"

Will frowned at his sister. "That's unusual. Most people don't use bills that large. Are you sure it's real?"

Maddie finished counting and wrote a figure on her ledger. "Eva Baumann does. You know money has never been an issue for her." She sifted through her cash box and pulled out the fifty, holding it up to the light. Looks real enough to me." She handed the bill to Will. "See for yourself."

He studied the currency for a few moments then held it up to the light and squinted at it. "Can I keep this? I'll give you the correct change for it."

Maddie shrugged. "Sure. Suit yourself."

"Why do you want that," I said becoming irritated. What was so important about his ex-girlfriend's money that he needed to keep it?

He leaned close and whispered, "I'll tell you later." Pulling out his wallet, he grabbed the correct change and tossed it on the counter. "If you girls are finishing up here, I'd like to take you all to dinner."

"I can't," Maddie said. "I've got too much to do tonight."

"Thanks for the offer, Will, but I'm too tired. I—I just want to go home," I said slowly. Though he didn't show it, I knew by his silence that my refusal had disappointed him. I slid the palm of my hand under the lapel of his suit. "Why don't I call home and ask Cook to make something for us?"

"Yeah," Francie chimed in. "I promised to call a few people tonight."

"Okay," he said and slid his arm around me. "I'll consider that a raincheck. When you call, don't forget to let Gerard know that Errol won't have to pick you up." He gave me a friendly squeeze. "*I'm* taking my girls home."

Right, I thought tiredly. I had a feeling I might fall asleep as soon as I got into the car, and he'd end up carrying me into the house.

On the way home, Francie stretched out in the back seat. "Wake me up when we get there," she said with a loud yawn.

I leaned my cheek against Will's broad shoulder. It felt good to snuggle up to him. As I began to drift off to sleep, a thought suddenly crossed my mind. "What was it that you wanted to talk to me about?"

"I need to check on something first, darling," he said slowly as though thinking out loud. "If my suspicions are correct…"

I lifted my head at the odd tone in his voice. "Then what?"

"Then that's the crop…" he trailed off, sounding like he'd slipped deep into his thoughts. "All of it."

I had absolutely no idea what he meant by that, but I knew I'd have to wait until we got to my house to find out. In the meantime, I closed my eyes and drifted off to sleep.

Chapter Twenty-Six

The next evening…

WILL

I arrived at Char's house in time for dinner. Gerard took my hat and ushered me into the library. I helped myself to a glass of whiskey from Char's secret liquor compartment while I waited for her to join me.

I was finishing off my second drink when she breezed through the door. I couldn't help staring at her. She had on a light pink, hip-waisted dress printed with dark pink roses. A wide sash tied into a loose bow draped her hips. A diamond and ruby comb sparkled in her dark brown hair.

I set down my glass and took her into my arms. "You look wonderful." The scent of her floral perfume filled my nostrils.

Placing her palms on my chest, she looked up at me with wide eyes and full lips drawn into a cherry-red pout. "Why didn't you wake me for dinner last night? Francie said that you and she had a lot of fun together."

I gently placed my finger under her chin. "You were so tired you didn't even stir when I lifted you out of the car and carried you up to your room. It was obvious you needed to rest. Francie and I didn't want to disturb you. Besides, I'm here now and I've got a little surprise for you."

Her pout transformed into a wide smile as she wrapped her arms around my neck. "Oh! I love surprises! What is it?"

"Harv's birthday is on the twenty-fifth," I said. "It's a Wednesday. He's turning sixty-five and he's having a big bash to celebrate."

Her smile faded. "Where's the surprise in that? He's been talking about it for a long time."

"He's holding it in a big venue out of town so everyone will be staying overnight," I answered. "It's Adrienne's day off from The Oasis and Harv has contracted her to headline the entertainment. Peter is bringing Louisa." I slid my arms around her waist and pulled her close. "Daniel, of course, will be there and I'm trying to convince Maddie to come too. Don't you want to celebrate Harv's big day with all your friends? With me?"

"Well, since you put it that way..." she responded with a shrug. "Where is this venue located?"

I drew in a deep breath, preparing myself for a fireworks storm. "It's at Breezy Point Lodge on Big Pelican Lake."

Her face paled. "What!?" She pushed me away. "That's close to where I... Why would Harv do that? Why would he want to go back to that area after what happened to me there?"

"The lodge's owner did us a huge favor so Harv's reciprocating," I said quickly, jumping to Harv's defense. "The resort was fully booked the night we drove up there to deliver the ransom money. Captain Billy put us up overnight in his home—all of us—and arranged a private dinner for us at the lodge. He never asked any questions. This is Harv's way of showing his gratitude."

"He's out of his mind!"

"Trust me, Harv knows exactly what he's doing," I said gravely and took her hands in mine. "We need to talk, Char. I'm worried about you. You're downcast all the time. You rarely leave this house." I slid my arms around her waist and stared deeply into her eyes. "Where is the woman who used to be so busy, so full of life? I want my sweet and sassy gal back."

She buried her face in my chest. "Yesterday, when Errol dropped me off in front of the salon, I literally ran from the limousine to the door of the shop, afraid that someone might come from behind and grab me. I know it's ridiculous to feel that way, but I can't seem to shake the feeling. The only time I feel safe going out is when I'm with you."

"You can't live like this, darling," I said quietly, desperate to make her understand. "You need to free yourself from the hold your fear has over you or it'll keep you a prisoner for the rest of your life."

When she looked up at me again, tears flowed down her cheeks. "But how?"

"You need to face your fear," I countered as I wiped a tear away with my thumb. "We'll go back to the place where it happened. Confront the problem head-on." I gave her a gentle shake. "You need to deal with it."

"I don't know what good that will do," she said with a sniffle. "What I *really* need is to find out who kidnapped me."

"One thing at a time," I replied though I couldn't agree with her more. I wouldn't rest until I'd uncovered the identities of the people who took her away. Char needed closure. So, did I.

The kidnappers thought they were clever, but they'd already made a fatal mistake. They'd begun spending some of Harv's counterfeit money at local casinos. It was just a matter of time before they were caught with the goods, and I intended to be there when it happened.

Chapter Twenty-Seven

August 25th

CHAR

The day of Harv's birthday party dawned bleak, cold, and rainy. Not a good omen, in my opinion. Chilled to the bone, I wore a white dress with black polka dots and a long white wool sweater with black trim and patch pockets. After an early breakfast, Will, Maddie, and I climbed aboard the limousine, and we set off for Breezy Point Lodge. Will and I sat together on the bench seat. Maddie made use of the twin jump seats that folded into place for additional passengers. A large, round hat box took up quite a bit of the empty seat next to her, along with several shoe boxes, a blue satin drawstring bag containing purses, and her jewelry tote. She wanted to get my opinion on which items to wear to the party tonight.

"This is exciting!" Maddie exclaimed as she checked her makeup in the mirror of a black and red, art deco powder compact. "I haven't been to a party of this caliber in ages! Everybody who is anybody is going to be there."

"How did you convince Ethel to manage the salon for you?" I asked curiously.

"I didn't have to," Maddie replied. "When she found out I'd been invited to Harv's party, she insisted on it. Ethel has done so much for us that I trust her completely. So, here I come!"

I slipped my black Mary Jane shoes off my feet and curled up in my corner of the seat, trying to work up some enthusiasm for the festivities tonight. I didn't want to go to Harv's massive extravaganza but more importantly, I really didn't want to go back to the area where I'd been held against my will. Unfortunately, I didn't have a choice. I'd promised Will that tomorrow I'd revisit the cabin where I'd been held and put the issue to rest once and for all. I knew he was desperate to help me come out of my shell, but I didn't have the heart to tell him I didn't think it would work.

Maddie pulled a flask from her handbag and held it up. "Anybody want a nip?"

Will grabbed his watch from his vest pocket and popped open the case. "It's nine o'clock in the morning. A little early for me."

I shook my head.

"Suit yourself," Maddie replied with a shrug. She uncapped the metal flask and took a swig.

A folded newspaper slipped off the jewelry tote and dropped to the floor.

Maddie snatched it up. "Gerard offered me today's paper on my way out the door. He thought we might want something to pass the time since it's such a long drive."

"I don't like reading in the car," I said, "but I'll take the daily crossword puzzle to work on later." It would be a nice way to wind down in my room after I slipped away from the party.

She flipped open the paper and began to browse through it as Will and I stared out our windows at the rainy countryside. The humming of the tires on the road lulled me into a relaxed state and I had just closed my eyes for a nap when Maddie gasped so loud it startled me.

Her flask fell to the floor with a thump as she swung around in her seat. "Oh, my gosh! Char, look at this! We're in the paper!"

I blinked in surprise. "What do you mean?"

Turning the paper in my direction, she leaned forward to show me a full-page article in the variety section entitled "Trailblazing Women." It featured images of me, Maddie, Ethel, and Sally.

"It's about time," Will muttered under his breath.

I turned to him. "What did you say?"

"Oh," he replied abruptly, "I said 'great timing' because it coincides with the opening of your shop. Congratulations!"

That wasn't his original remark, but I let it go to listen to Maddie. She read the entire article aloud so both Will and I could follow along. Interestingly, the female reporter who wrote the story seemed to know many specific details about the creation of both Anna's House and Madeline's Salon. The entire piece portrayed us as honest, hardworking women who wanted to help other women succeed. What it *didn't* say was that I'd been married to a notorious bootlegger who left me his fortune after he'd died during a shootout with the Feds. Not a word about my growing up dirt poor in Swede Hollow with an invalid mother and an alcoholic father who'd abandoned us.

I thought about that in amazement. For once, people would see the good things I'd done for others rather than judge me for the bad things that others had done to me.

"I need to send that reporter a sincere note of thanks," I said after Maddie finished. "She has no idea how much that article just made my day."

"Mine, too!" Maddie folded the paper and handed it to me. "I hope it drives a lot of new business to the shop."

Will gazed out the window, strangely silent, but wearing a wide grin.

* * *

We were getting close to Breezy Point Lodge when we sped by a log house. It looked familiar.

"We just passed the midwife's house," Will said as I craned my neck to see it through the back window. "I think it would be good for you to go back there and pay her a visit."

"But that place holds too many sad memories—"

"It's time to create new ones." He pulled the hand-held Dictaphone out of its holder on the wall. "Errol, turn the car around and go back to the house we just passed."

As we pulled into Ruth Hemsted's driveway, I reluctantly slipped my shoes back on and tied the sash of my long sweater. "I won't be long." I slid out of the car as Errol opened the back door for me. Luckily, the rain had stopped. A few streaks of sunshine poked through the clouds.

I walked to the house and knocked on the door, hoping she wasn't home. When it opened, Ruth stared at me through the screen door. "My goodness, Char," she remarked with a thread of surprise in her voice. "How nice to see you!" She opened the screen door. "Come in."

"I'm on my way to Breezy Point Lodge for a birthday party," I told her, tactfully letting her know I couldn't stay long. "So, I thought I'd stop by to say hello."

Poignant memories assaulted me as I stepped into her small, but cozy house of handmade curtains, doily-covered furniture, and the aroma of baked bread. I swallowed hard, willing myself not to get emotional over the unfortunate incident that had landed me here a month ago.

The few minutes I spent with Ruth elevated my mood immensely. Will had been right. Coming back to this place and having coffee with the woman who had lovingly cared for me felt oddly comforting and it gave me an opportunity to thank her once again for all she'd done for me. For the first time in weeks, I felt like smiling.

The sky cleared as we continued to the lodge and the bright afternoon sun shone down upon us. After a few miles, we went around a curve and passed the dirt road to Darla's farmhouse. The road straightened again. I stared out the window, watching the dense woods pass us by, vividly remembering the night I had walked this road in terrible pain, seeking help.

We passed an intersection with a clearing and a ramshackle building with moss growing on the roof. There were holes where the windows and doors used to be. Will drew in a tense breath and stared at the area. I wondered about his sudden reaction but didn't ask. Something had triggered unpleasant memories for him, too.

Whatever reservations I had about coming back here evaporated as soon as we passed the massive stone entrance and Breezy Point Lodge came into view. What a place! The huge lodge was constructed of massive pine logs and the adjoining hotel overlooked the shore of the sapphire waters of Big Pelican Lake. Past the lodge, dozens of cabins surrounded by pines made up a small neighborhood.

Automobiles of all types and colors lined the muddy, tree-lined road leading to the resort. I stared in awe at a large crowd of people spread out on the beach with blankets and umbrellas. Several men passed by the car with their young caddies in tow carrying golf bags. Errol pulled the limousine into the circular drive and stopped at the front entrance of the Lodge. He opened our door, and a wave of hot, humid air surrounded me. I removed my sweater before I climbed out.

"Wow," Maddie exclaimed as she stared up at the lodge. "I heard this place was amazing, but I had no idea it would look like this." She glanced at the buildings, wide-eyed with excitement. "It's so Jake!"

I spun around, taking in the activity around me. "I know what you mean—" I froze mid-sentence, halting at the sight of Eva Baumann coming out of the Trading Post in a fawn-colored dress. I turned to Will. "What is *she* doing here?"

She heard me and stopped short, her eyes narrowing when our gazes met. I spun away. I never forgot how rudely she had treated me the first time we met at the Oasis, and I didn't want to spoil my evening by dealing with her antics again.

Ignoring her, Will took my hand and guided me toward the lodge. "I don't know. Harv must have invited her." He kissed the top of my head and proceeded to pull open the wide front door. "Come on, let's get checked in. We don't have much time to get ready."

The cocktail reception started at six o'clock with dinner at seven. Birthday toasts and the cake would follow with a dance after that.

Will checked us in and escorted us to our rooms. Maddie and I had rooms adjacent to each other. Will's room was down the hall. "I'll be back at five-thirty to take you and Maddie for cocktails," he said. Holding the door open with his foot, he took me in his arms and kissed me deeply. "See you then, darling."

As soon as the door shut behind me, I kicked off my shoes, set my handbag on a small table, and flopped backward onto the soft bed with a huge sigh. It felt so good to get out of that cramped car. I wanted to take a nap but knew that as soon as my bags were delivered, I had to get ready.

A familiar scent distracted me. I sat up and looked around. A vase containing a dozen red roses sat on a small table with a card attached. I arose from the bed and pulled the card from the envelope. It read:

To my darling Char,

may this night be the best time of your life.

All my love,

Will

My eyes smarted with tears at the sweetness and devotion in his gesture. I was so lucky to have found a man like him and I knew it with every fiber of my being. I loved him so much!

Once my bags arrived, I opened my garment case and pulled out the dress that Maddie had insisted I wear; a sleeveless, champagne sheath covered with clear beads and gold sequins—the newest rage in French art deco couture. It had a V-neck in both the front and back and a flared hem. Maddie said it was the perfect dress for dancing the Charleston, but I had little interest in making a fool of myself by jumping around like a beheaded chicken in front of Harv's guests.

I carefully removed a large black velvet box from my suitcase containing the only jewels I'd brought. I hadn't worn the necklace in several years because the gems weighed heavily on my neck, but Maddie said it fit the dress perfectly. I opened the case and carefully removed a diamond necklace with a forty-carat, step-cut Columbian emerald pendant. The matching earrings, though smaller, were the same cut. The bracelet contained emeralds alternating with diamonds.

I put a couple of clips into my hair to reset my waves and then soaked for a while in a steamy bath, wishing I could stay in this soothing water all evening. A few minutes before five-thirty, I slipped into the luxurious dress and donned the jewelry. I had just finished touching up my eyelashes with the little brush from my Maybelline mascara box when Will knocked on the door.

"Come in. I'm almost ready," I said as I opened the door. He stood before me in a dark suit and a white shirt. His new gold cufflinks sparkled in the light. He must have just come in from the outdoors. The wind had slightly tousled his thick, dark hair. I stood aside to let him in. "Thank you for the flowers, Will! They're beautiful."

He didn't move. "You are absolutely stunning," he declared slowly, ignoring my remark about the flowers. "Those emeralds…"

"I hope you don't mind that I'm wearing them," I said apologetically. "The set was a gift from Gus." My fingers clutched the large pendant. "Maddie insisted I wear them with this dress."

"She made the right choice," he replied as he stepped into the room. "It's beautiful and the bright green enhances your eyes."

"I'll get my shoes on so we can get going," I said as I walked toward my suitcase. "I just hope Maddie's ready."

"She can wait," he said and shut the door. He gently took my arm and spun me around.

The urgency in his actions surprised me. "Why? What's wrong?"

"Absolutely nothing." Pulling an object from his trouser pocket, he went down on one knee and held up a black leather box. "Charlotte, will you marry me?"

I gasped and stared at the ring, so surprised I could barely speak. "Oh, my gosh, Will," I whispered. "Yes!"

"What did you say?" His handsome face took on a mock frown. "I didn't hear you."

"Yes," I countered with a laugh.

He cupped his free hand behind his ear. "Say that again?"

By now, neither of us could stop laughing.

"YES!"

He pulled the ring from the box and slid it on my finger. The large oval diamond sparkled brilliantly on my hand.

"It's beautiful," I said as I stared at the ring. "I love it so much."

He picked me up and swung me around. "I love *you*, darling."

"And I love you, Will," I said and slid my arms around his neck. "Gee, you took me completely by surprise. You planned all along to give it to me tonight, didn't you? That's why you insisted we come to the party!"

He lowered me to the floor, responding with a deep, passionate kiss. "I wanted to propose to you in a more romantic setting by the lake, but the rain took care of that."

"That's okay," I said happily. "It's just as romantic being here alone with you. The only thing we could have added was a glass of champagne."

"Got it covered," he said cupping my chin with his hand. "Let's go."

I slipped on a pair of burnished satin shoes and grabbed my matching handbag. "I'm ready. I can't wait to show Maddie my ring!"

To our surprise, Maddie had already left her room. She'd stuck a note for us in between the door and the jam.

We hurried downstairs to the cavernous dining hall, passing Leon Goldman and his bodyguards in the lobby. I hadn't spoken to Leon since the night we danced together at Adrienne's opening show at the Oasis and was surprised to see him here. I didn't know that Leon and Harv were such good friends—or that Leon and Will had become friends. The moment their gazes met, something unspoken passed between them as though they were confirming an earlier conversation or agreement. Knowing Leon, it probably involved roughing up a few people. It left me unsettled, wondering what was going on.

We entered a huge dining room filled with partygoers. Will took my hand and led me to a reserved table close to the dance floor. On the way, we were detained several times by people congratulating me on the article in the paper and praising my accomplishments. The first time it happened, I was stunned. After the way I had been treated at the Friendship Club ball, I hadn't expected anyone to mention it, much less laud me for a few good deeds. But after a total stranger approached me—someone who recognized me from my stint managing La Coquette—I began to realize something. The only difference between the people from Gus' world and Faye Delacorte's society crowd was their *attitude*. The ladies from the Friendship Club were no better than the women in this room so what gave them the right to judge me?

I didn't have an answer to that question, but I suddenly understood this: though I hadn't associated with most of them since Gus' funeral, the people in this room were still my friends. They accepted me for the person I was and didn't expect me to prove myself worthy of their group by meeting a set of rigid standards. The moment I realized where I really belonged, an invisible weight lifted off my shoulders.

Inside, I glowed with excitement to show everyone my engagement ring. I thought of the note Will had attached to the roses. Yes, this was turning out to be the *best* night of my life.

Chapter Twenty-Eight

WILL

I led Char to our table, anxious to show off my beautiful gal and her new ring. The table accommodated six—me, Char, Peter, Louisa, Maddie, and whomever she had invited to dine with us. As expected, she already had a friend, Boyd Nelson, sitting with her. Peter and Louisa had arrived before us, too.

Louisa saw us and jumped from her chair, making a beeline for Char. "Look!" She held up her left hand to show Char her new engagement ring. "Peter proposed!"

"Oh, Louisa, I'm so happy for you!" Char smiled and held up her hand. "Look, I've got one, too. Look, Maddie!" Maddie gave them both hugs of congratulations.

Once we were seated at the table, Char leaned toward me with a sly smile and whispered. "Did you guys coordinate the timing of your proposals or something?"

I chuckled. "Maybe…"

Boyd struck up a conversation with friends at the next table. At Peter's nod, we left the girls deep in conversation and made our way to the bar for a drink. We both ordered whiskey and water.

"Bottoms up, old boy," Peter teased and held up his drink to propose a toast. "To bachelorhood, or what's left of it."

We laughed.

"I'm going light on the coffin varnish tonight," I said getting serious. "If our plans go down the way we expect them to, we're going to need our wits about us."

Peter's smile turned into a tense frown. "I just hope no one gets hurt."

"Too late for that," I said and sipped my whiskey. "Plenty of people have already been hurt."

Peter leaned on the bar, rubbing his thin mustache. "How do you know for sure it's them?"

"How could I not?" I made a quick sweep of a pair of bodyguards watching over the person who employed them. "I'll never forget that day as long as I live. The tall one had a scar over his right eyebrow. Just like that guy over there." I cursed under my breath. "It's him all right."

Peter perused them briefly then turned back to me. "If it is them, they've been passing their *sour dough* all over town."

"Yeah, well this is where it ends." I set my empty glass on the bar. "All we've got to do is wait for them to start gambling and alert the guards securing this place."

Peter drained his glass. "What if they don't play at the tables here?"

I shot him a wry look. "Trust me. They will."

*   *   *

Peter and I arrived back at our table just as our waiter delivered a bottle of champagne compliments of Harv to celebrate our engagements. Peter and I signaled thanks to him as our waiter uncorked the bottle and filled our glasses. Harv sat at the head table close to the stage with a female companion. Seated around the table were his brother Marv and Marv's lady friend from Seattle, Captain Billy, and his wife. To his right, he'd seated Adrienne and Daniel. Adrienne looked as beautiful as ever in a deep red dress. I always enjoyed hearing her sing but didn't think I'd get the opportunity to see much of the show tonight. Neither would Daniel.

Though I tried to focus on the moment, my mind drifted elsewhere as Char and our party touched our glasses together and sipped champagne. Given the way Peter's blond brows knit together, he couldn't get our plan off his mind, either.

The dining staff served dinner at seven sharp, starting with a marinated olive and cheese platter and tomato bisque soup. I hadn't eaten since breakfast, and I was starving. When the main entrée was served, the tender roast beef au jus, herbed carrots, and roasted potatoes practically melted in my mouth.

"You must have been hungry, too," I said to Char. "You ate everything on your plate."

She leaned close. "The food was excellent, but we didn't have lunch today. I wonder what time they'll serve the cake. I'm dying for a cup of fresh-brewed coffee."

"Soon, I hope."

"Why?" she asked curiously. "Are you anxious for the party to get started? I don't think I want to stay that late."

Knowing what was likely to take place later tonight, I didn't want her to stay, either. If she knew why we were setting a trap and who it was for, she'd likely jump right into the middle of it.

At eight o'clock a small orchestra took their places on the stage and played happy birthday to Harv while colorful balloons and confetti rained down from the ceiling. A waiter rolled a cart containing a huge 3-tiered lemon-yellow cake across the floor and stopped in front of Harv's table. The crowd stood and cheered, calling for Harv to give a speech.

I let out an impatient sigh. As soon as we got through the usual dog and pony show of speeches and cutting the cake, I needed to excuse myself and scout out the casino. Peter, Daniel, and I would be coordinating with Billy Fawcett's security detail when the suspected kidnappers began to gamble with their counterfeit money. Harv's men and Leon Goldman's men were there in case we needed backup. Harv had decided to let Leon in on the scheme when he'd learned that some of the money had been spent in one of Leon's gambling rooms.

The mastermind of the kidnapping plot was my target. Leon had staked his claim to take down the actual kidnappers. If things went according to our plan, they would be in jail tonight. All of them.

*   *   *

As soon as Adrienne began her show, I announced that I wanted to get a special martini from the bar. Instead, I scouted out the casino. Captain Billy kept people entertained with roulette tables, craps tables, poker tables, and slot machines. The men I sought hadn't arrived yet, but it was just a matter of time.

By the time I returned, I found Peter and Boyd on one side of the table discussing the newest model of Cadillac. On the other side, the girls huddled together laughing and talking. I had planned to escort Char to her room, but Adrienne suddenly announced a "Ladies Only" Charleston dance.

Maddie jumped to her feet, grabbing Char and Louisa by the arm. "C'mon, girls. This will be fun. Let's go!"

Char started to make an excuse when Louisa stood up. "Yeah, Char. Let's dance!"

Char stared at her in surprise. "Louisa, I had no idea you knew how to dance the Charleston."

"I don't but it can't be that hard," Louisa replied with a shrug. "You and Maddie can show me the steps."

Maddie and Louisa slipped their arms inside Char's and walked her to the dance floor. Peter and I frowned at each other over the delay. We sat down and waited for their dance to end.

It didn't take much instruction for Louisa to figure out what to do and before long, all three women were laughing uncontrollably as they clowned around, kicking their feet high and swinging their arms to the music. I had been disappointed at first over the unfortunate delay, but watching Char gradually change back into her old self was worth the temporary wait. Her smile radiated when she laughed. Her gold dress shimmered under the lights and those emeralds...

The girls returned to the table out of breath and amazingly, full of energy. I stood up to take Char to her room, but she grabbed her purse and waved goodbye. "We'll be right back. Maddie wants to look around the casino."

"Not without me," I snapped. "Ladies, come back here! Peter, are you going to let your fiancée wander around the casino without a chaperone?"

Peter picked up his drink. "Not on your life. Let's go."

Peter, Boyd, and I followed the girls into the smoky casino, staying right on their heels. The wall-to-wall people made me nervous.

They wandered toward the back of the room to the poker tables. One table had a sign above it that read, "Ladies' Night Out." There were seven chairs. Four were occupied. The excited look on Maddie's face when she saw the empty seats made my gut twist.

She set her diamond and mother-of-pearl vanity case on the table and slid onto the seat of one of the chairs, patting the chair next to her. "C'mon, girls, let's try our luck at twenty-one."

Louisa bit her lip as she stared at the poker table. "I don't know how to play. I think I'll watch you instead."

To my dismay, Char placed her handbag on the table and slid into the chair next to Maddie. "Okay," she said glancing at the other female players, "I guess I can go for a round or two."

I moved close behind her. "Char, I thought you didn't want to stay late."

She smiled back at me. "I won't be long. Just a couple of minutes, okay? Maddie is counting on me to play." She opened her handbag and pulled out a folded stack of bills. After counting out her money, she slid the cash toward the cashier for an exchange of chips.

Someone slipped into the empty chair next to her. A tall, slender blonde wearing a shimmering black dress. Char locked into a cold stare with the last person to join the game. "Well, this night just got interesting."

Though I stayed silent, I winced at the trouble that could ensue between these two. Eva Baumann had joined the poker game.

Eva opened her handbag and grabbed a stack of bills. She counted out five twenties and handed the cash to the female dealer for her chips. Suddenly, another employee appeared and took the cash from the dealer. I glanced over at Peter. The operation had begun.

While they played, the women drank, smoked, and chattered like they were the guests of honor at a ladies' aid meeting. Paying little attention to their cards. Char, on the other hand, sat stoically studying her cards. As the night progressed, I couldn't believe my eyes. Char won hand after hand. Her luck kept on going until Eva ran out of money and threw her cards on the table.

"She must be cheating!" Eva snapped at the dealer. "Nobody wins like that!" Eva's bodyguards moved in close, staring at Char. Peter and I moved close as well, giving them warning glares to keep their distance.

"Collect your chips, Char," I whispered in her ear. "You're leaving."

"Look, I didn't cheat," Char whispered back. "All I did was apply basic strategy and pay attention to the cards that were played." She turned to the dealer. "Do you think I cheated?"

The red-haired dealer shook her head. "Not at all. It's obvious you know the game well."

"You must be either as crooked as she is or blind!" Eva picked up her cards and threw them at the dealer. "I demand my money back!"

"I learned from the best," Char said smugly. "I used to own a casino." She began to stuff her chips into her handbag, but she couldn't fit them all into it. She shoved some toward Maddie's dwindling pile and pushed the rest toward the dealer. "Thank you."

"It's getting late, Char," I said losing patience. "Let's go—"

"Better luck next time," Char said, taking a parting shot at Eva, "but I think you're going to need more than luck to beat me." She slid out of the chair. "Given the way *you* play, you're going to need a miracle."

Eva's face flushed dark red with anger and humiliation. "You think you're clever, but I got the last laugh."

Char patted her bulging handbag with her left hand, showing off her sparkling new ring. "I don't see you laughing now."

Across the room, Leon Goldman gave me the signal to get moving. "Peter," I said quickly to change the subject. "If you're escorting Louisa up to her room, will you show Char to her room, too? There is something I need to do."

"Absolutely," Peter said. "Are you ready to go, Char?"

I kissed Char goodbye. "I'll be by later to say goodnight."

I waited until Char had disappeared into the crowd with Peter and Louisa before I turned to Eva. "You and I need to talk." I pointed toward the back door. "In private. *Now.*"

Chapter Twenty-Nine

CHAR

I got halfway across the room when I realized I needed to go back to the poker table.

"Peter, I forgot my purse!" I cried over the din of laughter and the clang-clang-clang of silver dollar winnings being paid out of slot machines. "I need to go back."

Peter and Louisa stopped and turned around. "Hurry!" Peter said. "We'll wait here for you."

"Okay, I'll be just a moment." I hurried back to the table and found Maddie busily playing cards. She had stored my handbag on her lap.

"You forgot this," she said handing it to me.

"I know. Thanks for keeping it safe." I glanced around. "Where is Will?"

Maddie shrugged. "No idea. He was here a moment ago."

Not far away, Eva's bodyguards argued with Leon's men. I wondered why Leon's men were crowding around them. Something wasn't right. Suddenly, I understood why.

Eva and Will were sneaking out the back door. *Together. Alone.*

No wonder he wanted to get rid of me! "Hang on to my purse for a little longer," I said to Maddie. Something was going down and I planned to get to the bottom of it.

The door had closed behind them by the time I reached the exit. I opened it and slipped out only to find myself in a small, enclosed entryway. I opened the exterior door a crack and peeked out, waiting for my eyes to adjust to the darkness. I heard their voices before I saw them standing together, face to face at the corner of the building. Silvery rays of a full moon shone down upon their silhouettes. The sharp chirp of crickets and methodical lapping of the waves provided background music to enhance their little drama.

"Tell me the truth, Eva," Will said angrily. "What part did you play? You gave the orders, didn't you?"

"I don't know what you're talking about," Eva cooed as she slid her arms around his neck. "Now that I finally have you all to myself, let's not waste such a beautiful night talking in circles. I know you want me as much as I want you. You haven't taken your eyes off me all night." She tilted her head and kissed him. "You ditched your fiancée to be with me..."

I silently slipped out of the door, planning to catch them in the act when Will abruptly broke off the kiss. He pulled her arms from his neck and roughly shoved her away. "Don't play innocent with me! I know you were in on it, and I know why. You're broke, Eva. Your fiancé lost all his net worth and most of yours in bad stock market deals on Wall Street. It takes money to fund your princess lifestyle, so you needed to get more dough—fast." He gripped his hands on his hips. "You knew that without bodyguards Char was an easy mark. That's why you had her kidnapped."

What did he say?

My hand flew to my mouth to stifle a gasp. Eva Baumann ordered my abduction? How? I wanted to crash their little party in the worst way, but my desperate need to know more held me back. It took all the willpower I could muster to flatten against the building and simply listen.

"Don't be absurd," Eva snapped. "Even if I were capable of such a thing, why would I want *her* money? It's tainted."

"You might fool other people with that excuse, but it won't work with me," Will shot back. "You once said Char was richer than sin. The claim was a test to see if I'd deny it. When I didn't, your bodyguards kidnapped her and forced her lawyer to fork over three hundred grand in cash."

Eva uttered a sarcastic laugh. "For someone who was supposedly abducted and held for ransom, Char LeDoux isn't acting like it tonight.

Obviously, no one got hurt."

Will grabbed her by the shoulders. "Believe me, you have no idea what your get-rich-quick scheme actually cost her...and me."

The pain in Will's voice broke my heart. I had no idea he'd taken the loss of his child so hard. Amid my grief, I never once asked him how he felt about it or how he was coping with it.

Oh, Will, I thought guiltily. *I've been so selfish. I'm so sorry...*

Eva pulled his hands away and pointed her finger in Will's face. "Look, you can make up all the theories you want, but you have *no* proof."

"Yes, I do." Will reached into his pocket and pulled out a wad of bills. "The ransom money was counterfeit. This is the cash you gave the dealer for your chips. The serial numbers match."

My breath caught in my throat. She had the nerve to use ransom money against me at the poker table! That meant the money I won from Eva had been part of a crime—against me. I suddenly wondered if the money she'd spent at the salon on opening day had been some of it too. Was that why Will wanted the fifty-dollar bill she had used to pay for her products?

"S-somebody gave me that money," Eva cried as she backed away. "I didn't kidnap anybody, Will. I'm innocent. I swear!"

"You planned it, you provided the hideout, and you got your share of the payoff." He grabbed her by the arm. "It's over, Eva. You're coming with me."

"No!" She wrenched her arm away. "You're not a law enforcement officer. You can't arrest me. My father has a lot of influence in St. Paul and when he gets through with you, I guarantee your reputation will be ruined!"

Eluding his grasp, Eva ran away from him, passing right by me, but she was so intent on getting away, she didn't see me.

"Eva!" Will shouted as he started after her. The side door suddenly opened, and Eva's bodyguards burst through. They surrounded Will and began pushing him around.

"Where did she go?" One man demanded. "What have you done to her?"

The door burst open again and more men appeared—Captain Billy's security guards.

It was now or never. I slipped away amidst the commotion and ran like the wind after Eva Baumann. I caught up to her at the front of the building but didn't get a chance to confront her.

A fancy blue car sat in the driveway with the motor running. As soon as the valet, a tall, skinny lad with curly dark hair, got out and walked away, Eva jumped in and drove off.

"Hey!" he shouted as he ran after her. "Come back here Miss Baumann! That's not your car!"

I watched Eva drive away, vowing to myself to go after her. She got away from Will, but she wasn't going to get away from me.

We had some serious business to settle.

*　*　*

I didn't have a car and I sure didn't have time to look for Errol to chase after her in the limo. I had to find transportation *now*. Walking away from the lodge, I trudged along the car-lined road wondering what to do. A tempting thought suddenly crossed my mind.

It worked for her. Why not me?

Of course, I didn't plan to steal it, just borrow it. I stopped next to a new Ford Model T—the only car I knew how to drive. Looking around, I checked to make sure no one saw me, then I opened the door. Yes, the key was in the ignition, but then, why wouldn't it be there? Everybody left their key in the ignition so they wouldn't lose it. Me included.

I quickly cranked the Ford, started it up, and took off down the road. The rain had created deep muddy ruts in the ground causing the car to swerve as I navigated my way out of the resort, at the same time keeping an eye on the headlights of Eva's car.

At the edge of the resort, I turned left and gunned the gas as much as I could though I worried about sliding into the ditch. A few miles down the road, the headlights in the distance turned right. The turn-off was at a clearing I'd seen earlier that day, the one with the windowless shack. I turned down the dirt road and began to drive into the woods. In the distance, the car turned into a driveway and disappeared.

I stopped the Ford and turned it off, knowing I'd have to walk from there to avoid my automobile being seen. Slipping out of the car, I shut the door and started walking in the dark. Before my escape, walking alone at night through the woods would have given me the heebie-jeebies, but not anymore.

I hurried along the weedy shoulder of the road, swatting mosquitos, and looking for a blue car. When I found it, I hurried up the driveway to a sprawling one-story cinderblock house surrounded by mature trees. An odd sense of déjà vu swept over me as though I had been here before. Shrugging it off, I tried the front door and found it locked. Several lights shone in the living room. I didn't see Eva, but I saw her handbag laying on a parlor table.

Walking around to the back of the building, I suddenly froze. My eyes were accustomed to the dark and I had no trouble making out the small building attached to the house—the place where I'd been held captive. As I stared at the dark silhouette, the shock left me numb for a few moments but when I remembered Eva's orders had put me there, a surge of rage welled up inside of me. By sheer accident, I'd come full circle, but even so, I had no intention of shrinking back simply because this place had caused me so much pain.

I found the back entrance locked too. Luckily, the window closest to the door had been raised an inch. Just enough so that it would go unnoticed. I lifted off the screen and pushed the window upward. I found a single cinderblock next to the garage and set it under the window to stand on. After hiking my dress past my waist to get it out of the way, I hoisted myself onto the windowsill and swung my legs over the ledge, landing on the wood floor in a small, dark bedroom. I slipped my shoes off, straightened my dress, and tiptoed to the door. The kitchen and living room were combined into one beautifully furnished area with overstuffed furniture, braided rugs, and a wide, split-boulder fireplace.

The patter of footsteps sharpened my senses. I stepped back, watching Eva emerge from another bedroom. She'd changed out of her long black dress into a navy nautical top with white stripes, navy trousers, and flat shoes. More comfortable for driving a long distance…

"Going somewhere?" I said leaning against the bedroom doorframe.

She let out a small scream and whirled around. Upon seeing me, the shock on her face turned to pure animosity. "Where did you come from? And how did you get in? Leave or when my bodyguards get here, they'll drag you into town and have you arrested for trespassing."

"Fine. I'll show the coppers how I'm skilled at squeezing through small spaces," I replied sarcastically. "You know, like the hole I crawled through to escape when you held me prisoner in the cabin out back?"

"No one has stayed in that cabin for years." Her eyes narrowed with impatience. "Quit talking nonsense and get out."

"You're not going to get away with what you did to me," I said, ignoring her command as I slowly walked toward her. "I know you executed my kidnapping."

Her anger turned to a sneer. "Don't flatter yourself, *Mrs. LeDoux*. A doxie like you isn't worth the trouble."

I continued to advance toward her. "Oh, I know you didn't physically throw me into the trunk of a car and haul me up here, but you were in on it."

"Wrong. I wasn't here." She grabbed her handbag and moved toward the door. "This cabin isn't mine and it's the first time I've been here all summer."

"Then how did you come by so much counterfeit money? You bought chips with it at the casino." I stopped, cutting off her path to the front door. "You bought perfume with it at the salon. My guess is that you've been dropping it all over St. Paul and people are starting to catch on like Will did." I glared at her. "Soon everyone will know. Your face will be in the paper, but it won't be on the society page."

Disdain flickered in her eyes. "I don't have to listen to this," she snapped and tried to step around me. I blocked her way. She tried to shove me aside. "Get out of my way!"

I smacked my palms against her, knocking her backward. "You aren't going anywhere but to jail. It won't take Will long to track us here."

"Will has no idea that this place exists. Now get out of my way!" She picked up a large book on a parlor table and flung it at me. I ducked as it sailed past and hit the wall with a thud.

My anger boiled over. "If that's the way you want to play..." I picked up a ceramic ginger jar.

"No!" Eva screamed. "That's worth a—"

I hurled it at her. It smashed against the fireplace with a loud *crack!* and exploded into shards across the floor.

Eva stared slack-jawed at the broken vase. "How dare you! That was a precious gift to someone. You've shattered it into a million pieces! It will never be the same again."

"Now you know how I felt after I escaped my captors and collapsed in a farmer's yard," I said angrily. "Thanks to you, *I'll* never be the same again."

She rolled her eyes. "I have no pity for trash like you. Go back to the slums in Swede Hollow where you belong."

I snatched a hand-painted pheasant figurine and threw it at her head. She ducked, narrowly missing a blow to her scalp. "At least I'm not on my way to jail."

"Stop!" Eva screamed. She grabbed a poker from the fireplace tools and brandished it like a sword. "You don't have the right to destroy this house!"

I grabbed a heavy crystal candy dish filled with Brach's mints and lobbed it at her. "How does it feel to have everything crash down around you? You didn't care about that when your bodyguards tried to burn down my garage and rob my house, did you? When that failed, you resorted to Plan B. Robbing *me* of my freedom!"

"You deserve it for using Will as a stepping stone to overhaul your lousy reputation. I don't care how rich you are, you'll never be good enough for him!" She swung the poker wildly. I ducked and the poker slammed into a Tiffany lamp, knocking it off a table. It crashed to the floor, pieces of the special glass shade flying every which way. I jumped out of the way as the poker grazed my arm.

She moved closer to the door and unlocked it with one hand while she watched me closely. "I don't know what Will sees in you. You're crazy!"

I stopped, breathing heavily. "If you had endured what you put me through, you'd be crazy, too. Crazy for justice!"

She swung the poker again, forcing me to back up. I tripped over the fallen lamp and fell backward to the floor. By the time I scrambled to my feet, she had escaped. I ran outdoors to catch her, but she had already jumped into the car and started it up. The car hadn't sat idle long and luckily for her, it performed a hot start.

"You're going to pay for what you did," I shouted as she backed the car down the long drive, "to me, to Will, and our..." I couldn't finish. The word stuck in my throat.

I turned toward the house to get my shoes so I could drive *my* stolen car back to the lodge before the owners realized I'd taken it. I was muddy, exhausted, and ready to let the police deal with Eva and her ilk. Their crime spree was over. As for me, it was time to let go of the past and embrace the present. I was sick and tired of stressing over my problems. I had a lot to do to make up for the time I'd lost pining over them.

First, I had to find Will and tell him how much I loved him. Then I needed to apologize to Peter and Louisa for leaving the building without letting them know. Tomorrow, as soon as I got home, I planned to hug my son and thank God for blessing me with him. But then... I needed to call Sally about a sweet little girl who needed me as much as I needed her.

I prayed to God that she hadn't been sent to the orphanage yet.

Chapter Thirty

WILL

I took off after Eva but didn't get far. The casino door burst open, and her bodyguards surrounded me, overpowering me. The guy with the scar above one eye grabbed me by the shirt and shoved a gun in my face. "You got one answer, fella. Make it good or I'll blow your head off. Where is Eva?"

"She ran off," I said looking him straight in the eye. "She found out the ransom dough was counterfeit so she's leaving before the cops arrest her." The men cast worried looks at each other.

The door burst open again. Four of Captain Billy's security guards streamed out with guns drawn. I jerked away from scarface as they surrounded him and his partner, apprehending their weapons. These guys could take over now. The fate of Eva's accomplices was in their hands.

"Where's Baumann?" The lead security guard asked.

"That way." I pointed toward the front of the building. "I'm going after her!"

I had no idea if she'd gone up to her room and barricaded the door or if she'd told the valet to fetch her limo and driver, but time was of the essence. By the time I'd reached the entrance, I didn't see anyone but Peter and Daniel coming through the front door. They looked worried.

"Did you encounter Eva Bauman in the lobby?" I asked Peter.

"No," Peter replied, "but she's the least of your worries right now."

I stared at them, confused. "Why?"

Daniel frowned. "Char's missing."

"What?" I turned to Peter. "You were supposed to escort her to her room."

"She forgot her handbag and had to go back—"

I threw my hands up in disgust and let out a string of foul words. "You mean, you let her slip away." I sighed. I should have known better than to think she'd follow orders.

The young valet arrived with Leon's bodyguards. Harv's men were right behind them. "It was a Cadillac Towne Sedan," he told the men. "As soon as I walked away, she jumped into the car and drove off!"

I could hardly believe my ears. Char stole a car and drove away? "Which way did Mrs. LeDoux go?"

"Not Mrs. LeDoux," the valet insisted. "Miss Bauman!" He pointed toward the road. "She went that way. Mrs. LeDoux ran after her, but when she disappeared behind the parked cars, I didn't see her no more."

God only knew what would happen if Char somehow caught up with Eva. "I have to find Char," I said, "but we need a car."

"Come with us. We'll find them," Ray said to me. He was one of the bodyguards from Chicago that Harv had recently hired. "They couldn't have gone far."

We left the lodge with Harv's men in one car, and Leon's men in another. Areas of fog had begun to form. Between the fog and the muddy road, we couldn't go fast, and I worried about Char. Where was she? With Eva, or lying injured somewhere?

"If we don't see them on this road, I know of another place we can check," I said to Ray. "Turn on County Four. It's right at the clearing."

He turned at the county road and started down the dirt road. After a small curve, we came upon a Ford sitting on the side of the road. Both cars stopped, and Daniel jumped out to check it out. He climbed into the vehicle and then jumped out, shaking his head.

"Let's keep going," Ray said.

We encountered dense fog. I stared through the windshield wondering how I would find the place now. Suddenly, it came into view. "That's it! Stop!" I yelled as we drove past a long driveway with a cinderblock garage at the end. "There's a house back there and I think Eva is connected to the owner. She may have gone there."

We backed up and drove down the long driveway, but I didn't see the Towne Sedan. Surprisingly, the lights were on in the house. I wondered if Eva had hidden it in the garage. I blinked in shock when the front door opened, and Char walked out. I jumped out of the car before it stopped.

"What are you doing here?" I demanded. "Where is Eva?"

"Well," Char replied dryly, "I'm happy to see you too."

I really *was* happy to see her—and relieved—but I needed answers. *Now.* "Look, lady, you were supposed to go back to your room. Why didn't you listen to me?"

By now, a crowd had formed around us. Two men went into the house to look for Eva.

"Eva stole a car and I decided to follow her," Char replied. "It was my only chance to confront her with the truth."

"That Ford sitting on the side of the road," I said brusquely. "Are you responsible for that?"

"I needed a way to follow her, and the key was in the ignition so…" She shrugged. "I planned to bring it back. No one would have known the difference."

That got a laugh out of the crowd. I was the only one who didn't find it funny.

The screen door banged shut. "I don't know what went on in there," Ray said sounding completely baffled, "but it looks like someone had one heck of a tantrum." He came toward Char. "Care to tell us what happened?"

"Eva and I got into a fight. Then she took off. I'm pretty sure she won't be back." Char pointed toward the road. "She went that way."

"Let's go!" Ray yelled and the men climbed into their cars.

I slipped my arm around Char's waist. "Not you. We're going to take that Ford back to the lodge and put it back where you found it.

Hopefully, no one has reported it stolen."

We turned the lights off and shut up the house before we walked down the driveway to get the car. By the time we reached the Ford, a small farm truck ambled toward us, stopping next to our vehicle.

An older gentleman with glasses and thinning hair rolled down his window. "Say, if you're planning to go the way I came, you can't make it through now. It's been blocked off. A car slid off the road and rolled into the ditch. It looks like the rain washed out the shoulder. It's mighty soft lowland around there, what with the lake and all."

I gripped the steering wheel. "Did you see what kind of car it was?"

The old man shook his head. "Don't know much about them new ones, but it was some sort of fancy sedan. It's blue."

Char gasped.

I thanked him and rolled up my window. "I think we'd better check it out."

I drove about a mile down the road to a sharp curve. Several cars had parked across the road, blocking the accident from view, but from where I sat, I had a partial view of the scene. Headlights shone into the ditch where the men were trying to tip the car back to a sitting position. It was the same blue car that Eva stole.

I pulled up next to Harv's vehicle and rolled down the window. "What's going on?"

Joey, another of Harv's bodyguards rested his arm on the window. "Found the girl. And the car." He rubbed the black stubble on his chin. "It ain't good."

My instinct as a detective translated that last sentence to mean the situation was very bad. "What condition is she in?"

Joey's dark eyes studied Char peering over my shoulder. He slowly shook his head. "Me and Marco are on our way back to the lodge to report the situation to Mister Katzenbaum and call the police."

After Joey took off, I convinced Char to wait in the car while I spoke to Ray. I met him at the top of the embankment where the sedan had tumbled into the swampy ditch. "How bad is it?"

"We found the car on its side. She was under it," he answered gravely. "You don't want to go down there."

I nodded and turned away, numbed by the realization that the woman I'd argued with a half-hour ago was dead. I returned to the car and found Char sitting with her arms wrapped around her middle, staring out the window.

I slipped my arm around her shoulders and pulled her close. "Are you okay?"

"I was the last person to see her," she whispered. "I told her I wanted her to pay for what she did to me, and I meant it, but I wouldn't wish an ending like this on anyone. It's horrible."

"It's not your fault," I said gently. "Eva had a stubborn mind of her own. If she didn't get her way, she tended to get vindictive. She dumped me the first time around because I wouldn't take the old man's bribe. This time she decided to go after you. To destroy you and break us apart."

Char turned to me with sad eyes. "She almost succeeded."

I took her in my arms and kissed her. "You're a strong woman, Char," I whispered in her ear, inhaling the soft scent of her perfume. "That's why I love you. I'll never leave you."

She looked up, gazing into my eyes. "I love you so much, Will. Let's get married as soon as possible."

"You got it, baby." I let her go and started the Ford. "Now, let's get this car back to the lodge before anyone realizes it's gone, or we might be getting hitched in the county jail."

Chapter Thirty-One

Saturday, September 11th

CHAR

"Hold still so I can adjust this one more time," Maddie coaxed as she fiddled with my bridal headpiece. A cluster of pearl beads and a white ostrich feather adorned the thin strip of white satin and lace trim. I'd chosen my favorite pearl necklace and earring set to go with it.

"There," she said and stood back to admire her handiwork. "You look perfect. You make a beautiful bride, Char." She kissed my cheek. "I'm so happy for you and Will. I've never seen him so elated." She chuckled. "Or so nervous."

Our "immediate" wedding took two and a half weeks to set up. Not because I had second thoughts, but because I'd learned that Louisa and Peter were planning to get married right away, too. Louisa had decided on a private ceremony at the courthouse to avoid asking her mother for financial help. She had no intention of inviting her family.

I knew how important this day was to her and wanted to do something to help make it special. I approached her about holding the ceremony in my home and before I knew it, we were planning a double wedding. It didn't take long for that "small" gathering to get out of hand—especially once Maddie got involved. Between our friends, family, and a few close business associates, we had invited over one hundred people. We decided against bridesmaids, but we did ask Adrienne to sing one song for us.

My staff was "over the moon" with glee when they were told about the event, and they had worked tirelessly to make everything perfect. By the morning of the wedding, they had set up the great hall with chairs, flowers, and ribbons, and prepared the spot where the ceremony would take place. They had set up the terrace with torches, flowers, and a buffet for the reception.

The door to my room opened and Lillian entered, quickly shutting the door behind her to keep anyone who might be in the hallway from seeing my gown. She looked fetching in a dark green rayon dress with ruffled sleeves and a flared skirt. "Miss Louisa has finished dressing and will meet you at the top of the stairs when the music starts," she said.

"Okay, we're ready to go," Maddie told her in a shaking voice. "We're just waiting for Ethel to give us the signal."

Ethel had volunteered to coordinate everything going on downstairs and handle any issues that sprang up at the last minute.

"Stand up, Char," Maddie said to me, "so I can check your dress one last time to make sure everything is zipped and buttoned properly..." She'd been flitting around me all day like a nervous bird, fussing with my hair and applying her best brand of makeup from the shop. I, on the other hand, sat through the routine in a state of numbness, like it was all a dream. I had wanted this day to happen for so long. Now that it had arrived, it seemed surreal. In a few minutes, I would no longer be Gus LeDoux's widow. I had carried this identity for so long that it seemed strange to think it would no longer be mine. Would I feel like the same person after I married Will and possessed a new name?

I stood obediently while Maddie straightened my dress. I had chosen an art deco gown in white with a V neckline and ostrich plumage covering my shoulders. The front and back panels were uniquely accented with beads and sequins in a sparkling floral design. The scalloped hem had a beaded fringe.

"Char," Francie said as she burst into the room carrying a wicker basket filled with rose petals. "Papa's here! And he's wearing the suit you bought him!"

I'd asked my father to walk me down the aisle and I was surprised when he accepted. Over the summer, he'd been living in a home for alcoholics, struggling to dry out. He'd had a difficult start resulting in a few mishaps, but he'd promised me—and Francie—he'd be "straight" today.

"How does he look," I asked her quickly.

She sighed with relief. "He hasn't been drinking. I could tell if he had."

I took her hand in mine and swallowed hard, keeping my emotions at bay. My father's sobriety was the best wedding gift I could ask for today.

"Oh! What I really came to tell you was that Ethel said the bridal march begins in five minutes," Francie added, "and you're supposed to take your position at the top of the stairs!"

"All right then," Maddie replied in a squeaky voice as she picked up my wide bouquet of white carnations and blush roses, accented with trailing plumosa ferns and satin ribbons. "Here you are. Let's go—"

We entered the hallway, meeting up with Louisa and Sally. Louisa's future mother-in-law had designed and sewn an ankle-length, ivory-colored dress for her with lace sleeves. She wore a cloche-style lace cap with a delicate veil attached to the back that hung to her elbows. We held matching bouquets.

She smiled timidly. "I'm afraid I'm going to trip going down the stairs."

"You'll be fine," Sally said in a motherly way. "Keep your hand on the railing and take careful steps until you get to the landing. Your escort will take it from there."

Louisa and I each took our places at the top of the divided stairway. Francie joined Papa and Peter's father, Wendell Garrett, on the wide landing halfway down. When the music started, Francie began dropping the rose petals as she descended the grand staircase.

Louisa and I exchanged nervous smiles then we began our descent to *Felix Mendelssohn's Wedding March.*

I took Sally's advice and clutched the railing with a death grip as I slowly descended the first half of the stairway. Once I reached the landing, Papa extended his arm to me, his wrinkled face crinkling with a wide smile. His eyes glistened with pride. I gripped his arm and we both turned to face the altar opposite the stairs where Will and Peter stood waiting to receive us.

At Pastor Olson's cue, the congregation stood and faced the grand stairway. Gretchen, my nanny, stood in the front row holding my sweet little man, Julien. He wore a custom-made tuxedo that I'd had tailored for him.

Papa and I, Louisa and Wendell, began our descent together. Once we reached the altar, Papa kissed me and whispered, "I love you, honey." I had all I could do to keep myself from bursting into tears, but when he presented me to Will, I suddenly lost track of everything else.

Will looked so handsome in his black suit and milk-white carnation boutonnière. His black, wavy hair had been brushed to one side. His intense blue eyes beheld me with fascination and unabashed love as he took my hand. We turned to Pastor Olson to begin the ceremony.

Pastor Olson began with a warm welcome to the congregation and introduced us followed by a Bible reading and a short sermon. Then, Adrienne stood on the landing and sang a beautiful rendition of "It Had to Be You" in her deep, sultry voice.

Louisa and Peter said their vows first. When it came to our turn, Maddie took possession of my bouquet. Will and I faced each other holding hands.

"Repeat after me, Will," Pastor Olson said in his gentle, but commanding voice. "In the presence of God, I take thee, Char, to be my wedded wife. To have and to hold from this day forward. For better, for worse, for richer, for poorer, in sickness and in health. To love and to cherish. Till death us do part."

"In the presence of God," Will said to me in his deep, masculine voice. "I take thee, Char, to be my wedded wife. To have and to hold from this day forward. For better, for worse, for richer, for poorer, in sickness and in health. To love and to cherish. Till death us do part."

"Char, repeat after me," Pastor Olson said, giving me the same words to say.

"In the presence of God," I said smiling, but when I looked into his eyes, I saw more than his love for me. I saw a lifetime of unity and happiness. I saw adventure, travel, and yes, God willing...more children. "I take thee, Will, to be my wedded husband," I said boldly. "To have and to hold from this day forward. For better, for worse, for richer, for poorer, in sickness and in health. To love and to cherish. Till death us do part."

We exchanged rings. My hand didn't shake nearly as much as Will's did as he slipped the circular band studded with diamonds on my finger. Will's wedding ring was a simple gold band, exactly what he wanted.

"Louisa May Amundsen and Peter Rudolph Garrett," Pastor Olson said, "Charlotte Esther LeDoux and William Charles Van Elsberg, by the powers invested in me, I pronounce you man and wife. Gentlemen, you may kiss your brides."

We kissed to an exuberant round of applause then we turned to face the congregation.

"Ladies and gentlemen," Pastor Olson proclaimed, "I present to you, Mr. and Mrs. Garrett, and Mr. and Mrs. Van Elsberg."

As the crowd clapped and cheered, Will leaned close. "After this shindig is over, we need to talk. I've got a big surprise for you." He chuckled. "Baby, you're gonna *owe* me."

My heart skipped a beat. Really? It had to be a good one if he made a point to tease me about it at the altar.

"I can't wait," I said, laughing. I knew just how to pay him back. I had a *big* surprise for him too.

Epilogue

Friday, September 24th

WILL

"Will, when is this surprise you promised me on our wedding day going to materialize?" Char demanded as we rode home in the limo. "It's been two weeks since we returned from our honeymoon, and you still haven't coughed up the goods." She folded her arms and displayed that stubborn frown I knew so well. "I'm beginning to think it was just a bunch of baloney."

I laughed. I'd taken her to Big Louie's for an ice cream sundae to get her out of the house. I had to tempt her with something she couldn't refuse in order to follow through with my plan.

"Hey," I replied and slid my arm around her shoulders, pulling her close, "what about *your* secret? You haven't coughed up yours, either."

She gave me a sly smile. "I'm not going to until you tell me yours. You're the one who opened your big mouth first. So, put up or shut up, mister."

"Is that so?" I began tickling her waist. "Yes, boss!"

Errol pulled the limo into the driveway and glided the vehicle through the gate, waving at Chet. After the car stopped inside the carriage porch, we climbed out, still laughing and clowning around. At the top of the steps, we waited for Gerard to open the door.

"That's odd," Char remarked curiously. "Gerard isn't at the door." She rang the doorbell. "That's never happened before. I hope nothing is wrong."

"He's probably busy," I said waving the notion away.

The door flew open, and Gerard—the English guy who never smiled—stood before us with a huge grin on his face. Remembering his manners, he quickly reverted to his usual stoic expression and began profusely apologizing for his tardiness, but Char ignored it. The clamor of voices and laughter inside the house distracted her. "What's going on? Gerard, who is here?"

Her butler extended his arm toward the great hall. "Come in, My Lady, and see for yourself."

Char frowned at his vague answer, studying him as though he'd gone daft. "I will."

We went into the great hall to find the source of the noise and found everyone in the sunroom. Sally Wentworth sat on the chaise lounge in a bright purple dress holding a wiggly bundle in her arms. Char's staff had congregated around her, chattering, and making a fuss over her charge.

I trailed behind Char into the room and stood off to one side watching the expression on her face when she saw the child.

"Sally, I didn't know you were coming, or I would have stayed home," she said sounding flustered. "Have you decided to keep the baby?"

"No," Sally replied emphatically as she stood. "I'm handing her over to you. Congratulations, Char. Your application to be a foster parent was approved."

Everyone in the room cheered and applauded the good news.

Char gasped as she accepted the bundle, cradling the child in her arms. "Are you serious? But...I thought I was disqualified because of my marriage to Gus."

Sally nodded in my direction. "Ask Will. He's the one who got it approved."

Char turned to me; her eyes were wide with surprise. "Will?"

"I've been working on this since our wedding day. I knew how badly you wanted to foster the little girl, so I had a talk with Harv," I said simply. "He took care of it."

"What?" She shifted the child in her arms, pulling away the blanket to better see the baby's face. "You had Harv bribe government officials just to get my application approved?"

"No, that's not how it went," I said, shaking my head in frustration. "Harv met with them as your lawyer. He convinced them to approve of both of us. We're a team now, *Mrs.* Van Elsberg."

"Have you thought of a name for her?" Sally interjected into the conversation.

Char smiled down at the little dark-haired beauty. "Nora," she said lovingly. "I want to name her Nora Rose."

A chorus of oohs and aahs filled the room.

Hmm…I liked the sound of that name. "Good choice," I said. "It's perfect for her."

The baby's head turned toward the sound of my voice. Her bright, clear eyes focused on me with wide-eyed wonder.

"Oh, look, Will," Char cooed. "She's smiling at you. Do you want to hold her?"

Awkwardness and uncertainty gripped me at the thought of being entrusted with such a delicate creature. "Ah, I—I don't know anything about babies," I replied as I swallowed hard and nervously shoved my hands into my pockets. "I'm afraid if I hold her, I might break her. For now, I'll let you have that honor."

The women reacted with another chorus of sympathetic aahs.

Char leaned close and tenderly kissed me. "Thank you, Will. This is the best surprise you could *ever* give me. It was worth the wait."

"That's not even the best part," I said smugly.

Her jaw dropped in surprise. "There's more?"

"You don't think we'd gain approval for foster care and leave it at that, do you?" I replied with a wry grin. "Harv is going to call you about filing a petition for adoption."

The tears of joy cascading down her face melted my heart and reinforced why I loved this woman so much. She was sweet, sassy, and often frustratingly stubborn, but she never did anything halfway. She loved everything with her whole heart. Including me.

*   *   *

Sally left a few minutes later and the staff resumed their duties, leaving Char and Gretchen to care for little Nora.

Gretchen, a stout, red-headed farm girl from Wisconsin, had been caring for Julien since he was a few months old, and I had no doubt she could handle both Julien and Nora with ease. She and Char went up to the nursery to see if Julien had awakened from his nap and to change the baby's diaper.

"Oh, Char," I called out as they reached the landing on the grand staircase. I folded my arms and leaned against the sunroom doorframe. "Aren't you forgetting something?"

Char stopped on the landing, still clutching the baby in her arms. "Like what?"

"Like, ah…my surprise? I delivered the goods like I promised. Now, it's your turn."

"Just let me get the baby settled and—"

"Tell me now," I said teasingly. "I'm beginning to think it's just a bunch of baloney."

She told Gretchen to go on ahead, staring at me with a wry chuckle and a mysterious half-smile on her face, just like the one I saw on a painting once of an Italian gal called "Mona Lisa."

"I planned to tell you later when we were alone, but since you asked," she said, "I've decided to do something exciting with my life."

"What do you mean," I replied, curious. "You already have an exciting life here with me. What more could you want?"

Something about the daring sparkle in her eyes gave me pause. Oh-oh. My darling wife had something up her sleeve. Dare I ask what?

"I need a new adventure in my life," she said wistfully. "Something different and challenging."

"But, Char," I countered in amazement, "you have the shelter and the new cosmetics salon. And the children. You're so busy now, how could you possibly find the time to take on more?"

"Sally and her church have taken over the shelter," she said with a frown, "and Maddie is completely obsessed with running the shop so there is no role for me any longer in either place. I've got great managers overseeing both the Ford dealership and my soda shops so there is nothing for me to do in either of those businesses either. And I don't want to disrupt Gretchen's routine with the kids." She ended her little speech with a careless shrug. "I don't feel like I fit in anywhere. I'm just a spectator. So, it's time for something new. I've decided that I'm going to become a private investigator." She suddenly beamed with a wide smile. "I'm going to be your new partner."

I was positive I'd heard her wrong. "What did you say?"

"You and Daniel are going to teach me everything you know so that I can—"

"No. *No.* Absolutely not," I bellowed as the full effect of her words hit me. I walked across the great hall and stopped at the bottom of the staircase. "You are not going to be an investigator in my firm and that's *that.*"

"Why not?" she demanded, becoming indignant. "You just admitted to everyone a few minutes ago that we were a team!"

"It's too dangerous, Char."

"I knew you'd say that, Will," she said, seemingly undeterred by my refusal. "Actually, I'm glad you did because that means I can put my second idea into action instead." She let out a deep sigh of relief. "I'm going to start my own agency of *trailblazing women* and take female clients."

I gripped the newel post trying to control my temper. "Listen to me, darling. You don't have any idea what you're up against—"

"I'm aware it will be a challenge," she shot back sweetly, cutting me off. "I'll learn!"

She turned and ran up the stairs before I could get in the last word. I caught the stubborn look on my wife's face and knew that she was

238

determined to become the first female detective in St. Paul.

I knew better than to doubt her.

The End

Oh, my goodness, what is Char up to now?

A new husband, a new baby, and a new adventure await her as she builds

The Nightingale Detective Agency

in book four of the

Moonshine Madness Series.

Coming Soon!

To be the first to know—follow me on Amazon!

https://www.amazon.com/author/denisedevine

Want to stay in touch?

Sign up for my newsletter at **https://eepurl.com/csOJZL** and receive a *free novella of my exciting new series, West Loon Bay*. You'll be the first to know about my new releases, sales, and special events.

Want to meet more authors who write sweet romance?

Join my reader group at Happily Ever After Stories – Sweet Romance. If you like sweet romance and want to be part of a great group that has lots of fun and fantastic parties, visit us at:

https://www.facebook.com/groups/HEAstories/

More Books by Denise Devine

Christmas Stories

Merry Christmas, Darling

A Christmas to Remember

A Merry Little Christmas

Once Upon a Christmas

Mistletoe and Wine – *Coming Soon!*

A Very Merry Christmas (Hawaiian Holiday Series)

~*~

Bride Books

The Encore Bride

Lisa – Beach Brides Series

Ava – Perfect Match Series

Della – *Coming Soon!*

~*~

Moonshine Madness Series – Historical Suspense

The Bootlegger's Wife – Book 1

Guarding the Bootlegger's Widow – Book 2

The Bootlegger's Legacy – Book 3

The Nightingale Detective Agency – Book 4 - *Coming Soon!*

~*~

West Loon Bay Series – Small Town Romance

Small Town Girl – Book 1

Brown-Eyed Girl – Book 2

Country Girl – *Coming Soon!*

Cozy Mystery

Dark Fortune - Fortunes, Love & Fate Series

Unfinished Business

~ Girl Friday Series ~

Shot in the Dark – Book 1

The Accidental Detective – Book 2 – *Coming Soon!*

~*~

Audiobooks Galore!

Do you like audiobooks? Many of the above books are available in audio!

Narrated by Lorana L. Hoopes

Check out Denise's website for links to each audiobook

Monthly sales!

https://www.deniseannettedevine.com

Want more? Read the first chapter of each of my novels on my blog at:
https://deniseannette.blogspot.com